THE MERI

MAYA
KAATHRYN
BOHNHOFF

BAEN
FANTASY

THE MERI

Copyright © 1992 by Maya Kaathryn Bohnhoff

A Baen Books Original

Baen Publishing Enterprises
P.O. Box 1403
Riverdale, N.Y. 10471

ISBN: 0-671-72115-1

Cover art by Darrell Sweet
Map by Eleanor Kostyk

First printing, April 1992

Distributed by
SIMON & SCHUSTER
1230 Avenue of the Americas
New York, N.Y. 10020

Printed in the United States of America

The Six Who Came
Before Her Lay Buried
Beneath the Church . . .

She was just at the door when the Cirke-master, coming into the sanctuary by his side entrance, saw her and raised a loud cry: "Aha! Now I've got you! You'll do no more of your magic around here!"

Meredydd's first impulse was to flee, but she could almost see the crystal hidden beneath his robes. Instead she turned and faced him: "I've done no magic, sir. Whatever can you mean?"

"You were out picking weeds for your potions! Ruhf saw you clear as day. You and that little monster—"

At the mention of Gwynet, all thought of the crystal fled. "What do you know of Gwynet? What has he done with her?"

"Oh! Like likes like, is it? Well, he caught her out just as I've caught you. And now it's time for you to join your dear sisters under the Cirke, Wicke."

He was halfway up the aisle now; Meredydd could see the light of zeal in his eyes. . . . He took another step.

Primed to flee, Meredydd turned the door latch, then remembered the crystal. All she had to do was reach out and take it. She made herself wait.

But when his hand came clear of his robes, it wasn't the star talisman it held. It was a set of iron manacles.

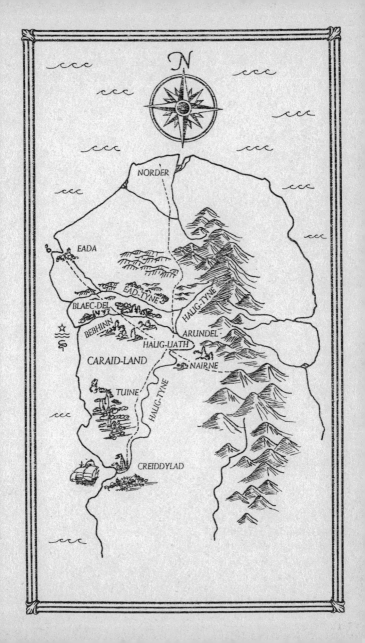

Chapter 1

There is a bridge between the finite and the Infinite. This Bridge is the Meri, the Spirit of the Spirit of the Universe, which men call God. Nothing may cross that Bridge: neither day nor night, nor old age, nor death nor sorrow nor evil nor sin.

Only the pure of heart may cross that Bridge, because the world of the Spirit is pure. In the crossing of this Bridge, the eyes of the blind will see, the wounds of the ailing will be healed, and the sick man will become whole.

To the crosser of the Bridge, the night becomes day, because in the world of Spirit there is everlasting Light.

  —The Book of the Meri, Chapter I, Verses 34–36

It was not lost on Meredydd-a-Lagan that she was the only girl at Halig-liath. It was brought home to her every morning at Assemblage where she stood, front and center, in the huge cobbled yard, surrounded by the other Prentices—boys, all of them.

It hadn't been so bad when she was younger; she had been almost indistinguishable then—cropped chestnut hair, tunic hung loosely on a slender, angular

1

frame. But she was fifteen now, and in the last year, many things had grown apace with height and hair.

This morning was particularly bad; she felt completely alien, awkward and unwelcome. In the warmth of a fine spring morning, she stood out from the others like a briar among roses—her bare arms hairless, her light tunic betraying mounds and bends and curves no other Prentice possessed. She sensed eyes on her as they murmured their congregational prayers and prepared for a day of lessons.

She dared to glance up at the Osraed in their gallery high up on the imposing stone wall of the Academy. They were looking at her too—Ealad-hach, Calach and her guardian, Osraed Bevol. She got Osraed Bevol to meet her eyes and he smiled. She forgot her awkwardness in an instant and filed away with the others for classwork.

"She's gotten to be such a tall girl," said Osraed Calach. "Taller than some of the boys."

"She's still a girl," Ealad-hach reminded him, and glanced at the silent, smiling Bevol. "She will always be a girl. She should be training in the domestic arts. Training to be the wife of an Osraed and the mother of Prentices."

"And why," asked Bevol, "should she do that when she could become Osraed, herself? She has absolutely no talent for the domestic arts, Ealad. None. But she is already practicing the Divine Arts with some skill."

"You should not let her practice."

"Why not? You let your personal favorite practice and Meredydd has shown far more natural talent and inclination than he has."

Ealad-hach wrinkled his knife-blade nose.

"Ah?" Bevol pressed, pointing a finger at that oversized feature. "Ah now, admit what you cannot deny. Meredydd is second to none in her class."

"And it goes to her head. A bad condition for a girl."

"*If* it went to her head and *if* she were an ordinary

child—of either sex—I would agree, but neither is true."

"The Meri will not accept a female Prentice, you know that."

"I know nothing of the sort. There is nothing in the Books that denies Prenticeship to girls."

"There is tradition—"

"Pah! Old folk tales, hearsay—"

Osraed Calach cleared his throat. "Do you intend to abandon your students in favor of this ancient argument?"

Osraed Bevol smiled and wagged his head. Snow-streaked copper, his hair and beard rippled with the motion, cascading over the azure of his robe. "I will never abandon my student," he said pointedly, and led the way from the gallery into the Academy.

Meredydd was not watching Aelder Prentice Wyth scratching illustrations of aislinn symbology on the whitewall. She was watching a spider apply warp and woof to the corner of an open window. The web had been taking shape for the entire morning and was nearly complete. Sunlight ran like blazing golden liquid down its pristine fibers—more delicate, more gleaming, more glorious than the finest silk. Meredydd imaged herself in a robe of the stuff—so fine and light.

She could see herself upon the sill, the size of a butterfly, lying back in the sleek, shining hammock, where bees would bring her nectar and ambrosia and the spider would play duans for her upon a harp of his own design. She could almost hear its song—light as down, shimmering, whispers of melody.

It was a shame, she thought, that the Arts didn't run to miniaturization. Then again, maybe they did and it just wasn't something the Prentices were permitted to know. After all, it wouldn't do to have them practicing Shrinkweaves on each other. The thought made her grin.

"Prentice Meredydd. Could you tell me what you

are studying that you find my lesson beneath your notice?"

She jumped quite nearly from her skin and blinked up into the Aelder's stern face. "Why—aislinn symbols, Aelder."

"Aye, that is what the rest of us were studying, *cailin*. But you, I think, were not." He straightened and turned toward the whitewall, and Meredydd thought how spiteful he was to remind her (and everyone else) that she was a girl.

Cailin, he called her—but only when Osraed Bevol was out of earshot. He had used the word once in the Osraed's presence and Bevol had referred to him as "boy" for a fortnight, refusing to dignify him by using either his name or his title.

At the whitewall, now, Aelder Prentice Wyth stood and lifted a bony, linen-clad arm to point at the group of symbols rendered there in blue oilstick. They were very well drawn, Meredydd had to allow. "Meaning, *Prentice* Meredydd. Give this aislinn meaning."

That was easy. "The horse," she said, "is life, events. Strong emotions. The rearing horse especially connotes difficulty in maintaining control of one's destiny."

Wyth's lips pursed. "And this?" His finger tapped a set of wavy lines.

"Water in motion," she replied. "Emotions, such as love or great passion are symbolized thusly. A stormy sea would indicate violent emotions or a fear of them—especially, a fear of passion."

"At least you studied."

"I always study, Aelder Wyth."

He peered at her, narrow-eyed. "A man dreamed," he said, "that he went upon Pilgrimage. And when he reached the shore of the Western Sea, he lay upon the sand and slept. When he awoke, a beautiful cailin urged him to rise up and follow her into the sea. He rose and walked after her and entered the water and *did not get wet*." He emphasized the last words with a smile and folded his arms across his chest. "Interpret this aislinn."

Meredydd glanced quickly about the semi-circle of Prentices and wriggled uncomfortably on her bench—not because she couldn't interpret the dream, but because she *could* interpret it and suspected it was the Aelder's own.

"Are you certain, Aelder Wyth, that you wish me to interpret *this* dream?"

"Why else would I have directed you to do so?" he asked sarcastically and drew a snicker from the other Prentices.

Meredydd set her shoulders and sat stiffly upright, steeling herself. "Pilgrimage—"

Wyth held out the bluestick. "Come to the wall and illustrate your Tell for the class."

She swallowed and gave the teasing spider web a last, longing glance, then rose and went forward. She took the bluestick, erased the existing symbols with the blotter and began her illustration.

"Pilgrimage," she said, drawing the symbol:

$$\underset{\text{\Large \raisebox{-2pt}{$\underset{\approx}{}$}}}{\overset{\displaystyle \star}{\text{---}}}$$

"—is the journey toward the heart's desire. The Sea $\approx$ is where the journey leads, to the Pilgrim's Post $\overline{\odot}$ from which the true seeker awaits the Meri $\underline{\star}$. The Sea is also symbolic of deep emotion; love, devotion, faith, passion. Sleep $\frown$ is forgetfulness or a lack of acceptance. The maiden who wakes the sleeping Pilgrim ∞ is someone or something which provides the catalyst for the continuance of the quest—a prodder, such as the conscience. The conscience wakes the sleeper and he enters the relationship $\odot$ with the Object of Pilgrimage but . . ."

"But?"

The classroom was so silent, Meredydd was certain she could hear the wind pass through the spider web.

At least, she could have if the breathing of the ten
other Prentices was not so deafeningly loud.

"But," she continued, "no effect is obtained."
There. It didn't sound so bad when you cloaked it in
academic terms.

"Sum up."

She turned the bluestick in her fingers and watched
it go round and round, then she pretended to study
the group of figures on the wall. "The Pilgrim attains
his heart's desire, but it has no effect upon him. He
. . . enters the Water of Life, but remains dry. I would
read this as a fear dream. Perhaps the dreamer is
afraid he will not be able to . . . absorb the bounties
of the Meri or perhaps he believes he does not need
to absorb them."

Aelder Wyth's face was whiter than his fine linen
robe. That he had not so interpreted the aislinn was
obvious.

"Terrible," he finally managed to say. "Prentice
Meredydd, you obviously need to improve your understanding of the aislinn symbology. Therefore, you will
read Aelf-raed's treatises on the Water Signs and present a written summation of your findings to me for
tomorrow's lesson. Then, I'll give you another dream
to Tell."

Meredydd's numb fingers nearly dropped the bluestick. Aelder Wyth had always been difficult to please,
but he had never shown such ego, nor had she ever
known him to be vindictive. She was about to protest
his out-of-hand rejection of her Tell, but his attention
was already elsewhere. He swiveled his head, his eyes
leaping lightly over the class. They landed on Brys-a-
Lach, known, in chatter circles, as "Aelder's Pet." He
was a big, handsome boy—a man at sixteen—and he
was almost as impressed with himself as Wyth was.

The Aelder Prentice smiled at his favorite student
and said, "Now, Prentice Brys, will you kindly interpret this dream? I will allow that Meredydd's illustrations are correct; you needn't repeat them."

Brys stood, broad-shouldered and impressive, and Meredydd sighed inwardly. It was so much easier for a comely young man to succeed in second level classes at Halig-liath than it was for a homely or undersized youth or—Heaven's help!—a girl. It was the system, of course. The first level classes were taught by the Divine Counselors themselves, the second level by Aelders—Prentices like Wyth who had not yet been accepted to become Osraed, and who most likely never would. The Osraed knew that good looks and physical charm had naught to do with prowess in the Art, but the Aelders were so fresh from the classroom themselves—

"It is clear," said Brys-a-Lach in a voice that would ring well from the gallery, "that the vision pertains to spiritual greatness. So devoted is the Pilgrim that he spends his last dregs of energy on the Path to the Quintessential Ocean and falls asleep, heedless of his own needs. Now, we also know that it is in sleep that an Osraed often receives instruction from the Meri, so this may also be interpreted as the Pilgrim opening himself to Her will. So spiritual is this Pilgrim that a special envoy is sent to awaken him to his destiny. So pure is he that he walks directly into the Ocean itself, without even having seen the Meri. So transcendent is he that the waters fail to discomfit him—even as the Book of Pilgrimages says: 'a knower is he who is dry in the sea.' This Pilgrim overcomes even the Ocean."

"But the whole point of Pilgrimage," blurted Meredydd, "is to *see* the Meri. Sleep does not symbolize greatness in any other context, why should it be any different here? Traditionally, it symbolizes lack of vigilance, lack of ardor, perhaps an inability to face reality. The ardorous Pilgrim would be wakeful and vigilant against the Meri's appearance. This poor fellow would lose his chance—the Meri could rise up and dance all about him while he snored in the sand."

The class found this a humorous image and burst into laughter. Red-faced, Aelder Wyth silenced them.

"A spurious interpretation—" he began.

"Nonsense," said Meredydd, forgetting all but the problem of interpretation. "A rational interpretation according to the texts. Furthermore, the Pilgrim is presumptuous; he enters the Sea of the Meri without the Meri's permission. He immerses himself in the Waters of Life and doesn't even allow himself to be touched by them or absorb their influences. This can mean only one thing: this Pilgrim misses the entire point of his own Pilgrimage. Extrapolating on that, I would say that the dream expresses the spirit's fear that this Pilgrim is drawing no spiritual benefit from his quest."

"Sagacious!" exclaimed one of Wyth's homely, undersized students—a freckled redhead named Lealbhallain. He applauded lightly and alone. Aelder Wyth and Brys-a-Lach both glared at him while the other boys ogled.

"So this Pilgrim has missed the point, has he?" asked the Aelder Prentice after a long, rending pause.

Meredydd shifted uncomfortably from one foot to the other, wishing Wyth hadn't left her standing, exposed, at the front of the class. "That is my Tell."

"This pointless Pilgrim is considerably chastened. The dream is mine."

There were a few gasps from those who hadn't already guessed this.

Aelder Prentice Wyth narrowed his eyes. "Do you wish to rethink your interpretation, Prentice Meredydd?"

If he sought to humiliate her, he did an admirable job, notwithstanding he had caught himself in the backwash. She felt very small and alone. She could take it all back, she supposed—wanted to with all those eyes on her. She glanced at Lealbhallain. His green eyes were enormous in his elfin face and he had caught his lower lip between his teeth. *He's probably holding his breath, too,* she thought, *and if I wait too much longer, he'll faint.*

"No, Aelder Prentice Wyth," she said finally, "I do not. I stand by my Tell. To do otherwise would be cowardly and self-serving."

He did not commend her for her integrity. She ended up with a triple reading assignment and the onerous task of sorting organic medicinals for the Apothecary. Poor Lealbhallain was commissioned to help her.

"You're very brave," he told her while they were up to their wrists in lakeweed. "I would have cried to have Aelder Prentice Wyth so furious at me."

"I'm not brave, Leal, just stupid and querulous. I should have . . ." She pulled lakeweed from the pail silently for a moment, trying to think of what she should have done. It would have been disobedient to refuse to interpret the aislinn outright. It would have been lying to Tell the dream as Brys had. Not that Brys was lying, of course. His Tell was different, that was all. But if she had given *his* interpretation instead of her own . . .

She sighed volubly. "I don't know what I should have done. Apologized to Wyth, I suppose. My Tell wasn't very flattering."

Lealbhallain gave her an innocently penetrating glance. "Was that the purpose of the Tell? To flatter Aelder Prentice Wyth?"

Meredydd chuckled. "No, Leal. It was not. But I suppose I could have apologized all the same. I'll have to ask Osraed Bevol what the correct course would have been."

Lealbhallain gave her a look of deep, admiring envy. "You are so fortunate, Meredydd, to have your own Osraed to ask."

She glanced down at the little piles of lakeweed that lay in puddles on the white crystal counter. "I know, Leal. And I wonder why that is, when I am so undeserving."

The boy's eyes widened. "Oh, no, Meredydd! I didn't mean—Why, you're a prodigy! You have so much natural talent—"

"No, Leal," she said, laughing a little at his zeal. "I have Osraed Bevol. That is what I have."

"And you said what, then?" asked Osraed Bevol, sipping his broth.

Meredydd laid the baps out on the table and glanced back toward the kitchen. "Bring the butter pot, won't you, Skeet? Then I said that there was only one thing it *could* mean and that— What?" she asked, seeing that the Osraed was shaking his head.

He set down his broth bowl. "How many times, Meredydd, must I tell you: there is never but one interpretation for any aislinn. Hm?" His crooked finger pointed at a spot in the air as if she might look there for the exact number.

She reddened. "Many times, Master."

"Correct. And this is a condition which also applies to other realities—to all things—whether spoken or unspoken. Even Pov knows this. Isn't that so, Pov?"

Skeet responded slowly to the use of his given name under most circumstances, but the Osraed Bevol was proof to his stubbornness. The boy let his great Master use the homely name that meant simply, "Earth," though everyone else, Meredydd included, must acknowledge him as fleet Skeet if they didn't wish to be completely ignored. Now, he smiled sweetly and set out the butter bowl.

"Aye, Maister. I do so know. Seventy times seventy meanings do a' things hae."

Meredydd sat in her place at the table and stared at her green-stained hands. "I let my horse rear up and carry me off, Master. I spoke out of turn. I should have let Brys-a-Lach have the last say about Aelder Wyth's aislinn."

The Osraed's dappled brows fluttered up his forehead. "Oh? Then did you think it the correct Tell?"

"Well, of course I didn't or I wouldn't have got so
. . . I spoke out of turn," she repeated and fell silent.

"You spoke up," corrected Osraed Bevol. "You
stood by your interpretation, which, while not the *only*
one, was at least spiritually appropriate. Prentice Brys
was currying favor, not searching for the truth." He
looked at her, eyes sharp, azure.

"Pardon, Master, but is it appropriate to judge
Prentice Brys's motive?"

Bevol pointed at her. "No, it is not. But it is entirely
appropriate for you to question my judgment of him.
And if it is appropriate to question my interpretation
of young Brys's motives, then it is appropriate to question his interpretation of a vision."

"I wasn't impertinent?"

"It was a classroom exercise, anwyl," he told her,
softening his criticism with the endearment. "You
were impertinent to cast your Tell as the only one,
but if Prentice Wyth had wanted to avoid embarrassment, he should never have used his own aislinn
as the subject for a reading."

Meredydd glanced up from her soup. Skeet was already half-way through his. "Perhaps he didn't expect
a negative Tell."

"Eh? Well, perhaps he's possessed of a superior detachment, hm? A man of rare humility." His eyes crinkled at the corners.

Skeet laughed, his own dark eyes glinting. "Aye,
rare," he said.

After dinner, Meredydd helped Skeet clear the
table. Sun still slanted through the kitchen window,
burnishing the pale cobbles, and she felt the pull of a
place to the east, almost in the fork of the Halig-tyne
where it gave birth to the dancing Bebhinn. She
glanced about as she entered the great hall, straining
to keep her footsteps light on the flagstones. The hall
was empty and she thought she could hear the Osraed
rustling in his parlor. She drew a soft cloak from the
pegs by the front door and reached for the latch.

"Be back in time for your studies," said Bevol's voice behind her.

"Yes, Master." She opened the door and slipped out quickly, knowing his eyes followed her down the path and up the lea. The solid oaken door was no impediment to those eyes.

He never told her not to go, however much he wished to, and it was beyond her to grant him that unspoken wish. So she fled eastward to the Fork, to the place where one river became twain.

It was called Lagan—"the Little Hollow"—and there had been a homestead there once. A fine homestead with an ample cottage and a big barn and a great forge. There was only burnt rubble, now, and tall grass and wildflowers that waved sorrowfully in the wind.

Every spring the mounds of shattered brick and stone and crumbled masonry were less apparent beneath the green carpet that encroached and obscured. Every spring the charred beams were more overgrown with vine and bramble. But the pain in Meredydd's heart was never overgrown and her rage was never obscured.

She picked wild roses from the tangle that embraced the fallen chimney. She pricked her fingers on the thorns and bled in penance for making Osraed Bevol so unhappy. What she could not do penance for, even by coming here and bleeding upon the thorns every day of her life, was her absence on a particular afternoon seven years past.

On that afternoon, a day of worship, Meredydd-a-Lagan had left her parents at the Cirke in Nairne and gone home through the Bebhinn wood. She had been told to go straight home and had promised to do just that, but the wood had wooed and won her before she'd even left the Cirke-yard.

Along the Bebhinn—so named for the musicality of its swift-moving waters—she had come across an amazing pool of the most beautiful, clear, sparkling water and had stopped there, as she was told never to do. After all, who knew what wolves or boar or wild dogs or other were folk inhabited the woods late on Cirke-dag? So warned her elders, who little understood that to a precocious little girl, such threats are promises.

She had taken off her shoes by the little pool and thrust her feet into the icy water and let the most wonderful aislinn images flow through her waking brain. She'd sat long, daydreaming. How long, she never knew. But in time and delight a tendril of mist had risen from the pool, captivating her with its graceful, spiraling pirhouettes. As she watched it, imagining it to be all manner of wonderful things, it assumed, finally, the form of a white-robed maiden.

This was a very wonderful and magical thing to a little girl, and it became more wonderful still when the beautiful mist-cailin spoke to her. Her voice was a musical whisper and it told Meredydd she would seek the Meri. She would become a Prentice.

It was such a startling, engaging idea—that a girl, a blaec-smythe's daughter, would study the Divine Art—that little Meredydd jumped to her feet in amazement, dropping her shoes into the pool. The white cailin dissolved back into a whisp of mist and the afternoon into sudden, cool twilight.

Looking frantically about, Meredydd suddenly realized that the sky was darkening rapidly toward evening. High above the trees, a burnished light flickered uncertainly in the mists of twilight.

Affording the lost shoes only a moment's mourning, she climbed carefully out of the pool hollow, climbed until she stood atop a slight rise among the ash and fir. Looking southeast, toward home, she could see what caused the pulsing, rippling light. Wild breakers of flame leapt above the crest of the lea, as if shattering upon an inland reef.

Her heart suddenly in her throat, Meredydd tore through the wood, heedless of her cold, bare feet, her eyes clinging to those leaping waves of incandescence.

She found the main path, broke from the verge of the wood and streaked up the intervening hill.

At the crest she was stopped as if by invisible hands and stared, terrified, into the vale. Lagan was ablaze. The forge, the barn, the cottage, all burned with the brilliance of the morning Sun. She could feel the heat even atop the hill.

Figures moved about the buildings, but they carried no buckets, went nowhere near the well. She made no sense of that, at first. It was only when she turned her eyes to the well itself that the full horror became clear. Lying beside it upon the ground were her mother and father, unmoving, unattended by the three dark-clad men who watched Lagan die.

Meredydd reached out her arms, straining forward, willing her feet to move. But they would not move and she hung there as if held fast, her hands stretched toward her home and family. Then, the men stirred. They lifted the limp bodies that lay by the well and dragged them toward the disintegrating forge.

Meredydd thought she had plumbed the depth of horror, but knew, with sudden conviction, that it had no depth. It was bottomless. She screamed, her voice sounding like the shrill of the hunting hawk. She screamed again and heard the tortured cry of the mountain cat in her ears.

The activity below ceased and the dusky people peered around, their muffled faces all eyes. One looked up the hill, paused and pointed.

Meredydd screamed a third time, her cry piercing her own heart like a lance and spreading on the hot wind of Lagan's destruction. The men stared as one man. Two of them retreated back a step, then two. The third turned away, then back, away, then back. Suddenly they were all three running away into the dark toward the river fork. They disappeared like a flock of daemons, trailing thunder from their horses' hooves.

As if released by the pressing hands, Meredydd fell

forward onto her face, tumbling several yards before
she could stop herself and clamber to her bleeding
feet. She moved down the gentle slope through wild
wheat that caught at feet and ankles. She fell and rose
and fell again, finishing her journey in the mud of the
barnyard, crawling on hands and knees to where her
parents lay.

There was blood on them. Blood on her mother's
sky blue dress. It spread in a horrid dark stain across
the bodice. Blood on her father's best white shirt—so
much that little white could be seen. She knew they
were dead without knowing how she knew and she
could contemplate no existence without them. They
were her entire world. Her goal was only to reach
them; merely to lay herself between them in the cool
mud and die.

The ooze sucking at her legs, Meredydd put out a
hand to touch her mother's face. Something blocked
the touch. Something in a long, soft cloak, now filthy
and soaked at the hem. Little Meredydd stopped, tee-
tering, her hand clutching, her eyes blurred with stinging tears, her mind unable to accept this intrusion.
Mewing like a kitten, she struck at the obstruction
again and again. A hand grasped her shoulder, gently.
She looked up, then, into the face of the Osraed
Bevol.

He touched a forefinger to her forehead and she
collapsed, face first, into the mud.

It was two weeks before she spoke. She cried
nightly, nursing her grief, fighting nightmares and day-
horrors. But the Osraed had loved her and cherished
her and instructed her. The deep pain passed and she
found consolation in loving the Osraed in return. It
also spawned an abiding rage—the first words the
eight year old spoke after her long silence were, "I
want them to die. I want to kill them."

It was Bevol who convinced her she must learn
powerful secrets to be able to even discover her parents' murderers, for no one knew who they were or

why they had attacked a peaceful homestead. And she, remembering the aislinn she had experienced at the forest pool, followed his urging and began the study of the Divine Art.

She'd learned many things in her tenure with Osraed Bevol, more, even, than the average student of Divine Art at Halig-liath. She had him to instruct her in the Telling of dreams and visions, the Healing, the Runeweaving, the secret duans, the speaking to the unspeaking. She could divine ailments and prescribe the cure; she could forecast the weather; she could follow the bees to their honey, then enlist their cooperation in retrieving it. She knew the courses of the stars and planets and the ways of animals, large and small. All these things she had learned and more, but she could not see the faces or know the names of the men who had killed her parents and changed her life.

She watched the blood bead, dark, on one pierced finger and brought herself back from the past. It was darkening now, and the breeze came cool and spicy from the Western Sea. Meredydd raised herself from the grave her parents shared, her hands absently arranging the flowers upon it. She stared a moment at the well that served as their headstone—pondered the weather-worn beam and rope. There was no time for the rest of the ritual today. It would wait until Cirkedag—the anniversary of the death of Lagan.

She got home just at dark, the lamps along the walkway coming on at her approach, the hall lighting as she opened the door. That had seemed an absolute miracle to her once, now it was only a welcome convenience—a fine bit of the Art, if she thought about it any deeper than that. But tonight she noticed the little lamps—noticed that their flames, though warm and bright, failed to make her feel that way. She stared at one fiery sprite in its glass enclosure and thought of the Meri.

"There is a bridge between the finite and the Infinite," said the Book of the Meri. "This Bridge is the

Meri, the Spirit of the Spirit of the Universe, which men call God. Nothing may cross that Bridge: neither day nor night, nor old age, nor death nor sorrow nor evil nor sin."

She would like to find a place where there was no night, no death nor sorrow nor evil nor sin. She would like to cross that Bridge—to see the Meri.

Osraed Bevol had seen Her, of course, many years ago on his own Pilgrimage. And now Meredydd longed for that privilege—Pilgrimage. It was something she'd almost taken for granted once, but now, as she crossed the threshold of adulthood, she realized it was not nearly so certain a destiny as she had imagined. She was old enough this year; it only depended now on her worthiness.

She had to pass on her marks at Academy, first of all, then the Osraed of Halig-liath must approve her. Once that was done, it devolved upon Osraed Bevol to determine if and when she was ready. She wondered if that would be soon. She wondered if she would be one of the fortunate few to see the Star of the Sea rise. And if she did set eyes upon the Meri, what gifts would she receive? What knowledge?

One thing she knew she wanted—the gift of Clear Sight. With that talent, with the knowledge and power of an Osraed, she would be able to look back and see the faces of those three masked riders.

"What does the flame tell you, Meredydd?" asked the Osraed Bevol from the parlor doorway. "What answers lie in the fire?"

She blinked and turned to face him, a royal purple salamander wriggling before her flame-enchanted eyes. "No answers, Master. Only daydreams."

He looked at her for a moment, then nodded toward the parlor. "I have tea on the fender. Come, it's past time for your lesson."

The room was fire-warmed and comfortably cluttered—books tumbled in symmetrical abandon like awkward crystals from every shelf and ledge, and everywhere lay evidences that this room belonged to a practitioner of the Art. A bird skull here, beside it a magnifying lense; a handful of colored crystals—poorly formed rejects; a bundle of old star charts. It was the books that reminded Meredydd of Aelder Prentice Wyth's assignment.

"What is it, anwyl?" asked Bevol, seeing that she had paused in the doorway.

"I was to read," she said, "the Aelf-raed essays on the Water Symbols. For Aelder Wyth. And write a paper on it . . . by tomorrow."

"You've read them."

"Two years ago."

"Have you forgotten the material?"

"No, of course not."

"Then—? All you need do is write a paper. What length?"

"He didn't say."

The Osraed shrugged. "Well, then?"

"He'll ask, first, if I actually did the reading assignment. I can't lie."

Bevol chuckled. "But you *did* do it. You merely did it two years before he asked you to. A most precocious student."

Meredydd laughed. "Ah, but he also wants me to Tell another dream. . . . Perhaps I'll be very ill tomorrow and the next day and by the time we are past Cirke-dag, Aelder Wyth will have forgotten all about my punishment."

"Doubtful."

"Then perhaps I can manipulate his dreams so the next one he makes me interpret is less controversial."

Bevol looked at her awry. "That is more feasible," he said and then waved a long-fingered hand at her. "Go. Go on and do your assignment. I must not interfere with Aelder Wyth. We will pursue our studies tomorrow."

Chapter 2

The mind is beyond the senses and reason is beyond the mind. Reason is the essence of the mind. But beyond reason is the spirit of man, and beyond this is the Spirit of the Universe, the Evolver of all.

Its form is not in the field of vision: no one sees That with mortal eyes. That is seen by a pure heart and mind and thoughts. Those who know That attain life everlasting.

—The Corah, Book I, Verses 30, 31

Meredydd dreamed. She was walking to Nairne on a mild spring day when she heard thunder on every side. The ground trembled beneath her feet, and from behind a wind blew. She whirled to see a huge, black horse bearing down on her, stones and divots raining upward from its hooves. It was upon her before she could even feel fear and swept her up onto its hot, broad back. It carried her away to Lagan, where it disappeared, leaving her alone at the ruined homestead.

In a heartbeat, she was walking to Halig-liath, taking the high road along the palisades just east of Nairne when, once again, the beast appeared, thunder rolling from beneath its hooves and hot wind belching from its distended nostrils. Again, it swept her up and rode her to Lagan and left her there, alone.

In a breath, she was on Pilgrimage, taking a road to the Sea. She had reason to fear the mad mount now, but Osraed Bevol was at her side and she thought, "He will protect me from the beast." But when the horse thundered down upon them, even Osraed Bevol was powerless to stop it. It swept Meredydd up onto its steaming back and delivered her to Lagan. There, she sat before the ruined forge and sifted the dust of the yard through her fingers, searching for something. It was important, that something, but she could not remember what it was.

Waking, she wondered at the dream, trying to interpret it. It seemed to her, when she held it against her waking life, that it was meant to reinforce her resolve—to remind her that she could not really leave Lagan until she had divined the identities of those responsible for her parents' deaths and exacted revenge. If no means of revenge presented itself now, no matter; she was certain the appropriate method would be revealed when the time was right. She never asked herself if she would be able to follow through with her vengeance. Her rage was silent, but fierce; she would do what had to be done.

She kept all this from the Osraed Bevol, of course, for she knew, as any student of the spiritual knew, that forgiveness, rather than revenge, was the Balance. Forgiveness was beloved of God. Meredydd wanted, more than anything, to be beloved of God, but she could find in her no forgiveness for her parents' unknown murderers.

She did not discuss her dream with Osraed Bevol, but during breakfast his eyes kept coming to rest contemplatively on her face and she soon convinced herself that he knew of it. Silence made her nervous, half afraid she'd blurt out what she was thinking, feeling. Rather than do that she began to prattle about the paper she had stayed up late to write. Osraed Bevol merely ate his bisquits and fruit and continued to regard her studiously; Skeet became quickly bored and left the table.

When she had run out of things to say about the paper, the Osraed patted his mouth with a napkin and said, "Meredydd, get a bowl down from the cupboard, won't you, please?"

She afforded him a wide-eyed glance, then hurried to do as he asked.

When she stood beside him with the bowl, he said, "Now, fill it with water."

Hesitating only an instant, she fulfilled that request, pouring from the tap of the little reservoir in the corner of the kitchen.

Seeing that she had finished that task, he continued, "Now, set the bowl here"—he tapped the table before him—"and bring me some salt."

"Salt, Master?"

He nodded. "Salt."

She went into the pantry for that, emerging with a little jar of sea salt which she brought immediately to him.

"Put a handful of the salt into the water."

She did, then waited for the next instruction.

He smiled. "It's time to go to school, anwyl," he said and pushed back his chair and rose. "Put the salt away and we'll be off."

Meredydd eyed him dubiously, wondering if she was supposed to ask what she had just done or simply laugh. But he was already on his way out of the kitchen, humming to himself and patting his hands together rhythmically. With a backward glance at the bowl of water, she returned the salt to the pantry and followed him from the room.

Theology was her first class that morning—Osraed Ealad-hach presiding. The subject was the Regeneration of the Meri, an important theme at this time of year with Solstice coming on and Pilgrimages being planned.

It was a subject which never failed to engender heated debates. Ealad-hach was a Traditionalist—Tradists or Trads, in Prentice vernacular. His students considered his views to be particularly hoary and called him Scir-loc or "White Hair." Meredydd had always wondered why he taught theology when the special knowledge given him by the Meri was in the field of Earth Sciences. It had always seemed to her that Osraed Bevol had a shrewder understanding of the scripture. His gift of knowledge was broader, encompassing sciences of earth, sky and spirit as well as the arts of healing and divining.

As a Tradist, Osraed Ealad-hach held that the Meri was, by Her very nature, eternal and unchanging. The Book of the Meri clearly stated that She shared God's very nature, and so Her regeneration occurred through Her selection each generation of new Osraed—Divine Counselors—who, after receiving Her inspiration, would then dispense Her wisdom wherever needed.

There was, too, the figurative or symbolic regeneration which She afforded to the faithful believer. According to Ealad-hach's personal theology, it was irrational and unscientific to suppose that the Meri literally regenerated.

" 'The Spirit was the First Being,' " intoned the Osraed at the beginning of the discussion, " 'the Creator of all, the Guardian of the Universe. The Vision of the Spirit, the Mother of all wisdom, It gave in revelation to Its first-born, the Meri.' That, of course, is Chapter One, Verse One of The Book of the Meri. You all know it, have committed it to memory; no doubt, some of you whispered it with me." He smiled beatifically and tapped his reading lenses into the palm of one hand. "We know too, of course, that the First Being does not change Its skin—figuratively speaking—or evolve. It is above egress and regress, beyond change. And it stands to reason that the Meri, being the 'first-born,' of the First Being, is also above and beyond all physical phenomena."

This observation led one of the Prentices to ask, as he was expected to, why, then, the Meri *appeared* to regenerate. Why every generation, or thereabouts, changes were noted by the Prentices singled out by Her for the role of Divine Counselor.

"According to the Book of Pilgrimages," the boy remarked, "there have been changes in the color and radiance of Her . . . aspect and even in the color of Her eyes and the expression in them."

"Ah," said the Osraed Ealad-hach, and the assembled Prentices rolled their eyes in preparation for the coming lecture. "If you had read your history with attentiveness, you would have noticed that the aspect changes of the Meri are connected with upheavals here, in Caraid-land, most especially those involving the spiritual conditions of its people and rulers. For example, our histories tell us of a great war that had embroiled all of Caraid-land and her near neighbors. The Royal policy so enraged the Meri that She changed aspect in the darkest days of the war and sent forth a legion of storms that destroyed most of Cyne Earwyn's navy and that of his enemy, as well. At the same time that She lashed the Sea to rebellion against human arrogance, She unleashed upon the Royal House at Creiddylad a plague of Osraed all Telling a future that frightened the Cyne into finding a peaceful solution to the war.

"And then," he reminisced, as if he could remember it himself, "there was the year that Cyne Liusadhe ordered all practitioners of the Wicke expelled from Creiddylad. Those embittered females then spread across the countryside, leaving evil in their wake. No sooner had they left Creiddylad than that city was struck by a plague that killed by the hundreds. That year the Meri changed Her aspect and elected only one Prentice to be Osraed for many Seasons. It was five years before another Osraed was chosen. And then . . . " His eyes fell on Meredydd briefly. ". . . there was at least one occasion upon which a girl went from Halig-liath as Prentice."

Startled, Meredydd raised her eyes and met his in what she thought must be an audible collision. Old Scir-loc merely raised his brows and moved to stand behind his workbench.

"Begging pardon, Osraed Ealad-hach," said Lealbhallain tentatively, "but if the Meri is, as the Book says, a child of the First Being and Its Vision, then is not the Meri a creation?"

Ealad-hach turned and speared the young Prentice with a practiced and accurate eye. "The Meri is identical with the Creator."

"But, pardon again, sir—but I have heard it advanced by the Osraed Bevol that the Meri is both a creature and an instrument of creation. 'The Lover and the Beloved have become one in Thee,' " he quoted swiftly, practically tripping over the words in his haste to get them out. "He explained to me that it is Her spirit that is transcendent, but that Her body, being a physical phenomenon, must be subject to the Universal laws of integration and disintegration, and that—and that She—She . . ."

The look with which Osraed Ealad-hach fixed poor Lealbhallain had so intimidated him that he simply stopped speaking.

"It is the Osraed Bevol's *opinion* that the Meri's body is a physical phenomenon. It is not an opinion that *we* share. Do *you* share that opinion?"

Lealbhallain swallowed noisily, drawing a snicker from his confreres. "Well, sir, I . . . That is, it would explain . . . certain . . . things . . . sir. About the Meri, I mean."

"And do you deem it necessary that the Meri be explained? She is the Meri. Perhaps She need not be explained at all. Perhaps She is inexplicable."

Prentice Brys-a-Lach and his pet, Phelan Backstere, both hummed and nodded sagely, patting their fingers together in silent applause.

"Then why do we even discuss the subject?" asked Meredydd, before she could think better of it. "Why aren't we simply told, 'The Meri is as the Meri is,' and have an end to it? What good does it do to study something that will not permit study?"

Ealad-hach, a tall man, raised himself to his tallest and looked at Meredydd over one high ridge of cheek bone. "Are you being impertinent, Prentice Meredydd?"

"No, sir. I'm being frustrated. The Corah tells us we must seek out knowledge with open minds and that when the conscious spirit commands the mind, the mind can think all thoughts. *All* thoughts, not just two or three, not just thoughts of here and now, but of spiritual things. Thoughts of the Meri. Thoughts of the First Being."

"So, you think you can study your way into the Meri's good graces, do you? Recall, Prentice, what the Book of the Meri tells us on that score; Chapter Two, Verse 5: 'One does not reach the Meri through much learning. Nor is She reached through the intellect or religious teaching. She is reached only by those chosen. To Her chosen, the Meri reveals Her glory. On Her chosen She bestows Her kiss.' Her *chosen*, Prentice Meredydd, not the well-studied or the thoughtful or the hard-working."

"Yet," argued Meredydd, "Osraed Morfinn, in his 'Commentaries and Meditations,' says, 'If men thought of God as much as they think of the world, would not all attain liberation?' Is that a purely rhetorical question, then? Are we not intended to think of God; to think of the Meri and to strive for understanding? And in striving for understanding, must we not question our own beliefs to make certain they conform to the truth?"

Ealad-hach fiddled with the sleeve of his robe, winding a stray strand of thread around one finger. "What is your point, Prentice?"

"Merely that if the Meri is, indeed, our living Link

with the Creator, then the fullest knowledge of Her should be sought."

"If you will recall," said Osraed Ealad-hach, "this discussion began with the advancement of a theory, by Prentice Lealbhallain, that the Meri has a physical nature which is—how did he put it—subject to the physical laws of integration and disintegration. Do you support his theory?"

"I support no particular theory, Osraed. I have yet to be certain."

"You are of an age for Pilgrimage, Prentice. Don't you think it prudent to be certain of what you believe you will find at the end of the Journey before you get there?"

"I suppose—"

Ealad-hach pounced. "I think you must do better than suppose, Prentice. I think you had better be certain that it is not a merely physical creature you seek."

"I never suggested that She *is* merely physical. I simply shared my perceptions of the Corahtic references."

"Your theory, Prentice Meredydd, will appear on my desk tomorrow morning. I will meditate on it over Cirke-dag, while you meditate on the nature of the Being you claim to worship and adore—oh, and along with that, Chapter Twelve of the Book of the Meri."

Meredydd's cheeks flamed. "But Osraed! I advanced no theory, I—"

"No, you advanced careless, inconclusive thinking. It might serve you to recall another passage from the Book of the Meri. The one in which we are told that the Meri is not reachable by the careless. I want more than perceptions from you, cailin. I want conclusions!"

"Only if they match your own," Meredydd muttered.

"What?"

She blushed all the way to the roots of her hair. "Nothing, Osraed. Nothing."

"I thought," murmured Lealbhallain during a break

between sessions, "that you were being open-minded, not careless."

They stood in the circular concourse where the three great wings of Halig-liath's academy met, waiting for the Osraed Ealad-hach to vacate the classroom. It was cool there and the breeze was fanned by the passing of a myriad lively young bodies. Their laughter, talk and scuffling was carried upward into the shallow conical vault where it circled like an invisible but noisy flock of birds before fluttering out through the open casements.

Meredydd sighed, savoring the caress of air against her still flaming cheeks. "Thanks, Leal. I wish *you* were the Osraed. I'd have much better marks."

"What's the matter, then, *Prentice* Meredydd?" Brys-a-Lach appeared unexpectedly at her shoulder, making her jump. "Don't know how to handle old Scir-loc, of a sudden?" He grinned at his crony Phelan, who had materialized behind Lealbhallain.

"You shouldn't call him that, Brys. It's ... disrespectful."

"Eh?" said Brys, feigning deafness. "Eh? Wha's-at? What shouldn't I call him, cailin?"

"Scir-loc!" she whispered fiercely.

Brys made a comically horrifed face and glanced over her shoulder. She could hear Phelan wheezing frantically behind her. She turned, a scowl creasing her face, and saw old Scir-loc himself, barely a yard away and glaring at her. His bony face was red as a chicken's wattle and she could almost see him shaking in rage. He said nothing, but turned on his heel and disappeared into the Northern Wing.

Meredydd whirled on Brys. "You—you unscrupulous ... fish! How can you be so—so mean-spirited and still dare to call yourself a Prentice?"

"Oh, Meredydd!" Brys cooed. "Please abuse me further. It tickles my ears royal to hear you use such words for me. *Unscrupulous fish!* By the First Being, you make me quake! I dare call myself a Prentice because my father says I dare."

She started to coil herself for another attack, but saw Aelder Prentice Wyth entering the classroom just down the North Wing hall. "I don't want to be late for class," she said and shoved past him. Lealbhallain followed close behind.

Today Aelder Prentice Wyth chose to discuss the use of symbology in riddles. Riddles had always seemed to Meredydd an absurd way of imparting information, and she'd decided they were more of a mental game than any part of spiritual discipline. Osraed Bevol had never stressed them in his private tutoring, but she had always done reasonably well with them anyway.

Wyth began with that hoary old poser, "What has four legs in the morning, two legs at noon and three legs in the evening?" Everyone's hand went up except Meredydd's. She was exercising her mind in the excellent web supplied by the window-frame spider, climbing, sliding, swinging. It vibrated beneath her like ship's rigging in a stiff breeze, chanty-singing, strong and resilient.

"Did you hear me, Prentice Meredydd? Prentice Brys says you are daydreaming and not paying a bit of attention to me. Is this so?" Aelder Wyth stood nearly atop her.

Meredydd blinked. "No, sir," she lied before she could stop herself.

"Good. Then you will be able to tell me what enters a trap but is never caught."

She could hear the web whispering lightly from the window, a breeze brushing its silken fibers. She strained to hear what it said, then smiled up at Aelder Wyth. "The wind," she said. "The wind enters a trap but is never caught."

Aelder Wyth was not impressed. His long, angular face displayed a tight displeasure out of keeping with such a minor incident. "Remove that mocking grin from your face, cailin, and tell me the answer to this riddle: that which flies gives birth to that which does not fly; that which does not fly gives birth to that which flies."

It was all Meredydd could do not to roll her eyes. "The riddle describes the life cycle of a bird. The bird gives birth to an egg—which does not fly—and the egg, in turn, gives birth to another bird—which eventually flies."

Aelder Wyth walked about the room, then, calling out riddles to other students. They were simple ones for the most part, and only Phelan guessed wrongly what was always behind you, but which, turning, you never saw. (The answer, of course, was the back of your head, and Phelan should have known it, but he rarely paid any attention to anyone but his lord-god Brys, and very likely had missed Wyth's lecture on the Form and Logic of Riddles.)

It took the class a minute or two to twit Phelan adequately and Meredydd thought Wyth was finished with his puzzling, when he came up behind her and said, "I have a white house with no doors and windows."

Startled, she squeaked and said, "You have an egg!"

Brys echoed the squeal, then guffawed. Phelan giggled inanely and the other Prentices snickered. Aelder Wyth, for his part, speared Brys-a-Lach with his sharp, over-large eyes and said, "What can you beat without leaving a bruise?"

Brys grinned. "An egg."

The class was suddenly so quiet Meredydd could hear the spider web trying to trap the wind. Then she laughed, explosively and loudly, unable to withstand the mental image of Brys beating a defenseless egg to prove he could do so without bruising it.

"Silence!" demanded Wyth and the class complied, their eyes dancing between Meredydd and the red-faced Brys. "Will you share the joke with us, Prentice Meredydd?"

She choked back her laughter and tried to appear contrite. "It was only that Prentice Brys's poor egg would not only be bruised, it would be an omelette."

There was a prolonged wheezing sound like air escaping a bellows, then the boys burst into raucous laughter again. High up on Aelder Wyth's cheeks, two spots of bright color glared.

Meredydd drew an essay assignment. Brys got no reprimand at all. She felt scalded after that, and sat silently at her bench, huddled a little as if that might make Wyth forget she was there. She dreaded the Dream Tell session and prayed Wyth would run out of time and have to relinquish them for dinner. But he didn't. He got to Aislinn Interpretation with fifteen minutes to spare and immediately brought the entire class's attention back to Meredydd.

"Prentice Meredydd, did you do your reading assigment?"

"Yes, Aelder Prentice Wyth. I did." She did not, as she had meant to, mention that she had done it two years ago.

"And do you feel ready to interpret another aislinn?"

"Yes, Aelder Prentice Wyth." *Untrue,* she thought, *I'll never be ready.*

"Very well, here is the dream. Class, please take notes."

Ten bark pads came out of ten satchels. Ten writing sticks poised. Meredydd swallowed.

"To the wall," he ordered. She went.

"I dreamed," he said, making no game of it this time, "that I had set off to Nairne on Cirke-dag. On my way to worship, a great, black horse came and swept me away to . . . the House of Secret Pleasures in Lin-liath."

There was a murmur of amazement from the class and Meredydd, the figure of a horse half-drawn under her hand, froze.

Wyth's eyes grazed the murmurers' faces. There was immediate silence. "His eyes," he continued, "held fire and his hooves struck sparks from the earth. No sooner had he left me outside this ... place, than I was walking to Halig-liath. The same animal appeared and carried me again to Lin-liath. Then, I found myself on Pilgrimage, walking to the sea. I had just sighted the waves, when the same black beast took me back to that infamous House. I awoke. Tell me this aislinn."

Meredydd blinked at him, squeezing the bluestick so hard it snapped between her fingers. "I can't Tell the dream, Aelder Wyth."

"Oh? And why not?"

She was sweating now, cold, clammy sweat that clung to the middle of her back and made her scalp want to wriggle. "Because it's the same dream I had last night. Except for where the horse carried me, it was the same dream."

Aelder Wyth gaped at her. The other Prentices followed suit, looking like a nest of startled owls. Meredydd might have laughed under other circumstances, but under Wyth's incredulous, riveting stare, she could do nothing but gape back.

Wyth's mouth shriveled into a prunish-looking dent. "You're lying," he accused her. "You're only trying to shirk your assigned task. This dream is *mine* and you will interpret it!"

"Please, Aelder—"

"Obedience, Prentice Meredydd, is an attribute of the godly." He fixed her with the gimlet eyes of a ferret—so sharp, they prickled her face. She would interpret the dream, they said, or she would stand, forever, at the whitewall.

Obedience. Even to a bully like Wyth Arundel. Meredydd wondered when he had become such a tyrant and why. She wiped the bluestick's oily hue from her fingers and picked up one of the broken halves. Then she emptied her mind of all but the images in their dream.

"The horse," she began, "strong emotions, the passionate movement of life." She finished the horse symbol.

"Going to Cirke symbolizes the worshipful attitude, contemplation, devotion to God." She drew that symbol next to the horse.

"The horse sweeps the dreamer away from devotion, worship and contemplation to . . . to this House of Pleasure. This can only . . . I mean, this would seem to symbolize physical gratification, material distractions and the like. We see the horse"—she pointed to the first symbol—"also in conjunction with Halig-liath—the Holy Fortress—which symbolizes education, learning, scholarship, spiritual advancement." The symbol for Halig-liath appeared on the whitewall.

"The final major symbol in the aislinn is Pilgrimage." She drew the symbol beneath the one for Halig-liath.

"Pilgrimage is the summit of our goals. It represents the best in us. Our highest aspiration. The horse keeps the Pilgrim from reaching this ultimate goal. I would interpret this dream as either a fear expressed by the spirit or a warning issued by it, that the passions of life may intrude between the dreamer and his devotion, his worship, his spiritual education and, ultimately, the attainment of his highest goal. That they may carry him to physical excess rather than spiritual fulfillment."

Meredydd stopped speaking and waited, but Wyth, his eyes intent on the blue-on-white images, was silent. Brys-a-Lach was not.

"I think Meredydd is entirely off the path. Entirely. May I do a Tell, Aelder Prentice Wyth?"

Wyth glanced at him momentarily, then nodded.

Brys stood, thrusting himself upward into a shaft of sunlight which caught and held him as it fell from one of the many mullioned windows. In his fine, white tunic, he gleamed—a broad-shouldered, golden haired angel, an Eibhilin. The Sun worshiped him more beatifically than even Phelan could do.

"I believe," he said, voice deep and challenging, "the vision means practically the opposite of what Prentice Meredydd's analysis indicates. Note, carefully, that no matter how many times the horse carries the dreamer away from devotion, education, aspiration—and I am willing to acknowledge the correct interpretation of these images—he returns to his quest. If the horse takes him from Cirke, he returns to the higher path to Halig-liath. If it steals him from there, he takes yet a higher path—the one to the Meri, his ultimate goal.

"It is clear, therefore, that what the spirit is communicating to the dreamer is a tale of his own spiritual indomitability and persistence. He is so strong, he overcomes his passions and the swift course of physical life and returns to his spiritual pursuits."

Aelder Wyth pinned Meredydd to the whitewall with his dirk-sharp eyes. "What do you think of this analysis, Prentice Meredydd?"

She quailed, wishing she could make herself say, "Oh, it's obviously correct, sir. How stupid of me, sir, to think otherwise. Forget everything I said!" Unfortunately, she could not make herself say that, and so what came out instead was, "I think there is a slight chance it could be correct, but . . ."

"Yes?"

"It is the spiritual pursuits that are being interrupted by the passions, not the other way around, as Prentice Brys suggests. The dreamer ends his course at . . . at Lin-liath, not at Halig-liath."

Aelder Wyth continued to study her, his eyes hooded. "You said you also had this dream. Is this true?"

"I am not in the habit of lying, Aelder. I had this same dream last night, with one major difference."

"Yes. The place the horse delivered you. Where did the horse take *you*, Prentice Meredydd?"

She had his full attention, Meredydd knew—eyes, ears, senses—all were trained on her. The other Prentices might not have existed. Something of importance was happening here, but she was at a loss to understand what it was. A tension had seized her, tickling the back of her neck, making the hair stand on her arms. She rubbed at them.

"It took me to the ruins at Lagan."

Wyth nodded, pulling at his lower lip, staring at her, still. She realized that tiny lines radiated out from his eyes and creased the corners of his mouth and she wondered how they had come to be there when he was only eighteen.

When she thought she would scream at him to say something, he moved, turning away from her. She thought he seemed . . . sad. Then he spoke and she decided she must have imagined it.

"Your behavior is presumptuous; your interpretation spurious and . . . vicious. You may be seated." He waved in the general direction of her bench.

"Vicious!" she repeated, not moving from the whitewall. "How can it be vicious? You gave me a dream to Tell. I interpreted it as best I could. How is that vicious?"

"You knew the dream was mine."

"The dream was *mine*."

"You use it to make personal attacks—"

"You are being unfair! The object of the Tell is to gain wisdom and insight, not gratification. If you can't be fair-minded and detached from your aislinn, then you shouldn't give them up to be Told."

"I shouldn't?" His eyes narrowed.

"No," Meredydd continued, recklessly, "you shouldn't. It's not fair to me—to any of us. Why have you done this? Twice, now, you've given me your own dreams to interpret. Why? Why have you given them to *me*?"

Her voice rang shrilly in her ears, making her sound almost hysterical, making her cringe. Aelder Prentice Wyth retreated behind his workbench and took up his books.

"I can no longer tolerate having you in my class, Prentice Meredydd. I shall seek to have you transferred to another class for Aislinn Interpretation."

He left without a backward glance, leaving Meredydd standing, white-faced and shaking, before her peers. They ogled at her for a moment, then rose silently in ones and twos and headed for the Refectory for the midday meal. Only Lealbhallain stayed, waiting for her to move or speak.

Finally, she did. "Did I bring this on myself?"

Leal blinked his springleaf eyes. "No, Meredydd. You only did what was asked of you. And you did it honestly. I don't think your interpretation was at all spurious. And I didn't think you were grinning, either—especially not mockingly."

"Then what is wrong with me? I seem to be constantly in trouble. This year has been so difficult. Everyone treats me ... differently than they used to. Osraed Ealad-hach is impatient with me; Aelder Wyth acts like he hates me; the other Prentices look at me strangely and whisper like old fishermen."

"I don't do that," Lealbhallain assured her. "I don't do any of those things."

Meredydd smiled at him. "No, you don't. That's because you see me as a friend—a person—not as a girl. They all see me as a girl now—inferior. A lot of people don't think girls should be allowed to study the Divine Art."

Leal stood, seeming strangely unsteady. His chin came just to her shoulder, but he tried to lift himself a little at the heels so as to look at her more on a level. "It's a hard thing to challenge tradition, Meredydd. You're a rare person—a rare girl to have such talent."

She moved past him to her workbench, where she collected her satchel of books. There was cat-sparkle in her eyes when she turned back to look at him. "Am I? Am I that rare? Who's to say there aren't hundreds of girls hiding their talents beneath their aprons? Look, Leal, if girls are so rarely talented in the Art, why do we hear so often of some woman being charged as Wicke?"

Lealbhallain blanched. "Oh, but that's not the same thing, surely!"

"Isn't it?" She grimaced and made a dismissive gesture. "Well, that's as it may be. But why should it be such a strange thing for a female to be Osraed? The Meri is female."

"She's not a *human* female," remarked Leal.

Meredydd hung her satchel over one shoulder and turned to face him, hands on hips. "And so?"

Lealbhallain blinked and his mouth popped open. "It doesn't seem strange to me," he assured her after a moment of awkward silence. "I believe in you, Meredydd. I believe you will make the most wonderful Osraed ever."

She put a hand on his shoulder and let the fondness she felt for him show in her eyes. "How lucky I am to have such a loyal friend. Thank you, Leal."

He quivered strangely beneath her hand, like a fawn she had once petted. His eyes held the same innocent panic. She laughed and patted the shoulder.

"You need to eat," she told him and steered him toward the door.

They left the classroom and went back up the long flagged corridor to the concourse. From there they wound down a flight of steps to the high, wall-hugging gallery from which the Osraed watched their morning exercises, and along it to the broad staircase that led down to Halig-liath's courtyard. The courtyard was robed magnificently in sunlight. Each cobble gleamed warmly, welcoming the pliant feet of Prentices to their ageless, baked surfaces. As they descended, Meredydd let the warmth in through her eyes and tried to put aside the sense of helplessness that paced in tiny circles within her breast.

After their meal, they would have Osraed Bevol for their lessons on the heart and soul of the Art—the laying on of inyx and the Weaving of Runes. It was Bevol who taught them the discipline of meditation and the spirit of prayer. Who taught them how to use the tools of their craft—crystals, herbs, vapors, aromatic incense—to focus their faculties. It was Bevol who would lay her helplessness and frustration to rest.

The thought of her guardian made her feel immeasurably better and she was about to turn to Lealbhallain with a light comment, when she heard the whispers.

"She . . . Wicke . . . something to Wyth." A soft chuckle followed, oozing up from the hollow beneath the stone steps.

She knew, somehow, that she was the Wicke of the discussion, knew, too, that she should hurry on, get to the Refectory where rumors that she had called the Osraed Ealad-hach "Scir-loc" and had enraged Aelder Wyth so much he had expelled her from his class would cause all heads to turn and all eyes to stare.

She suddenly had no desire for food. She slowed and softened her steps and strayed toward the stone balustrade. Beside her, Lealbhallain glanced warily about.

". . . wager it's not a House of Pleasure that subtle and crafty horse takes him to," said Phelan's voice, high and reedy. "I wager it's *her* house."

"Tha's where my horse'd take me," mumbled someone else.

"Mine would follow her to that blasted ruin of hers. The grass there is hip tall and the earth is soft and warm and sweet with the perfume of flowers." It was Brys's voice, low, musical, suggestive of things Meredydd understood only instinctively. It tickled her spine, but not pleasantly.

"That's not all at Lagan that's soft and warm and sweet," said Phelan, and she could hear the sly grin in his voice. "Ho-ney-suck-le." He chuckled, but it cracked and turned to a squeaky giggle.

"She goes there, you know," said Brys.

"Everyone *knows* tha'," said the third boy. "She goes Cirke-dag in the month, ye know. The month they're killed."

"On Cirke-dag," repeated Brys. "I could follow her. I wonder if I did . . ."

"You wonder what?" asked Phelan.

"G'on," urged the other. "*Say* it."

"I should be ashamed," sighed Brys.

"You should, but say it anyway."

"I just wondered if I could get her to lie down in that deep grass on that warm earth and . . ."

"Aw, come *on!*"

"And show me what makes her tunic—" There was silence, then a wild trio of giggles, gasps and guffaws.

"She do billow mysterious!" wheezed the mumbler.

Meredydd's face blazed, hot and red. Not even daring to glance at Leal, she fled down the steps and across the square to the Refectory, knowing she would now find the prying gazes there a cooling comfort and wishing fervently that Brys would forget how to use his tongue.

"I will speak to Aelder Prentice Wyth, if you like." The Osraed Bevol studied Meredydd's troubled face with patient eyes.

She shook her head and scuffed the toe of her sturdy leather shoe through the pathside grass. "If anyone speaks to him, it should be me."

"There are those who will say this is proof young women should not be given the Divine Education. Especially not alongside young, impressionable men."

Meredydd glanced up at him, her eyes bright. "Is it my fault my body has *billowed* in this fashion that Brys and his cronies find so amusing? Is it my fault, when the First Being has written it into my physical nature?"

The Osraed smiled. "No," he said, "not your fault. But many would say it is your limitation, your weakness."

She opened her mouth to say she had no limitations, but blushed, realizing that was untrue. "How is it *my* weakness when it affects *them*?" She shook her head. "My limitations have nothing to do with the shape of my body."

"No? What have they to do with, then?"

She had to think about that. She thought about the dream, about how she had translated it for Aelder Wyth. They had gone several yards along the ridge toward home before she answered his question. "Passions," she said. "Attachments."

"Ah. And what are these passions of yours, Meredydd? Are you also curious about the shape of Brys's garments?"

She was appalled and then amused. Accordingly, she blushed, then laughed, then went silent. "You know, Osraed, better than anyone, what I am passionate about. It makes me wonder . . ."

"Wonder what?"

"If I interpreted the aislinn properly. Perhaps it doesn't mean the same thing for Wyth that it does for me. After all, our spirits may not speak at all the same symbolic language."

Bevol's brow wrinkled. "An Osraed cannot go about interpreting aislinn with attachment. Purity of heart and mind is necessary to the Art, but difficult to bring to it. This is why the Meri chooses so few to serve Her."

"She didn't choose Wyth. Why did She not?"

"Only She knows the answer to that ... and perhaps, Wyth, himself. Perhaps this dream reveals much about him. But, it is really not your affair. Wyth fulfills his role at Halig-liath. He imparts his knowledge to the younger Prentices. He is eligible for Pilgrimage again this year at Solstice. He is already scheduled to go in the last week of the Season. And perhaps the Meri will choose him this time."

Meredydd nodded, feeling a sudden, almost fond pity for the Aelder Prentice. He had been a good teacher for the last two years, and she had to allow he'd taught her much about the forms and intricacies of the Dream Tell and the symbolic language of the human spirit. It must be only his own sense of inadequacy, she told herself, that made him occasionally surly. She could well imagine what it would feel like to be passed over for the station of Divine Counselor when you had spent your entire life in pursuit of that goal. And, a cold voice within told her, *it is something you may come to know firsthand.*

"If Her servants won't accept a female as Osraed," she asked Bevol, "will the Meri?"

"The Meri isn't human, Meredydd. She is another order of creation altogether. She is as perfect a Being as can inhabit any form of flesh, even Eibhilin flesh."

Meredydd looked at him, eyes pleading. "You know the futures, Master. Will I see her?"

"You know I cannot answer that. Let me answer something else instead. It is a glorious afternoon. Let us have our lesson here on the way home, eh?" He glanced at her aslant, his eyes robin's-egg bright and sparkling. *Come away from that path,* they said.

She sighed. "Yes. That would be nice. What are we studying today?"

"What is most worthy of study?"

"The First Being."

"Do you really believe this?"

Meredydd stared at him, then glanced away, her

eyes skittering ahead down the path. What a question!
Did she believe—? She thought. It was a good question, espcially in view of the lines her life had followed. She could have become bitter about her
parents; bitter and angry with any God who could let
them be extinguished while she was left behind alone.
Well, not alone, certainly. She glanced at Bevol again.
He was still watching her.

"All my life I have been taught to believe there is
a Spirit in the Universe," she said.

"That is no answer."

"No." She walked on, letting her gaze ripple over
land and sky, grass and tree, earth and cloud. "Yes. I
believe. But I feel sometimes at a loss to understand
exactly What it is I believe in. It is difficult to know
Something so subtle. It's not like knowing another
person."

"Isn't it? Do you fancy that you know all there is
to know about me, anwyl? Do you know the essence
of Bevol?"

She blushed. "Of course not. But envisioning the
invisible . . ."

"Takes more than good eyesight. It takes all the
physical senses, tuned to their purest pitch. And it
takes more. It takes senses that are just as subtle as
that which they must be trained to sense. Do you
recall this verse? 'When the conscious spirit commands the eye, the eye can see all forms. When the
conscious spirit commands the ear, the ear can hear
all sounds. When the conscious spirit commands the
tongue, the tongue can savor all tastes. When the conscious spirit commands the mind—' "

"The mind can think all thoughts," Meredydd finished with him. "Corah, Book One, verse Twenty. But
how does the conscious spirit know of the existence
of the Spirit of the Universe when It cannot be seen?"

Osraed Bevol stopped in the middle of the sloping
path and pointed off to the side. "Bring me a pine
cone from that tree."

There were only the dried and brittle husks of cones lying about the foot of the tree so Meredydd ducked beneath the low-hanging boughs and plucked a fresh one from the first cluster she could reach. She returned to the path and held the golden little cone out to him.

"Break it."

She hesitated only a moment, then easily crushed the little thing in her hands, exposing its interior. She looked to Bevol for comment.

"What do you see in it?"

"Very small nuts, Master. Pine kernels."

"Break one of them, anwyl."

She did that, biting with her fingernails into the tough, pulpy husk, splitting the pine nut in twain.

"What do you see in it?" asked Bevol.

"Nothing at all, Master."

"Anwyl, from that unseen essence of the seed that you hold in your fingers comes this tall pine tree. Do you see that essence?"

"No, Master."

"But you know it is there."

"Yes. I can see that it must be there, because the tree is the evident result of it."

"Believe, anwyl, that such a subtle and invisible essence is the Spirit of the Universe. That is Reality. That is what men of religion call God—the First Being from which grew this all." His arms made a sweeping, all-encompassing azure gesture. "The essence of the tree finds expression in the tree. The Unseen finds expression in the visible Universe." He studied her a moment then said, "Home, now. Your old Scir-loc is hungry."

Meredydd gasped, knowing he had heard the rumors. "I didn't call him that! Brys-a-Lach tricked me into saying it because he knew Osraed Ealad-hach was standing right behind me."

Bevol chuckled. "And told me all about it." The chuckle easily became a laugh. "Ah, such an impertinent, impudent Prentice I have raised. I am a discredit to my station."

"He didn't say *that*! Oh, Master, I am so sorry!"

"What have you to be sorry about? You didn't do anything to apologize for except allow Brys to vex you . . . twice in one day. You allowed him to distract you, anwyl. I saw the way you were in class this afternoon. You heard half of what I said, you mixed your powders poorly, you mumbled your inyx and you forgot half the words to a duan you had memorized a month ago."

Meredydd now mumbled an apology for all of that, feeling his eyes on her, only half-filled with humor.

"Master," she said, when they were winding down the wooded slope behind Gled Manor, "Last night I joked about manipulating Wyth's dreams. I have to allow, I did think of it half-seriously. Did I do that? Did I put that dream into Wyth's head?"

Bevol made a wry mouth. "What do you think?"

"I don't know. Perhaps dreams float above us in a great pool and we merely reach up and take them out. Perhaps we both selected the same dream."

Bevol nodded, his eyes now on the gate to their large back garden. "Perhaps you did," he said.

When they came through the back door into the kitchen, Skeet was waiting for them with a bowl of water clutched in his hands and a sour expression on his face.

"What is this?" he asked, sloshing the water at them. "Why is it left here where poor Skeet can get into it?"

The Osraed Bevol's white brows fluttered to perch beneath his broad-brimmed hat. "Why, whatever is ailing 'poor Skeet'?"

"I find this bowl of water and take a sip and—gack!—it's all salt, it is!"

Bevol turned to Meredydd. "Do you see salt in that water, anwyl?"

She put down her satchel of books and took the

bowl from Skeet's hands, glancing into it. "No, Master. I see no salt."

"But didn't you put salt into the bowl only this morning?"

She smiled. "Yes."

"Well then, perhaps you should take it out again."

The smile deepened. "But I can't, Master. It's dissolved into the water. I can't even see it."

"I can surely taste it," Skeet interjected.

"Can you taste it, Meredydd?" asked Bevol.

She touched her fingertip to the water, then put it into her mouth. She nodded, grimacing. "Yes, very much so."

"It is salty?"

"Yes."

"And what do you see?"

"I see only water."

The Osraed Bevol nodded. "And is the reality that there is only water in that bowl?"

"The illusion is that there is only water. The reality is that there is salt in the water; salt that cannot be seen but which can certainly be tasted." She glanced at Skeet, but quickly turned away again so as not to laugh and wound his immense pride.

Osraed Bevol chuckled and slapped Skeet resoundingly on the back. "When one brings the right senses to bear, anwyl, one can taste a good many subtleties in life."

Chapter 3

If you seek the brave, look to those who forgive.
If you seek the heroic, look to those who can return
love for hatred.

—The Corah, Book II, Verses 50, 51

The next day at Halig-liath was torture for Mere-dydd. It seemed to her that there was no one who did not stare at her—no one who did not smirk or whisper or snicker when she walked the halls. Osraed Ealad-hach said nothing of that embarrassing scene in the concourse, but he was more acid than usual. Her new Dream Tell instructor, the young Osraed Ladmann, treated her coolly—virtually ignoring her in class—and no one but Lealhallain seemed to be inclined to talk to her. Even Osraed Bevol seemed odd during the afternoon Craft class. He was too quiet, his eyes lacked their usual waggish glint and he, like everyone else, seemed to be watching her.

And then there were the whispers. She told herself she wasn't going to let herself overhear them this time, that she was going to walk straight past the doorway they issued from without listening. But, of course, that was impossible.

"Naw, Brys ain't here today. That Meredydd, she's a' fault."

That was yesterday's mumbler. She could see him now, reflected in the polished, faceted panes of the classroom door, surrounded by a group of five other boys. Scandy-a-Caol was his name—son of Nairne's newest and most prosperous collier. Though raised up-country in the town of Eada, he was late of the Cyne's capital, Creiddylad, which the histories called "Jewel of the Sea," and he rarely let any of his classmates forget that he had lived in such a superior place in terms of size, population and culture. All had heard about the grandeur of their former home—a house that even required the attentions of an actual *servant*.

Meredydd had no doubt that when he went down-coast to visit his mother's family there, he regaled them with tales of Caraid-land's spiritual center and used his tuition at Halig-liath to impress. Scandy was, above all else, a tale-bearer, and just now he was bear-ing the Tale of Meredydd, Wicke of Gled Manor.

"How do you figure?" asked one of his current audience.

Scandy squinted up one eye and leaned into the group. "She threw an inyx on him, sure as water's wet."

"Go ride a pig!" protested someone. "What ails him?"

"It's his tongue, it is. All numb-like. His throat makes sounds, but his tongue just flops between his teeth like a dying fish. He can't use it for naught."

The audience was impressed. They made apprecia-tive noises and vowed not to do anything to anger Meredydd-a-Lagan.

"Aye, that Meredydd be Wicke, sure as Colfre is Cyne," said Scandy awfully, and Meredydd, chilled to the bone, fled to her class.

She had thought it. She remembered thinking it—a stray thought, only: *May you forget how to use your tongue, Brys-a-Lach*. Just that. But if she had really done this thing, how did she now go about undoing it?

She was almost physically ill when the day was over, her stomach tied in a myriad knots. Her one consolation was that she no longer had to do Aelder Prentice Wyth's last reading assignment. It was small consolation when she felt her life was suddenly out of her control—as if all the progress she had made at Haligliath, her reputation as a good student and conscientious Prentice—all was being undone in a matter of days. She had always had good marks, her teachers had liked her, thought her precocious and bright. Until now. Now, she began to wonder if she would even pass Osraed approval for Pilgrimage.

She was in her Medicaments class when Osraed Calach came with a summons. She was to come with him immediately. She knew what that meant—an appearance before the Academy Council. Fear wound its coils around her heart. Dear God, would they really accuse her of practicing Wicke, of casting inyx on Brys?

Fending off the prying eyes of her classmates, she tried, with her own, to grasp the Osraed Calach's and seize his thoughts. But he would not look at her. He escorted her, silently, down the near-empty corridors toward the concourse.

When she could no longer stand the nerve-twisting whisper of their feet, the solemn flutter of his robes, she asked, "What have I done?"

He glanced at her then, and she thought she saw a spark of sympathy before he snatched his eyes away. "Perhaps you have done nothing, if you must ask," he said.

They traversed the long, broad central gallery with its upswept arches and came, at last, to the Osraed's Council Chamber. Inside, Osraed Bevol awaited her, seated at a long, polished table of heavy, dark reddish wood. Seated beside him was the Osraed Ealad-hach, while a woman she recognized but couldn't name sat in a high-backed chair at one end of the council table. That the woman disliked her, she was immediately aware. Dark eyes hurled darts of venom at her from beneath a hat made up of rich folds of colorful cloth.

Calach led Meredydd to the center of the chamber and left her there, facing the long table. He went swiftly to his own seat beside the other two Osraed.

Meredydd stood, mute, before them. A patina of lucent color from the tall stained-crystal windows spread itself over her like a web of light, pinning her to the floor. She brought herself stubbornly upright, forcing her head up and shoulders back. She would not quail. She had done nothing wrong. Leal would swear she had not called the Osraed Ealad-hach "Scirloc," that she had done nothing intentional to rag Aelder Prentice Wyth. She would simply deny that she had done anything to make Brys-a-Lach lose his voice.

The silence continued, eating its way into her resolve. She felt sweat trickle slowly down her back. Still, no one spoke; the woman in the rainbow hat poked at her with angry glances. Ealad-hach was the only one of the three Osraed who would look at her and his gaze did nothing to promote ease. Calach was fidgeting with his sleeves and her own Master, Bevol, was evidently immersed in meditation.

I will scream, she thought. *I will demand to know why I am here. I will cry. I will run. I will hide.*

The silent scrutiny ended suddenly when the Osraed Bevol sighed audibly and said, "Please, brothers, what are we waiting for? Aelder Prentice Wyth will be in class for several minutes yet and we're serving no one by sitting here behaving as if Meredydd did not exist. My Prentice should know why her studies have been interrupted."

Ealad-hach's eyes skittered sideways to the woman in the high-backed chair. "Very well, I will explain to Prentice Meredydd the circumstances which caused her to be summoned here." He moved his eyes to her—rigid, icy. "You are accused, cailin, of attempting to seduce Aelder Prentice Wyth, ostensibly to procure higher marks from him."

Seduce! Meredydd was not even sure she understood what the word meant. Cold to the core, all she could do was stare at the Osraed through the veil of calico dust motes that swelled around her and attempt to move lips, tongue and diaphragm all at once. It was difficult, but she did just manage to whisper, "I don't understand."

"Listen to her!" cried the seated woman. "Listen to her voice! It's the voice of a siren! Have you any doubt?"

Meredydd turned her startled gaze to the woman's lurid face and recoiled from the hatred displayed there.

"Please—" began the Osraed Bevol, but Ealad-hach cut him off.

"How do you answer this accusation, cailin?"

Meredydd swung back to face him. "I answer that I don't understand the charge, Osraed. What am I supposed to have done?"

"Liar!" cried the woman. "You know what you've done! You have distracted my son from his spiritual pursuits, shattered his meditation." She stood and faced the panel of Osraed. "Wyth was to be eligible for Pilgrimage this Solstice. This is his last chance at that—his last chance to see the Meri and pass Her approval. This creature threatens his hope of ever becoming Osraed."

"I threaten no one!" protested Meredydd. She turned beseeching eyes on her own Master. "Please, Master! I've done nothing wrong! I thought Aelder Prentice Wyth despised me!"

Ealad-hach cut her off with a scathing glare. "You will allow Moireach Arundel to state her complaint, Prentice Meredydd, and you will not interrupt her."

Meredydd fell silent, lowering her face into the shadow of her hair, trying to hide her fear and outrage.

"A moment," said the Osraed Bevol, quietly. "Moireach Arundel, on what do you base your complaint against my Prentice?"

"On *what*? On my son's behavior—distracted, morose. He writes her name in his journals, he dreams her dreams—or so he tells me. He's been arriving home late these past weeks, telling me this or that at Halig-liath has held him. But it's not Halig-liath that holds him, Osraed. It is *that* wanton. He's been following her home. Standing in the grove before Gled Manor, waiting to see her in the window where she studies, waiting for her to come out."

Bevol's eyes, narrowed, picked at her. "Who told you this, Moireach Arundel?"

"I've heard the talk in Nairne—the talk the boys bring home with them. It much excites them, little as they understand the danger in it."

"And Wyth told you about the dream?"

"Yes. I asked him what it meant; he wouldn't answer me. He could see how it had distressed me. But I *know*, Osraed Bevol. I *know* what it means. It means *she* has bewitched him." Her finger pointed, graceful, arrogant in ringstone dazzle.

Meredydd raised her eyes to Moireach Arundel's face then—met her eye to eye through the shaft of swirling motes—golden, blue, crimson. Hatred flashed there, brighter than the gems on her fingers. A hatred Meredydd was suddenly convinced was born of fear.

"Is this what happens when tradition is shattered?" asked the Osraed Ealad-hach rhetorically. "The Art is strong, carried on by men of honor and purity of purpose. But when a girl appears within these sanctified walls . . ." He glanced askew at Bevol.

"History should have warned you, brother. A female is not fit for the Divine Art, not fit to tread the Path to the Sea. Thoughts of earth and fire boil in their breasts and cloud their minds. Water, Bevol, water is pure until it comes in contact with earth or fire. Then it is sullied or boils away."

"It seems to me," said Bevol mildly, "that Meredydd is not the one whose mind is clouded. If Aelder Wyth has reacted to her in this way, how is it her fault?"

"She is fire!" protested Ealad-hach. "And like fire, she burns, bright and fair and fetching. The fire enchants the moths; the moths are enticed to their own destruction."

Bevol shrugged, the corners of his mouth turning upward. "And is that the fault of the flame? The intelligent man uses flame as a light to guide his footsteps, as a beacon to call the lost to safety, as a spark with which to start his fire and warm his soul."

Calach nodded, pursing his full lips. But Ealad-hach ignored the remark.

"Perhaps, brother, if you remove this cailin from Halig-liath now, history will not repeat itself."

The words drew Meredydd even as they chilled her. What had history to do with her and in what way was she repeating it? The remark brought to mind something Ealad-hach had said in class about a cailin going as a Prentice from Halig-liath. Curiosity pushing her fear aside, she might even have asked, but the door behind her opened and light from the outer hall fanned across the gleaming floor. Meredydd felt the coursing of dread up her spine and knew the latecomer was Wyth.

He approached slowly, quietly, treading upon the polished stone as if it was as slippery as it only looked, circling wide to Meredydd's right—away from his mother. He bowed respectfully to the Osraed.

"Mother," he said, almost whispering the word. "Mother, what are you doing here?"

Moireach Arundel glanced from her son to the Osraed Ealad-hach. "I am here to see that you become an Osraed instead of a fool. Here is my son, Osraed Ealad-hach. Ask him if what I've said is not true."

"You mother charges that Prentice Meredydd is distracting you from your calling," said the Osraed. "That you are . . . enamored of her. Is this true?"

Aelder Prentice Wyth's face was the color of a hen's egg and gleamed damply in the broad shaft of dappled light he shared with Meredydd. "I . . ." he said, then his mouth worked for a moment in silence. He glanced wildly at her out of the corner of his eye, then dropped his gaze to the floor between his feet. "I'm . . ." He stopped, took a deep breath and tried again. "My feelings for—that is, my feelings about the Prentice are . . . very strong. I don't know if enamored—"

"You see!" said Moireach Arundel. "See how he stumbles and stutters? She has clearly bewitched him."

"What?" Wyth looked so startled, Meredydd nearly laughed aloud—might have if she was not grimly aware of where she was and why.

"Your mother charges, specifically, that Prentice Meredydd has attempted to seduce you with an eye on higher marks in your class. That you, only yesterday, expelled her from your class—" Ealad-hach sent Moireach Arundel a significant glance. "—would seem to support the idea that the cailin's presence . . . disturbs you."

"No! No, it's not true!"

"She does not disturb you?"

"She does, but—" He shifted nervously from one foot to the other. "But it's not *that*. She's *never* tried to—to seduce me. Please, believe that. I—" He turned his face toward the accused, causing a banner of red light to fall across it. "She has done nothing."

"Then you deny that you are attracted to her?" asked Calach.

Moireach Arundel rose. "My son is accused of naught. He is not on trial here."

"Moireach, no one is on trial here," said the Osraed Bevol. "We merely wish to ascertain if there has been any breach of religious covenant or Academy regulations."

"Practicing Wicke is a breach of religious covenant, is it not?"

"There has been no proof that Wicke has been practiced by either of these young people. Your son contests that there has been any wrong done."

Moireach Arundel pointed at Meredydd. "She is a thief. She steals my son's life. That is the wrong she has done."

"No, mother! No. I. *I* have done wrong." Wyth turned his face to the three Osraed behind their table. "I have abused my position as an Aelder at this Academy and I have abused Prentice Meredydd—humiliating her when I could, censuring her when I could not. I would have been pleased if she had tried to seduce me, but she didn't."

Meredydd gaped at him, not believing, for one moment, what she was hearing. His mother made a strangled mewing sound and Ealad-hach cleared his throat.

"Then you do admit," he said, "that she has distracted you from your pursuit of the spiritual. That her presence has interfered with your preparations for Pilgrimage."

"My passions have interfered with my pursuits, Osraed Ealad-hach." He glanced warily at Meredydd then. "She tried to warn me. I didn't want to hear it, so I ejected her from my Dream Tell class. She only told the truth."

"Ah!" exclaimed Moireach Arundel. "But she spoke to him in dreams. Surely that is Wicke."

"It is also a facet of the Divine Art, Moireach," said Calach mildly.

"It was my dream," said Wyth. "I gave it to her to interpret. It was stupid of me, I realize. She could hardly interpret it any other way but what she did. It wasn't . . . flattering and I was angered and ashamed. It was I who misbehaved, not Meredydd."

Meredydd glanced at the Osraed. Ealad-hach was frowning and seemed uncertain, Calach was looking bemused and Bevol was smiling. Cheered, Meredydd smiled, too.

Moireach Arundel shrieked. "Smug, vile creature! My son is ruined and she grins like a glutted cat!"

"Your son is hardly ruined, Moireach," said Bevol reasonably. "In view of the circumstances, he has acted with honesty and courage to admit so much. I think perhaps, he should apologize for abusing his authority as an Aelder and apologize to Meredydd, as well, for whatever he feels merits apology."

Moireach Arundel was livid. "Apologize? To *her*?"

Wyth ignored her. "I am sorry, Osraed. I accept your punishment—whatever it might be."

"We will have to consult," said Calach, glancing at his fellows.

"And what about her?" asked Moireach Arundel, waving a hand at Meredydd. "She is not guiltless."

"Yes, she is," said Wyth. "She has never encouraged me."

"Her very presence encourages you! It isn't natural, Osraed, for young men to hold such intimacy with the cailin. Especially not here, not in such a holy place. Halig-liath is sacred ground, intended for sacred pursuits, not earthly ones. Having her here encourages the pursuit of the flesh. The boys strive to catch her wanton eye rather than the eye of God; they seek her grace, not the grace of the Meri. She should be removed."

"That is for us to decide, Moireach Arundel," said Calach. "But we shall take your words under advisement." He made a graceful gesture that pointed her to the door and she left in a sweep of burgundy robes.

"Aelder Prentice Wyth," said Osraed Calach, "there have been rumors of your behavior with regard to Prentice Meredydd. Not all of which have reached your mother's ears, I think. The rumors hint at a certain attachment to her person. Perhaps you should contemplate whether the goal of this attachment is an honorable one."

The red blaze down Wyth's elongated face deepened to crimson. "Yes, Osraed," he mumbled.

"We must consult," said Ealad-hach. "You are both excused."

Meredydd fled the chamber as if a horde of snapping beasts had risen out of the floor in pursuit. She thought Wyth might have called to her, but she didn't stop. Home she ran, burning up her humiliation before it burned her up.

"You must remove her, Bevol," said Ealad-hach. He no longer sat, but paced the chamber, rubbing his hands as if the aged joints contained premonitions of inclement weather.

"Why? Because one Prentice has fallen in love with her? She is a lovable girl, Ealad."

"That she is a girl is precisely the problem. She shouldn't be here at all. She doesn't belong here."

"Nonsense. Her natural talents alone make her a candidate for Osraedhood. Why else do you think I enrolled her at Halig-liath?"

"Ah, to raise my ire. You have always been a changer-up, Bevol."

"And you have always been a Trad—don't look so shocked at me, you old Scir-loc. Yes, and you deserve that appellation, too, by the Stone. The Cyne may be set before it, but you, old fellow, are set *in* it. And in your ways."

Ealad-hach bristled, notwithstanding the criticism was delivered with wry humor. "Someone has got to be set here, Bevol, for you are like the wind."

"It is my namesake."

"More's the pity. You blow this way and that and fail to see the danger in this situation. Your girl is talented, aye. I've seen that. But if you meant to do her a favor by encouraging her, you've erred grievously. If one of my daughters had shown such a nature, I'd have schooled her in how to tame it. For what is praiseworthy in a man is sinful in a woman."

"Tradist nonsense," observed Bevol.

"A rational view of the Scripture," countered Ealad-hach. "The Scripture does not once refer to the Prentice as 'she.' "

" 'He' is merely the common pronoun. Would you rather the Prentice be refered to as 'it'?"

Ealad-hach pointed a long finger at Bevol. "This is not a humorous matter, brother. Your girl is drawing censure from every quarter. The Moireach Arundel is not the only parent who has expressed displeasure at Meredydd's presence here."

"And are we to be swayed by public opinion, then?" Osraed Calach, who had been watching the verbal duel in total silence, finally spoke up. "I had rather thought we were intended to shape it."

Bevol nodded. "Your scriptural argument was much better."

"Then I shall return to it. There is no scripture that makes a place for a woman in the Art."

"And there is no scripture that denies her one."

"Brother, a man with the Art is Osraed. A woman with the art is Wicke. It is as clear as that. Our histories show the evil that comes of allowing cailin to pursue those talents which, I grant you, they may perversely display from time to time. When the Wicke were driven from Creiddylad in the reign of Liusadhe, their wickedness, when set loose in the land, drove the Sea to a boil and the Meri to a change of aspect. Because of those embittered women, entire villages were lost to the waves and Creiddylad was swept by plague."

"If you choose to interpret it that way . . ."

"In what other way can it be interpreted?" demanded Ealad-hach.

Bevol shrugged. "Perhaps the Meri was enraged with Cyne Liusadhe for expelling the Wicke in the first place and the plague occurred because they weren't there to stop it."

Ealad-hach fixed him with a baleful glare. "You

come so close to blasphemy at times, Bevol, I wonder you ever became Osraed."

"And you come so close to stagnation at times, I wonder you continue to be ambulatory. Meredydd stays."

"She will cost us, Bevol."

"She stays."

"She is Wicke, Bevol. You know it."

"She is a cailin. Sweetly rebellious, intelligent and strong. She has a good heart. She would make a splendid Osraed. You," he added, pointing at Ealad-hach's razor beak, "should be thankful we have her here at Halig-liath."

Frustrated, Ealad-hach turned to Calach. "What do you think? Do you side with me or with Bevol?"

Calach's pale brows crept beneath his fringe of straight colorless hair. "I don't side with either of you. For the sake of Meredydd I would like to see her stay. Her tenure here will not be long; she's of an age for Pilgrimage and she certainly passes on her marks. For the sake of Halig-liath . . . I would like to see this all laid to rest . . . amicably."

Ealad-hach glared at Bevol. "She must go."

Bevol merely studied him, wide-eyed. Then his eyes traveled around the room, stopping here or there as if distracted by a glint of light or a flash of color. "Well," he said, finally, "there is one way for her to leave that I might agree with."

"And that is?"

"Let her go on Pilgrimage at the Solstice."

Ealad-hach ogled at him. "Have you so little love for your Prentice? You must realize what will happen to her."

"Yes, she could see the Meri."

"As Taminy-a-Cuinn saw the Meri? Do you wish her to share that unfortunate's fate?"

Bevol smiled and smoothed his beard. "What do you know of Taminy-a-Cuinn's fate? Only what you've read. Only what you've interpreted—just as you interpreted the tale of Cyne Liusadhe's unhappy Wicke."

"I did *not* interpret!"

"No, of course not. Come, Ealad, surely you see that the easiest way to settle this dispute is to send Meredydd on Pilgrimage."

"Sacrilege."

"Sense. Surely the best judge of what the Meri wants in an Osraed is the Meri, Herself."

Ealad-hach paused in his pacing and favored his brother with a dour stare. Calach glanced back and forth between them, eyes narrowed, speculatively.

Finally, Ealad-hach nodded—once and curtly. Then he left the chamber in a swirl of green robes. Bevol, looking after him, smiled. So did Calach.

"Scoundrel," he said, and left the room by another door.

Meredydd came down from her room to help Skeet prepare dinner. He didn't ask why she had come home so early, or why she had run up the stairs as if daemons were in pursuit or why he had heard her crying. Skeet did not pry. But he did listen. When Osraed Bevol came home some time later and took Meredydd aside into the parlor, he hunkered on the staircase just beyond the door and pricked his ears. The information that went in to those ears would never find its way out, but it served his understanding.

"They want to dismiss me from Halig-liath, don't they?" asked Meredydd. She turned it into a statement, feeling somehow that if she said it first, it would hurt less.

Bevol's brows climbed. "They? 'They' are Ealad-hach, Calach and myself at this juncture. This is not yet a matter for the Cyne's Council."

He was teasing her, making the situation seem less threatening than she felt it. She tried to smile by way of thanks, but it was a weak effort.

"Meredydd, I will not lie to you and tell you that

Ealad-hach is your ally. He is openly opposed to your presence at Halig-liath. I'm sorry about that. I honestly thought he had gotten used to you, but this last year or so things have . . . changed a bit." He made a wry face and punctuated it with a glance that indicated where the changes lay. "Calach, on the other hand is quite sympathetic to you, and I . . . well, my position is rather obvious. Ealad-hach has suggested that I am prejudiced in the matter and that it should therefore be brought up before the Osraed Body."

"He hates me," murmured Meredydd.

"He is a conservative, anwyl, opposed to the idea of females at Halig-liath on the basis of tradition. He always has been. I thought you might have swayed him a bit; you were such a winning child and sympathy for your . . . predicament was high." He shrugged. "Evidently, he has swayed back again."

"He thinks we're evil," observed Meredydd. "How can he believe that? He's married. He has daughters of his own."

Bevol smiled wryly. "Daughters who will never see the inside of Halig-liath. They will learn the domestic arts and marry and perhaps raise sons who will obtain that privilege. No, to Ealad-hach it is a matter of context. In the proper context, women are good and fine and noble. Outside of that context, they contribute to evil results."

"It's not my fault—"

"It is no one's fault, anwyl. It is not even poor Wyth's fault. He is attracted to you. There's nothing wrong in that. He fought it valiantly. In fact, he fought it unreasonably. And he used the wrong weapons. Now, *that* was his fault. He should never have brought his own dreams to you. He should never have let his temper speak louder than his intelligence. But even at that, those are things he may be forgiven by those who must offer forgiveness."

He gave her a significant look which, for the moment, she ignored. "Will the Meri reject him again because of this?"

"For possessing a young man's heart? I think not. But I'm not the Meri. She will either accept or reject Wyth's spiritual suit on the basis of his merits. It's not for me to approve him."

Meredydd found the patch of emerald velvet on her tunic suddenly very interesting. She rubbed it with the tip of one finger, barely aware of its texture. "So I am not to be dismissed?"

"Not at this juncture, although . . ."

Her eyes seized his face. "What, Master?"

Bevol cocked his head to one side. "Ealad-hach wishes to bring the matter of female Prentices in general and you, in particular, up before the Body so that all the Osraed in Caraid-land may have a voice."

Meredydd swallowed convulsively at the thought of facing all of those men—young and old, austere and jovial—of standing under their scrutiny.

Bevol read her expression. "Does that frighten you?"

"Yes."

"You could always withdraw. Ealad-hach is rather hoping that's what you'll do—leave Halig-liath of your own will."

"Leave?" Meredydd rejected the idea with surge of anger. "I have been a good student at Halig-liath. I've spent six years of my life there, learning, growing. Halig-liath has been part of my home. It's given me a purpose and a goal which I will not lay down simply because some people object to the form my body has taken. I love the Art, Master. You say I have a talent for it. I love the Meri and I want the right to seek Her approval, regardless of whether I have the approval of others. I have made a commitment, haven't I? I'm covenanted, aren't I? How can I not live up to that covenant?"

Bevol averted his eyes, studying the fire now, instead of his Prentice's flushed face. "You are a cailin. No one will think less of you if you withdraw."

"*I* would think less of me! You would, too, Master. And the Meri—it's Her grace I crave, not Ealadhach's, not Aelder Wyth's, and certainly not his mother's. If I withdraw, aren't I admitting that what Ealad-hach believes is true—that cailin are somehow . . . inferior?" She shook her head emphatically, chestnut hair rippling with the motion. "I will not withdraw, Master. They will have to throw me out."

Bevol pursed his lips, but not before she had seen the smile. "I suspected you might say something like that. So, I made a counter suggestion that, since the Meri is the ultimate authority on who should or should not be Osraed, She be consulted."

"How can that be done? She has never treated the issue before now."

"Solstice approaches quickly. It is possible that if the Prentices who go on Pilgrimage this Season are instructed to contemplate the admission of females to Halig-liath, the Meri may illumine them on the point. Of course, there is a very easy way to settle the question of your own continuance."

Meredydd licked suddenly dry lips. "And that is?"

"We could let the Meri decide your fate. You could take Pilgrimage this Season. In fact, I believe you could be the very first to leave at the Solstice."

"But I'm not ready!" She felt her cheeks light up with sudden blood. "I'm not fit to be Osraed, Master Bevol. I'm failing in school; I'm the cause of discord; I manipulated an instructor's dreams and benumbed a fellow Prentice's tongue. I'm wicked. Impossibly wicked."

There was such fevered passion in the claim that Osraed Bevol, overcome with the humor of the situation, laughed at her. "Oh, so wicked are you, anwyl! You're so wicked and this blind old Osraed so dimwitty, that he can't perceive the stain."

She started and stared at him. "Oh no, Osraed Bevol! I didn't mean to imply—I— There, you see? I've done it again. Blundered. Blathered." She made futile little gestures with her hands.

"Nonetheless, wicked cailin. I think perhaps it is time for your testing and proving. I think we'll walk Pilgrimage at Solstice."

Meredydd quelled her initial panic and tried to consider the situation rationally. After all, what had she been training for these past six years? She smoothed the front of her tunic and cleared her throat. "And the other Osraed will agree with this?"

"Agree? Ealad-hach is most eager to see you go— and fail."

A pang of fear, a bolt of ire, a twinge of unease. Fail! Fail, would she? And who was Ealad-hach to predict her failure? He was one of the Meri's chosen, that's who he was. Someone who had passed Her test. Someone to whom She had imparted particular knowledge.

"Of course," observed Bevol, watching her face, "Ealad-hach is a scientist. The ways of minerals are more clear to him than the ways of the human spirit."

Meredydd didn't even smile. "Solstice is only a week away."

Osraed Bevol rose and stretched. "Aye, but dinner is right now, or my nose deceives me." He ushered her out, glancing only idly at the empty spot on the stair that had held Skeet's warm hams a moment earlier.

That urchin met them in the big dining nook, grinning and sassing and a little peeved that Meredydd didn't notice his wit through her thoughtful, fretful haze. He served up and fell silent.

"Master," said Meredydd at length, "Osraed Ealad-hach spoke of history repeating itself in me. What did he mean by that?"

"Ah," said Bevol. He put on his pensive face and gazed at Skeet's dark head. "The record of Halig-liath has it that many years ago—over a century now—another girl studied at Halig-liath. She was Taminy. Taminy-a-Cuinn, daughter of the Cirke-Master—what was his name? Ah—Osraed Coluim—Coluim-a-Cuinn. According to the records, Taminy was a good student. As good a student as you are; as good as her male classmates and possessed of a natural talent in healing, especially. Legend has it that she sang a duan so perfectly, she rarely had recourse to herbs or waters or even crystals. And it was said that when she did use the crystals, she made them burn so fiercely that those looking on couldn't watch for fear of being blinded. Legend also has it that she was pretty enough to turn the heads of Prentices and Aelders alike. Turn them so far that there was a great falling away among the boys. Some never went on Pilgrimage; some were withdrawn from Academy by their parents until Taminy should be removed; some decided they really weren't suited to the contemplative life of scholarship or the rigors of service. A few committed acts that were . . . completely against every principle written down for us in the Corah."

Meredydd's brow crinkled in alarm. "And Taminy caused all of this?"

"That was what many people thought. And, in the end, the Osraed Body agreed with them and sent Taminy home in disgrace."

"What happened to her?"

"Her father, the Osraed Coluim, appealed the matter all the way to the Cyne's Council, but the Chancellor, an Osraed of Tradist bent, persuaded the Cyne—Thear, it was at that time—that it was a matter of religion, not a matter of state. Osraed Coluim did the only thing he could do, for his daughter's sake; he took her on Pilgrimage against the strict wishes of the Osraed Body. He came back without her. He claimed she walked into the Western Sea and drowned herself. The Body said it was her punishment."

Meredydd sat, stunned, horrified. "Will that be my fate, as well?"

"What—merely because it was hers? Superstition ill-befits an Osraed, Meredydd-a-Lagan. If you aspire to the station of Divine Counselor, you must leave superstition behind."

"But—"

"Your Pilgrimage, if you recall, is being openly encouraged."

"Yes, by Osraed Ealad-hach. Isn't it superstition that causes him to despise me?"

Bevol pointed at her with a chunk of bread. "*Fear* you, Meredydd. He fears you. Because of this . . . faery tale. On account of Taminy, he fears *you*."

"Why? What do I represent? What did she represent that he should fear it?"

"Change." He waved the bread up and down. "Eh? You see? Forward movement. Upward movement. Advancement. He is an old man. Old men have trouble adapting to these things."

"But he's Osraed."

"And are Osraed perfect, Meredydd?"

She swallowed a tiny sip of soup, her eyes on his face. "I . . . had thought so."

"Well, they are not. Osraed are human, anwyl. No human is perfect. Of created beings, only the Meri is perfect, for She is a creature of a different order. She is Eibhilin, a Being of Light."

Meredydd found her eyes drawn to the mark upon Bevol's broad forehead. Between his brows it sat, an odd starburst pattern which proclaimed to all who saw it that he was Osraed, chosen by the Scion of the First Being and His Sign upon Earth. The Kiss of the Meri, it was called, and from Halig-liath and from other Holy Places beyond even Caraid-land (or so Osraed Bevol said, though it was not Doctrine) Pilgrims flowed to the Sea. They came by the score, but only a handful received that Divine Kiss.

Meredydd was still thinking of that Kiss an hour

later, as she stared into the rippling rivulets that fled
up the chimney of their cluttered parlor.

"Master, tell me again how the Meri came to you."

"How She came to me? Would it not be more in-
structive to hear how I came to Her?"

"I suppose that's really what I meant."

He chuckled and tugged lightly at her hair, plaited
now, in preparation for sleep. "That journey begins at
birth, anwyl. Perhaps even before."

"Please?"

"Ah, well."

She felt him settle back in his fleece-padded chair
and wriggled her fire-warmed toes against the fender
in anticipation.

"My Pilgrimage was a rather long one and contained
four tasks. To find a rod of iron in a heap of grain, to
find someone who needed healing but would not tell
me so, to follow a riddle path to a dell where my Path
to the Sea would be given me, and, once on that Path,
to not deviate from it by a hair's breadth for any reason under the sun. I passed the tests—"

"But cannot tell me how," finished Meredydd. "May
I guess?"

It was a ritual by now, this guessing game. He nodded and she went on as if she had heard that motion
of old bone and muscle.

"You used a magnet, didn't you—to find the rod? I
said a bellows the last time, but that was wrong, I'm
sure. It must have been a magnet. And the riddle—
well, since you won't tell me what it was, I can't guess
at that. But the person you healed must have been a
mute, because, of course, they *couldn't* tell you that
they needed healing. And I think that in order not to
stray from the path, you blindfolded yourself and had
your Weard lead you."

"Two of three," he said. "Not bad."

"What went missing?"

"The thread of my story. Now, I completed my
tasks—although I was not sure I had or that I had

done them correctly—and I came out to the Sea where I had been led. I found my Pilgrim's Post, my Weard took up his station behind me, and I sat in the sand and waited. My mind was only as calm as it could be, my heart was hungry with anticipation and quivering with dread. After all, more Prentices are shunned than embraced. The pull of sleep was strong, but I struggled to ignore it. I had intentionally seated myself in a tidal pool and an icy wash of water reached me at the times my drowsiness was at its worst.

"On the second night of sitting so, I saw a bright ripple beneath the waves, parting them like a gleaming knife, like a flame in the water. And out of this lambency, the Meri rose, radiant, beautiful, all of grace and Light. She gazed at me with great green eyes like emerald coins and I gazed back. Then, when I thought my breath had stopped in my lungs and I began to sway with delirium, She swam toward me and came up out of the water and met me eye to eye. Then She set her lips—if lips they were—to my forehead.

"I felt different, suddenly—transformed. I was calm, assured, joyous, but still full of wonder. I knew things I'd never even suspected before. I saw what holds the stars in their courses and makes the planets dance in their orbits, paying court to their Suns. I knew the names of lands I'd never visited. I knew what makes some men hate and fear and other men love. I knew that the best of all treasures was the love of God and that it was also the best of all gifts. I knew that the first thing a true man or woman must possess was a pure, kindly and radiant heart. I knew the will of the First Being for Caraid-land and for Nairne and I knew Its will for me. I saw myself giving the Pilgrim's Tell before the Cyne in Creiddylad. I saw Halig-liath with me in it. I saw bits and pieces of my future." He paused for a moment then said, "And there is something else I saw which I have never mentioned before. I saw a little girl in a burned out steadyard, struggling in the mud to reach the dead body of her mother."

Meredydd whirled about to face him, nearly thrusting her feet into the fire in her haste. "You saw *me*?"

He nodded, stroking her hair as if to calm her, his own hair and beard gold-slashed copper in the firelight, his face ruddy.

"Why didn't you ever tell me?"

"It did not seem . . . important."

"Do you know how my Pilgrimage will end?"

"Does anyone's Pilgrimage ever end?" he asked philosophically.

"Do you?" she persisted.

"I hope it ends with you giving the Pilgrim's Tell before Cyne Colfre." He read her expression, then said, "Anyone can see the beginning of a thing. Only God sees the end clearly."

"Do you?"

"No, Meredydd."

She searched his face, then turned back to the flames, content that he would never lie to her. They sat in silence for a moment, then Bevol said, "You will not go back to Halig-liath until the Solstice Festival at the end of the week. I will prepare you for Pilgrimage, myself."

"But, your classes—"

"I will hand them over to my second. He can handle the academic testing."

Meredydd nodded, her chin rocking on drawn up knees. One week. One week from now, she would be on her Path to the Western Sea.

Chapter 4

Bend and you will not break, for the bent can straighten.
The emptied can be filled, the torn mended.
Want can reward you, even as wealth can bewilder.
The wise man finds the Balance:
Without becoming inflamed, he is kindled;
without defending himself, he is defended;
without laying claim, he is acclaimed;
without competing, he finds competence.
How true is this: Bend and you will not break.
                              —The Corah, Book II, Verse 90

Cirke-dag dawned cool, breezy and with the threat of rain. Cloaked against that threat, the inhabitants of Gled Manor made the twenty-minute walk to Nairne, arriving at the Sanctuary to mill in the Cirke-yard with their fellow worshipers. Meredydd kept her head high in spite of the glances she reaped from the parents of her classmates—most especially from those who were close to Moireach Arundel and her son.

There was nothing of the siren about her today, drabbed in a stole and a woven dress that, knee slit, fell nearly to the ankles of her leggins. Every scrap of

68

skin was covered but for hands and face, her hair formed a chaste, shining coil about her head. She ignored the prying eyes, fixing her own on Halig-liath. Crowning the escarpment at the eastern end of town, it dominated Nairne like a dowager Cwen supreme astride her stony mount. Mist rose off the Halig-tyne, curling serenly at the foot of the cliffs, rising to wrap itself about the angles of wall and spire, softening the arrogant profile.

I might never set foot there again, she thought and felt a keen sense of loss. Ah, but at least there would be the Farewelling—the climax of the Solstice Festival when the Pilgrims were feted.

Skeet tugged at her tunic now, telling her it was time to go in. She took her eyes from the Holy Fortress and turned to climb the wide Sanctuary stair. Aelder Prentice Wyth stood just above her on the steps, his hair flying in the spring breeze, his long, angular face stark and troubled. She blinked and turned aside before he could speak to her.

Though she fled into the Sanctuary, she found no solace within. Eyes still prodded her, accused her wrongly. Across the aisle from where she sat with Osraed Bevol and Skeet, Prentice Brys and his family glared at her. Brys's neck was buried in scarves that were pungent with medicaments and herbs. She could smell the camphor strongly even from here. The corners of her mouth twitched impulsively and she raised her hand to cover it, bowing her head and praying earnestly for his speedy recovery.

The Cirke-Master, Osraed Saxan, gave a teaching on tolerance and understanding, but it fell into hard soil. Those who regarded Meredydd-a-Lagan, accused seductress and Wicke, with icy disdain continued to regard her that way. She could feel the eyes on her, curious, judging, condemning. At the end of the Teaching, as the last note of the last lay rang off, Meredydd excused herself and left the Cirke.

She was halfway across the Cirke-yard when she

heard someone calling to her. For all she wanted to bolt and run, she stopped and turned. A sigh of relief escaped her; it was Lealbhallain. She waited for him to catch her up and smiled at him.

"A friend! You are still my friend, aren't you, Leal?"

He frowned, the freckles across the bridge of his nose mingling into a ruddy-gold blotch. "How can you ask that, Meredydd? I am always your friend. You were running away," he accused her. "Aren't we going for our Cirke-dag stop by the backstere's?"

Meredydd looked down at the toes of her shoes. "Are you sure you wish to be seen with me?"

"Always."

His loyalty made her feel willful and free. She nodded, raising her head. "Aye, then. Let's have our pastries, by all means."

They performed the ritual just as always, crossing the Cirke Bridge to the south side of Nairne and strolling all the way to the quay to give the backstere a chance to get back from Cirke. Then they strolled back into town again past closed shops and opened tearooms and public houses. Business halted on Cirke-dag, but eating and socializing did not, hence shops that provided fuel for either of those pastimes shut down only during worship and opened immediately after to receive their throngs of customers, some of which were not seen in Nairne from one Cirke-dag to the next.

At the backstere's they got creamcakes and resumed their walk, heading back again along the river, which dissected the little town into uneven halves. Meredydd's eyes found new beauties in the streets of Nairne today—in the fresh-washed cobbles and white-washed storefronts with their gleaming windows and hand-painted signs. And the smells of Nairne were also beautiful—baked goods and Cirke-dag dinners from a myriad houses, spices and flowers and, from the river, the perfumes of tarred planking and wet earth and stone.

"What are you thinking, Meredydd?" asked Leal-bhallain when she had been silent for a very long time.

She pecked at the half-finished creamcake. "I'm wondering what I'll do after."

"After?"

"I'm going on Pilgrimage at Solstice, Leal."

"What? Why?"

"Osraed Ealad-hach . . ." She paused. No, she really shouldn't lay this at his door—that would be backbiting. "Osraed Bevol thinks it would be a good way for me to prove myself at Halig-liath. To prove I'm not what people are saying I am." She glanced at him sidelong. "You've heard the rumors."

He nodded, watching the flagged walkway in front of them. "Aye. You must know I don't believe it. By the Kiss, Meredydd, I *know* none of it's true. You're no Wicke. You've done naught to Wyth or Brys or anyone."

She laughed. "Bristles!"

He glanced at her reproachfully. "I'm your friend, Meredydd. I'll always defend you."

Impulsively, she put her arm through his. "I'm fortunate in my friends," she told him and he smiled brilliantly for her. "Tell me, Leal. Have you ever been to Creiddylad?"

He blinked at the sudden change of subject. "Aye."

"Is it really a jewel?"

He shrugged. "I suppose you could say it was. It's a big town and fine and rich. Except the poor parts. It's not like here, where there's some a little rich and some a little poor, but most living goodly lives and making sure the poor stay only a little that way. In Creiddylad, there's deep poor. Folks that can barely scrape by. They've no land, you see. They're all crowded into little—" He waved his free hand with its bit of creamcake as if trying to prod a word loose from the air. "Warrens," he said finally. "Aye, they're almost like that—like rabbit hutches. And all these folks crammed in there with no land of their own so they can't farm up victuals for the family table."

Meredydd was stunned. If the report had come from anyone else, she wouldn't have believed it, but Leal would lie to her no more than he would abandon her. "But that's awful. And how can it be, with Cyne Colfre living right there?"

"Well, father says there are reserves set aside from tariffs and the like that are supposed to help care for these folk and set up workshare for them, but he says that hasn't been working so well of late. Father says it's greed—unscrupulous administrators turning the monies to their own use. Used to be that Creiddylad was like Nairne and the other villages, where the landed folk took care of the unlanded folk, at least that's what Father says. He says it *must* change, of course, but who could change it?"

"I would think God could; the Meri could. Perhaps we should ask after it when we go on Pilgrimage, instead of worrying about our own estate."

Leal nodded. "I think you must be right. But why do you ask about Creiddylad?"

"Like I said, I was thinking of what to do after. I don't know if I could stay here, because if I fail, Nairne wouldn't have me. They'll believe the stories and I'll have no life here. I thought maybe I could go to Creiddylad. Maybe there'd be something for me to do there. It sounds like there's a lot to be done there," she added.

Lealbhallain scowled—actually scowled—at her. "Oh, you'll go to Creiddylad, all right, Meredydd-a-Lagan. You'll go there to give the Pilgrim's Tell to Cyne Colfre. Mark it."

They had reached the riverbend by now and wandered along the quay, watching the little boats bobbing on the quiet waters and the fishermen sitting so patiently on their piers. But when they sat on a stone balustrade in the shadow of the palisades, it was Haligliath that drew Meredydd's eyes—drew them up to the warm stone walls and the staunch parapets. She could see the outer wall of the concourse from here and the high gallery above the hidden courtyard. In one week, she would say good-bye; she prayed it was not forever.

She left Lealbhallain on the corner of his street, not wanting to cause him any trouble with his family, and left the streets and avenues of Nairne behind her. The rest of the day was hers and she knew exactly what she would do with it.

Ritualistically, she took the anniversary path—the one that left the Nairne Road and ran to the Bebhinn Wood. The one that led to a place where a younger Meredydd had squandered irreplaceable time. Every year to the day she had done this—retraced those childish steps—but never had that woodland pool seemed the least bit magical. It was a joyless place of sodden grass and sorrowing trees and never, since that day seven years before, had it held anything that should have made an eight-year-old girl stop, enchanted, to while away her mother and father's last hours—hours that should have been her last, as well.

The day was pied now, blue-gold and silver, as clouds scudded landward like legless sheep in an infinite pasturage. Meredydd glanced up at them through jostling limbs and wondered at worlds she knew, from Bevol's teaching, existed beyond them, flung like jeweled chick-seed across the void. She knew, too, that the void was not a void, but teemed with stars and galaxies and gases and nascent worlds and ancient ones thronging with life—all seeking the same Goal. Her thoughts swung to the Meri and to the Meri's Kiss and she wondered what form the Meri took on those other worlds.

A limb brushed wet fingertips against her neck, making her pull her thoughts back down to Earth. She had reached the pool and stood at the top of a berm in the path, looking past a drape of moss into the hollow. She stepped forward and down, brushing the moss aside, and was astonished.

Every blade of grass was verdant velvet and mounted by a tiny bead of water. Up from and over the emerald-strewn ground, evergreen shrubs waved jeweled fans, while their taller sisters and cousins danced in clinging, silvery finery of the sheerest moss. The pool itself lay in the setting like a giantess's pendant—glittering peridot, sapphire, topaz, diamond deep and clear. Meredydd could see all the way to the bottom.

The sight amazed her for only a moment before she felt a soul-plumbing thrum of fear. She skirted the pool quickly, saw a tendril of mist rise and thicken, and ran, unreasoning, up the path toward Lagan.

Meredydd . . .

Did the wraith whisper it? Did her ears even hear it?

The part of her that cared to know was submerged in sudden terror. What would she see when she reached the top of the hill? Was that smoke or only a stormcloud lying dog-low on the horizon?

She broke from the woods and leapt into the waves of winter wheat that bowed across her path, wind-worshiping and golden. It slowed her and she dropped her stole, then picked up her skirts and bounded on, eyes locked to the crest of the hill. She was winded by the time she reached it and her hair had escaped from its careful coil and fallen, unplaited and reckless, to her shoulders. She crested the waves of grain and filled her eyes with the scene below. For a second it was flame and shadow; for a heartbeat it was smoke and fear. Then a cloud cleared the Sun and it was a sleeping ruin, swathed in new green, looking less than melancholy in its spring colors. Lagan was not in mourning.

Heart in her throat, skirts gripped in white-knuckled hands, Meredydd tottered down from the hill, eyes tight on the spot where their bodies had lain, where there was now only fresh grass and tiny blue flowers.

She crossed the yard, wind cooling her flaming cheeks, and went through the broken doorway into the house. It was only a foundation now, cracking and disintegrating, inhabited only by wild things and wild grasses. Vines overgrew the chimney, moss overlaid the crumbling walls.

She looked. She searched. She lost herself in the tiniest details. Perhaps this year her maturing eyes would find what they had never found before—a clue to the why and the who of the death of Lagan.

Her ears snatched a sound out of the unquiet air and she raised her head, gazing around to the four corners. To the west, the hillside swam in wheat; northward, the Bebhinn rushed over its bed of shattered rock, fresh from its rift with the Halig-tyne; to the east and south, the Tyne Road was empty of anything but several sheep that had crossed the long bridge from Arundel. She watched them for a moment as they dipped their heads to drink of the Holy River's slow stream, going back at last to cropping Lagan's grass.

The river captured her for a moment. It was a stately river, circumspect, mannerly and genteel. It whispered, giggled, perhaps, but never kicked up its heels in laughter and song like its daughter, the melodious, spirited Bebhinn.

Meredydd shook her head, ending the reverie. That must have been what she heard—just the sheep crossing the bridge—tiny, sharp hooves on wood and stone. She sighed and left the house to pick some wild flowers at the forge. They grew well there in the ashy soil. She was on her way to the graves with some wild roses when she saw in the wet earth near the well something that had not been there when she arrived—hoofprints.

She puzzled. They were well-shod hooves, but not large. The prints were deep. An average horse—a larger than average man. The puzzlement slipped through unease toward fear and she froze, flowers in hand, staring at the prints. When the horse snorted directly behind her, she leapt up and away, landing with her face toward the intruder. She squinted up into the gleaming sky.

It was Aelder Prentice Wyth who slid from the fine leather saddle. He looped reins around the carved wooden pommel with its gilt edging and faced her across her parents' grave.

She stared. He stared. Then he mumbled.

"What?" she asked. "What did you say?"

He took a deep breath and watched his family's sheep approach the ruined walls of Lagan and said, "I said, I'm most truly sorry, Meredydd, for all that's happened. I heard Osraed Bevol say you'd be no more at Halig-liath and I can only believe that it's my fault. Mine and my mother's."

"I'm leaving Halig-liath to go on Pilgrimage," she said, clutching her flowers to her breast. "Next week, at Solstice. Osraed Bevol thinks that's best. He believes only my acceptance by the Meri will win me acceptance in Nairne."

"Pilgrimage? Already? But you're only fifteen!"

"Nearly sixteen. I'm eligible to go and Osraed Bevol must think I'm ready or he wouldn't suggest it."

"But . . . do you want to go?"

She thought about that momentarily. Thought about it for the first time, really. Did she want to go? Wasn't she afraid of going—afraid of finding out what qualities she possessed or failed to possess? Was she so confident of her success? Did she need to be?

"Yes," she said. "I do want to go. I've studied most of my life to go. I've dreamed about it, longed for it." That much was true. She had dreamed—daydreamed mostly—before she understood the full meaning of Pilgrimage, before she understood it had nothing to do with glory and celebrity and adventure. Now she merely dreamed.

"Dreamed," repeated Wyth, nodding. A grimace tugged his wide mouth awry. "We both dreamed. Although my dreams are more nightmares. Pilgrimages that fail, mostly. Pilgrimages that end in my rejection, in my death. Sometimes I die of old age, waiting and waiting for Something that will never come. Sometimes I never even make it to the Sea. I wonder why—why did the Meri reject me? What do I lack when I love Her so? Is it . . . because of my father?"

Meredydd shook her head with sudden impatience and stooped to lay her flowers on the grave. "A father's sins are visited on his son only if the son *allows* them to be. If you are lacking something, the lack is yours, you didn't inherit it. And if it's yours, you can remedy it."

"He took his own life, Meredydd."

"Aye. So don't allow him to take yours, as well."

He almost smiled. "Such good counsel."

She glanced at him sharply and was surprised to find him sincere. She made a gesture of denial.

Aelder Wyth glanced at the ground between his booted feet. "I lied to you about my dream. The horse never took me to Lin-liath. It took me to Gled Manor. To your house."

Meredydd flushed with embarrassment and glanced about, seeking an avenue of escape.

"You *have* seduced me, Meredydd, although unwittingly. No matter where I send my thoughts, they return always to you. In class, I know, I act as if I had the wisdom and authority of an Osraed. I don't have anything like that wisdom. And I shouldn't have the authority I've been given—not over you. Not when I only abuse it."

He took a sudden step over the graves, meeting her face to face and startling her into a tiny retreat. He caught her hands to keep her from fleeing further.

"You should teach *me*, Meredydd. I should be your Prentice."

She disentangled her hands and took another step away. "Don't say this! You're misguided, Aelder Wyth. You squander your attentions on me—"

"No, not squander. Listen to me, Meredydd. I have

a fine estate. I'm an Eiric already at eighteen. But Arundel is too big, by far, for my mother and sisters and myself. It will be mine alone when the sisters marry. When I come back from Pilgrimage, Meredydd, if the Meri has me, if you will—"

Meredydd's heart clenched into a tiny, terrified knot. "No, Wyth!"

"Why not?"

"I'm only fifteen."

He laughed. "Nearly sixteen, you told me."

"And what of my own Pilgrimage? If the Meri has me, I'll have so much to do. So much work. And She might bid me go out of Caraid-land to do that work."

"You don't have to go."

"Disobey the Meri?"

"I mean, you don't have to go on Pilgrimage. You could marry me at Solstice, instead."

"I *will* go on Pilgrimage, Wyth Arundel."

"Yes, yes. Aye. All right." He waved her anger back with placating hands. "If you wish so much to go, then go, of course. And when you return, I will let you continue your studies."

"*Let* me! You could have no choice!"

"Of course, I could have a choice. A husband—"

"I have no husband. I'll not have you as one."

His distress was evident. "Why not?"

"Good God, Wyth! How could I marry someone who would stand there and speak of *permitting* me to do the Meri's will?"

"I take it back. All that I said. I'm wrong. Of course, the will of the Meri is paramount."

"Wyth, I don't *love* you! I don't know what love is, yet. My parents had it. Osraed Bevol and Aelwyn Meara had it, may God bless her soul. But I've too small a vessel for so deep a thing as that. And what I do have is full of the Meri. She fills my cup, Wyth. There's no room in it for you."

"But She's a spirit. I'm a man. The filling is different."

A man at eighteen. So serious—gangly, over-tall body drawn severely upright, deep set eyes so somber, lips so tight. A man.

Meredydd laughed. "Oh, Aelder Wyth, I hope when we've both visited the Sea we'll understand what a man is—or a woman, for that matter. Now, take your sheep along home, please. They're eating my roses." She started to turn away.

"My roses, you mean."

She swung back. "What?"

"*My* roses. Lagan is mine now. Has been this last five years—part of Arundel."

She gaped at him. "By what right—?"

"By mart forfeit. After . . . after the fire, you'd gone with Osraed Bevol. He never claimed the land as your guardian—"

"So your family did? But five years—"

"Mother said it was needed. Our pasturage had got so worn we needed extra for the increased herds. And if we held Lagan the hands could take them through direct on the Tyne Road to the market in Creiddy-lad—not have to take the long way around to catch the road above the palisades. Father had started the claim but . . . well, mother did it on his behest, or mine, I suppose. You weren't of an age to lay claim yourself."

"But so *soon*. They'd just been buried."

"Aye. But Osraed Bevol could have contested our claim for you. It was a surprise he didn't, really. After all, you'd need a dowry." He glanced away from her, shrugging. "But then, he wasn't your blood kin, not even your legal guardian then, I think. I really don't know what happened, Meredydd. I was just a boy, after all."

"You hold Lagan." Meredydd shook her head.

"I'll give it to you," he said, slipping closer to her. "I'll build you a house here. A house with a thousand rose bushes."

She waved him to silence, her inner turmoil taking

all her attention. All these years she'd assumed Lagan was just as it had been—home. But the family of Lagan no longer existed. Her home no longer existed.

"Then I've been trespassing."

"No! You couldn't be a trespasser here."

"But your mother—"

"She doesn't know. She doesn't know a good many things. She thinks you're some sort of . . . Dark Sister and she thinks you've Runewoven to make me lust for you. She thought you knew Lagan was part of Arundel and were scheming to get it back. She doesn't know what I know, Meredydd—that you're an angel and innocent of deceit and that I love you."

"Please, Aelder Wyth, stop saying those things. I'm no angel. I'm hopelessly flawed in ways you can't begin to imagine. I have to go." She turned.

He reached for her. "You hate me. Because of Lagan. Because of my mother's foolish accusations. Because of my stupid bungling—"

"I don't hate you, Wyth. I don't," she assured him and tried to put the whole force of herself behind her eyes. "But neither do I love you. And don't tell me I could learn," she added when he opened his mouth to protest. "I have far too much to learn already."

She made good her escape this time, or nearly so, for he mounted his horse and followed her up the hill.

"Let me ride you home," he said, his horse prancing beside her.

She kept on, not even looking at him. "No, Wyth. I have thoughts I need to order and exile. And your mother might see us and God knows what she might think."

That brought him up short. He reined in his mount at the top of the hill and glanced furtively around. Then he watched her trudge away from him through the tall wheat, over and away toward Gled Manor.

"I *will* see you again, Meredydd," he called. "I won't give up."

She stopped halfway down the hill, Nairne-side, and

turned on him. "It's the Meri you should be making that promise too, Wyth Arundel. And see that you keep it!"

Back she swung and marched away, skirts trailing, hair streaming, leaving him alone atop the hill.

Chapter 5

Transformation takes place in one's mind.
Therefore the mind must be kept pure, for what one
thinks, he becomes.

—The Corah, Book II, Verses 3, 4

The Sun had shifted outside the window and fallen
across the pages of her book, making reading difficult.
She rubbed her suddenly burning eyes and started to
move away from the gleaming wash of sunlight. She
was startled when the Osraed Bevol dropped a large,
blue crystal down upon the open pages. Caught in the
shaft of white light, it sprayed vivid azure rain across
the pristine paper, drenching it.

Meredydd gasped at the beauty of it.

"Now," said Osraed Bevol, "tell me about the crystal in my hand."

She turned and looked at him questioningly. He
held his knotted fist before him, closed and impene-
trable.

"But, Master, how can I tell you about what I cannot see?"

"I have told you, I have, in my hand, a crystal."

"But I can't see it," she repeated.

He pointed with his other hand at the book on her desk. "What is that?"

She glanced at the blue glory. "A crystal."

"Tell me about crystal."

She did as she was told, studying the glittering gem as it sat upon the book. "It is gleaming, glittering. It takes the light of the Sun and refracts it and spits it in all directions. It is beautiful, colorful, vivid."

"Is that all?"

"Well . . ."

"Pick it up."

She did as commanded and discovered the crystal was cool to the touch even though it had been sitting in the direct Sun. She felt of it with her fingers, caressing the facets; she tapped it with her fingernails.

"It is cool," she told him. "And hard and has sharp planes and angles." She held it up to her eye and gazed through it at the sunny garden outside. She saw a myriad gardens. "It changes the world one looks at through it. It multiplies the world."

"And does this describe what I hold in my hand, as well?"

Her eyes pried at his expression, trying to divine what point he was making with her. "Well," she said, "if what you hold in your hand is a crystal, I suppose it might. . . . Well, yes, of course it does. Except that it might be a different color, or perhaps it has no color at all."

The Osraed smiled and set the second crystal next to the first. It was a completely clear gem, but when the Sun struck it, the white light shattered into a myriad of colored shards, strewn with the azure ones across the pages of Meredydd's book.

"By knowing a piece of crystal, anwyl," he told her, "all that is crystal is known, since any differences are only words and the reality is crystal. Just so, by knowing a piece of iron, all that is iron is known, since any differences are only words and the reality is only iron. And just so, by knowing love, all that is love is known, since any differences are only words and the reality is only love."

He sat down across from her on a short three-legged stool. "Now, tell me how this applies to your Pilgrimage."

Meredydd gave the matter a moment of thought, then replied, "The Pilgrim must be observant and learn from the things she observes about other things not observable."

"All right. Now, I have asked you a question; you may ask me one."

She had a question, the one sitting topmost in her mind. "What do I do first? Tonight, I mean."

"You go to your Farewelling."

"I mean, after that."

"That would be getting ahead of yourself. First, you go to your Farewelling."

This Solstice Festival was different than all other Festivals. That it was the eve of her own Pilgrimage (an eve she had never really expected to see, she now realized) charged it with an excitement she had never known before. The aloof behavior of her fellow Pilgrims and the avoidance of people she had once thought of as friends injected an element of pain.

The festivities began in the great courtyard at Haligliath where a formal ceremony took place in honor of the Pilgrims. There were eight this Season. Her classmates Brys, Scandy and Lealbhallain were among them. She was not cheated of her moment on the dais beneath the Osraed's high gallery. Osraed Bevol bestowed upon her a pale crystal; Ealad-hach, his mouth twisted as if he had sucked an unripe crabapple, handed her the Scroll of Honor; Osraed Calach set the traditional wreath of flowers upon her hair.

Then, in the gathering darkness, the celebration moved down along the palisades to the Nairne Road in a long, snaking, noisy parade. Pipers and drummers played before the honored Pilgrims and a crowd of well-wishers trailed behind—every ambulatory man, woman and child in Nairne beating, shaking or tootling something to frighten away the evil spirits that few, if any, believed in. They paraded through the Cirke-yard, crossed the Halig-tyne at Cirke Bridge and proceeded up the main avenue of town toward the river bend.

Along the quay, the parade disintegrated into a merry rabble. The pipers and drummers continued to play while the Pilgrims were led out to dance. Cailin came to the quay-side green, bedecked with ribbons and flowers, they each chose a Prentice from the group of Pilgrims to dance with them. But there was no one for Meredydd. The first girl onto the grass went straight to Brys-a-Lach and shot Meredydd a sidelong glance eloquent with ridicule.

"None'll dance with a Dark Sister," she said and led her partner away.

"I will," said a voice from the milling throng.

Meredydd turned. It was Lealbhallain, of course. She shook her head. "What will people say?"

"What they are already saying—that you've failed with Aelder Wyth and so you're seducing me."

She gasped. "Are they really saying that?"

"Aye. And that you did it with creamcakes and a love duan." He smiled and held out his hand. "Come out with me."

"But there'll be a cailin waiting to dance with you."

"You're the cailin I wish to dance my Farewelling. Come out with me," he repeated.

She curtseyed and accepted the hand, then, walking proudly beside him onto the dancing green. They drew many eyes as they turned upon the close-cropped sward. Curious eyes and unfriendly ones. Meredydd kept her own on Leal's face, fearing to see any hint of distress at the attention they garnered. But there was none. He smiled and laughed and, in all ways, put her at ease.

And she was at ease, she realized. She was enjoying

her Farewelling. Loving the mirth and the music and the dance. Glad of her loyal partner. They had done four quick outings together, and were dancing to a slow tune about a lovelorn shepherd, when she saw Wyth Arundel standing at the edge of the watching crowd, his eyes burning through the air between them. Involuntarily, she stiffened, causing Lealbhallain, who had been dancing quite close to hold her at arm's length and search her face.

"What is it, Meredydd? What's wrong?"

"I don't want to be watched anymore, Leal. I'm sick of everyone staring at me."

He stopped dancing and looked at her, then turned his head. When he turned back again, she knew he had seen Wyth.

"The fire pageant is about to start," he said. "Let's go find a place to watch."

They left the green, Lealbhallain still holding her hand, but she could feel Wyth watching and she knew he was following.

They found a good place along the balustrade from which to watch the pageant, and when the first bright streamer of light shot up above the ramparts of the holy stronghold, its mirror image cleaved the dark waters of the Halig-tyne. Meredydd gasped with delight just as she did every year. The fireworks went on for some time and, in the play of light on water and cloud, she forgot everything but the wonder and delight of the Solstice.

Forgot it, that was, until after the fire-show when she and Leal wandered the quay. A hand on her arm pulled her from a pleasant absorption in the contrasts of dark and light—of night and torch-flame—that dappled water, land and air. She turned and found Wyth Arundel gazing solemnly at her, his mouth a grim rebuke.

"I must speak with you, Meredydd," he said, and afforded Lealbhallain a dark and meaningful look. "Alone."

Leal started to speak up, then thought better of it and looked to her for comment. Confused by the sudden intensity of the two faces now turned upon her, by the milling crowd and the flickering light, Meredydd could only glance from one boy to the other, her brow knit. Finally, she shook her head.

"What have you to say that can't be said before Leal?"

Wyth's eyes shot to the other boy's face. "Anything I would say to you is for your ears only. Please," he added, "I really must speak to you."

Meredydd sighed and nodded. "All right, then. I'm sorry Leal. I'll bide a moment with Wyth. Don't leave me, though. Wait a bit?"

Leal tossed the Aelder Prentice a challenging glance. "All night, if I must," he said and jerked his head up-quay. "I'll be at the backstere's stall." And he moved off, his back staff-straight.

Wyth took Meredydd's arm, then, and led her to the very edge of the cobbled street, to where the stone balustrade overhung the sparkling water and boats bobbed below in the shifting darkness. She could hear them there—creaking, whispering, the river slap-slapping against their brightly painted hulls.

Wyth spoke. "You mustn't go, Meredydd. You mustn't go on Pilgrimage."

She goggled at him. "What can you be talking about? Of course I must go."

He captured both her hands. "Meredydd, please, it's too dangerous."

"No more so than for you or Leal."

"Yes! Much more! . . . Have you not heard of Tami-ny-a-Cuinn?"

She eyed him warily. That name again. "Aye," she said. "I've heard of her."

"Then you know how dangerous this is. You may never return."

"Nonsense."

Her calm rebuttal seemed to throw him into a conniption of alarm. "No, Meredydd, *not* nonsense, *fact*. I tell you, if you go on this Pilgrimage you will *never* return. You'll be destroyed, just as Taminy was destroyed. The Meri will not be sent a cailin Prentice. She will not tolerate it. And if you go, and if you don't come back, then I . . . Oh, I think it would kill me, Meredydd!"

"Nonsense," she repeated, annoyance growling in her stomach. "How can you spout such rubbish, Wyth Arundel? You're losing hold of yourself altogether. You're a Prentice and the object of your life is to attach yourself to the Meri, not to me. Kill you, indeed! What rubbish! Let me ask you this: what would you say if I was to tell you I'd marry you . . . *only* if you did not go on Pilgrimage this Season?"

His mouth was open, ready with his answer, when the tail of her question lashed him. He faltered; his mouth closed; his eyes widened. "You wouldn't ask it."

"Wouldn't I? Well, if I'm the wicked spoiler your mother and half Nairne thinks I am, that's just what I'd do. So give me your answer, Wyth Arundel. Will you give up the Meri and take me instead?"

He stared at her as if she had just turned into something completely incomprehensible. Then he shook his head. "I couldn't do that, Meredydd. I could not."

"Well, if you won't give up your life to me as I live, why should you do so if I die?"

Wyth turned his head to gaze across the river at the great white cliffs that rose, starkly, on the nether side. His face was in shadow and Meredydd could see only the glitter of mirrored light on his eye. His shoulders shook lightly and she was afraid, for a moment, that he was crying. But the sound that escaped his lips was not a sob, it was a chuckle. Meredydd's mouth fair fell open in astonishment.

"You'd try a saint," he said. "You're a wicked girl, Meredydd, not to let me romance you." He turned his face back to her again, his eyes wistful, but not solemn. "So very, very wicked." He ducked his head quickly then, and kissed her lightly on the mouth.

She went to find Leal with her fingertips still pressed against her lips, her eyes moist with inexplicable tears.

It was late when she and Skeet and Osraed Bevol wandered home. Meredydd was exhausted, Bevol was mellow and quiet and Skeet was Skeet. Bubbling over with all that he had seen and heard and done, he regaled them with tales of this or that prank and the music and the jugglers and the magicians and . . .

Meredydd smiled and started wearily up the stairs, when she had a sudden thought. She swung back to face Bevol who was watching from the bottom of the steps.

"This is the night. The first night of the Season."

"Indeed."

"Well, what do I do?"

"You sleep. And you dream."

"And then?"

"That would be getting ahead of yourself. First, you dream."

She did dream. She dreamed of starting on her Pilgrimage with both Skeet and Osraed Bevol. She dreamed of woodland paths and grassy meadows that she knew, somehow, lay to the north. But as the dream progressed, Meredydd was overcome by the fear that she would forget it and not be able to tell Osraed Bevol what had happened when she awoke.

She began to run each sequence of events over and over in her dreaming mind, striving to memorize each footfall, each fork, each stand of trees or slant of trail. But the effort drained her and she soon suspected that the Path was endless and that she would tread it forever, never coming any closer to her goal.

She could conceive of only one solution: She must wake up and write down what she had seen. Yes, that was it, she must wake up. But her body refused to

obey the dictates of her will and she found herself
stranded between dreaming and waking.

If I can't wake and write, she thought, *then I must
sleep and write.* And so she dreamed of her journal
and a writing stick and began to scribe the substance
of her journey painstakingly upon ephemeral pages,
watching her own progress on the Path through and
between the words she wrote.

Now the dream advanced and the dream-Bevol gave
her a task to perform. She was to go to a certain
woman in a certain village and return to him with an
amulet. There would be several amulets to choose
from, but the dream did not tell her which to take or
how to choose. It showed her only going to the woman's house, seeing the talismans lying on a bed of velvet, and leaving with one of them clutched in her
hand. All her attempts to see the amulet failed and
she returned to Bevol with no sense of accomplish-
ment, but only uncertainty.

She kept writing, watching the characters of her
dream between the curls and angles that appeared
beneath the tip of her scribe.

Osraed Bevol gave her a riddle for her next task.
She wrote it down carefully. The riddle, she knew,
would take her to a place. But she didn't know the
place or why she went there. She knew only that there
was in the place something of that magical glade along
the Bebhinn, and the very thought of it disturbed her
so much that she woke, weary and confused and realized her dream note-taking had been for naught.
She had forgotten Bevol's riddle and everything that
followed.

"I feel as if I've failed already," she confided over
breakfast. "I tried so hard to remember the dream,
but the book I was writing it in wasn't real. It's all
gone."

Osraed Bevol studied her for a moment, then asked,
"What was the first thing you recall?"

"We began the journey together. You and Skeet and I."

"Ah. And where did we go?"

"North, into the countryside . . . Northwest."

"Then that is where we shall go."

Meredydd was dubious. "Are you sure?"

"Is that what you dreamed—northwest?"

"Yes."

"Well, then." He turned to Skeet, who had watched their exchange with much interest. "Provision us for Pilgrimage, Pov. You know what to bring and what to leave. And you, Meredydd, bring two changes of clothing and anything else you think a Prentice might need along the road. Don't forget a cloak. Evenings are cool."

Meredydd did as directed, wondering when the sense of magic would come, the intimation of destiny, import, purpose. Feeling only tired and muzzy, she dressed in a long-sleeved sous-shirt and light tunic with leggins of silk and soft ankle boots. She packed a cap as well as a cloak and brought several extra pairs of stockings. Taking seriously what Osraed Bevol had said, she packed the crystal conferred during the Farewelling, along with some small sachets of medicinal herbs.

Thus prepared, she tucked a favorite book of meditations into a pocket of her pack and met Bevol and Skeet in the kitchen. Skeet wore a backpack obviously teeming with provisions and Bevol, in leggins, sousshirt, jerkin and jacket, looked more like a local jagger than an Osraed.

"How long will we be gone?" Meredydd asked as they left Gled Manor and took to the road, headed west toward Gled-Nairne Crossing.

"As long as it takes," said Bevol, "which depends entirely on you."

Meredydd did not find that thought a particularly comforting one. She imagined them trekking endlessly, while she tried to remember and decipher her dream—a dream that would only recede further with time. The only thing even vaguely comforting about the situation was that Bevol himself was acting as her Weard; he would observe her, care for her, but would offer no more guidance than he was instructed to in his own dreams.

The Nairne road was a broad pebbled way that cut north to south across Caraid-land through field and farm and wood. As they reached the Gled-Nairne Crossing, Meredydd gazed south toward the place where the roofs and spires of Nairne itself peeked out of its stole of trees. She missed it already, and the sight of Halig-liath guarding the waking town loosed a cascade of thoughts and a clutter of emotions having mostly to do with embarrassment and loneliness and separation. And Leal. Dear, loyal Leal. And Wyth. Sober, serious, earnest Wyth.

"Master," she said as they put their backs to Nairne and home. "I told you that Aelder Wyth spoke to me last Cirke-dag."

"Ah, yes. You said he apologized . . . and offered you marriage. You accepted the first and refused the second, if I recall correctly."

Guilt flashed through Meredydd's heart. "There was more. I didn't tell you everything."

"Oh?"

"He told me his family holds Lagan."

"Yes. Indeed they do."

She stared at him. "You knew?"

"Of course I knew. I was your only guardian. They had to inform me of the claim."

"And you didn't contest it?"

"You said you never wanted to see the place again."

"I was a child!"

"Yes. A very stubborn, adamant child. And I was not your blood kin; I was only the Osraed who had performed your Name Tell. I could not speak for you. You spoke quite loudly for yourself. The very thought of Lagan caused you great pain and you let it be known."

"You didn't tell me Arundel claimed it."

"You never asked."

"Five years, he said. They've held it for five years. They must have claimed it right after . . . right after his father killed himself."

Osraed Bevol said nothing.

"Which happened only a fortnight after my parents were murdered."

Still Bevol was silent.

"Wyth said his father had started the papers for the claim. . . . I only just thought—Master, did Rowan Arundel kill my mother and father?" How could she, she wondered, as the words twisted themselves between her lips, say it so coldly? Why was she not screaming, crying? Why was she still walking along this road as if it was all in the world she could do?

Skeet's eyes, dart sharp, skittered back and forth between his Master and Meredydd, resting finally on the old man's face.

"I don't know," said Bevol finally.

"But you're Sighted," she protested. "You could weave a Past Tell and *see* if he did . . . couldn't you?"

"But I did not."

"Why?" She stopped, now, and faced him.

"What would it have served? What would have been accomplished? That a little girl be poisoned with fear and hatred?"

"He could have been brought to justice!"

"If he killed your parents, then he was brought to justice, Meredydd. By his own hand. He laid his punishment at God's feet. What would you do—have his sin visited on his son? His daughters?"

Meredydd gazed, unfocused, at the pebbles in the road. Fine they were, round and smooth. "It has been," she said and began walking again.

She believed the Osraed when he said he didn't know if Rowan Arundel had murdered her parents (to gain prime pasturage and a right of way?). Even if he had woven a Past Tell, he very likely would have seen no more than she had seen. Cloaked and masked men silently carrying out their appalling task in a firelit yard. But there was one thing he definitely could assess—would have to have done so as a member of Halig-liath's Osraed triumvirate.

"Why did Wyth's father kill himself, Master?"

"What would you make of it if I told you it was guilt? Consuming and terrible guilt."

"Was it guilt?"

"It was. The man's soul was in tatters. He could not face himself. He chose to face God instead."

"What should I make of it, Master? That he was party to killing my parents?"

"That is a possibility, since only his family gained by their deaths."

The thoughts. The thoughts that crawled and scuttled and flew through Meredydd's head. They were night thoughts, dark-winged and sharp-clawed, and they battered for release like bats seeking escape from a cage. When the trio stopped for the night in the woods hard by the banks of the Bebhinn, she was in torment, for she had held those thoughts captive all day. Now, in the comfort of camp, they tumbled out before her eyes where she was forced to hold them up against firelight and appreciate their loathsomeness.

Revenge. That was the word. The third Cirke-dag of every month she had gone to Lagan's ruin seeking a clue, a sign, some way of knowing who stood to receive her revenge. She'd studied the Divine Art half in the hope that it would aid her in that pursuit. That through her talents and acquired skills, she would be able to weave a Past Tell and find the destroyers of her innocence and the stealers of her life.

It was an unworthy goal; she knew it. She knew it most cuttingly when Osraed Bevol's eyes were on her, as they were now. But wasn't it justice she wanted to serve? Wasn't it nobler than vengeance? Wasn't it a just retribution?

"Meredydd," said Bevol softly, so that only she could hear. "There is no duan for vengeance, did you know that? There is no Runeweave in the Divine Art for retribution. Only Wicke offers that consolation. Only a Dark Sister can accept such a mission."

I can't hear you, she thought. Thwarted, now. Her requital was thwarted. These years she had poked about the corpse of Lagan, seeking her sign, her clue, and the murderer had been dead, himself. Out of her reach, damn him! Out of the reach of her passion to be the cause of his destruction.

Ah, the frustration. She had had her revenge in her hand just a week past, when the son of her parents' murderer had stood right in front of her and offered up his heart and soul. Had she but known, she could have spurned him viciously, made his life hell, tortured him with what she suspected. Or better, she could have accepted his offer of marriage and destroyed him slowly from the inside out, day by day.

She wondered if his mother knew the truth. Wondered if the hatred she'd felt from the woman had its source in the results of her husband's greed—or in her own. If she had only known, she might have woven a Truth Rune for Moireach Arundel . . . if only she had known. She recalled the scene in the Osraed's Chamber, but recalled it differently. Instead of Meredydd the Meek, standing naively before her accusers, she was the Avenger of Lagan, hurling a counter-accusation, pressing for a Runeweave that would force the truth into the open. A far different Moireach Arundel would that be, cowering on the polished floor. What would Wyth think of his mother then, when it was shown without doubt that Meredydd was innocent?

Innocent?

She cowered herself then, cringing away from the stuff of her own thoughts. Not innocent. Vicious. Cruel. The same Meredydd Wyth thought gave such good counsel: The sins of the father are visited upon the son only if the son allows them to be. And Wyth *had* allowed them to be—without her help. He stewed each day in shame that did not even belong to him; stirred the fire beneath his personal cauldron with feelings of inadequacy and failure and became enamored of Lagan's sole survivor—his father's legacy.

It was very quiet in Meredydd's mind suddenly, and her heart lay hushed in her breast. She did not want Wyth to suffer. She took no joy, at this moment, in knowing that he did suffer, and on her behest. Her desire for revenge tasted bitter on the back of her tongue and she was glad that the Osraed Bevol had not marred her years with him by telling her all he knew of the death of Lagan.

Meredydd closed her eyes. They burned from the dry heat of the fire and the wet heat of her tears.

"Master," she said, "I'm glad there is no such duan. No such rune."

She moved to lie down then, exhausted, and felt Bevol take her shoulders and guide her drooping head to his breast. Across the firepit, Skeet blinked and nodded and mumbled the melody of an old prayer duan. But Meredydd neither saw nor heard him. She had fallen down a well of sleep so deep even dreams could not escape.

He stood at the top of the stairs, his back to the long stone flight, his face pressed against the mullioned window. His eyes were focused through one of the flat panes that alternated with the faceted lead-crystal ones. The window looked north, over the kitchen roof, across the garden, above the sash of trees along Halig-tyne. He could see the river pasture from here, see the sheep dotted like fleecy mushrooms over the shadow-strewn meadow.

He moved a step to the right and the green world

outside fractured into a dizzying collection of tiny pictures—each a realm complete. He tilted his head and the little images reeled and danced, bright, in shades of green and azure and cloud white.

He was wishing for other colors when the dark banner intruded into his lead-crystal world, appearing out of the darker green of the treetops. He squinted and caught a splash of orange, searing against the new backdrop of sooty gray. He stepped back to the left and the myriad worlds coalesced into one. A world of green and blue and white riven by a pennant of near-black that soared above the tyne-wood.

The tongue of orange licked again at the dark stain and the boy gasped. How pretty it was, that glowing tongue, how eloquently it dispelled his boredom, how delightfully it changed the unchanging world outside the windows of Arundel. He moved back to the faceted pane and watched the play of flame and smoke, his eyes finding more delight in the way the encroaching twilight spread the radiance of the fire out upon the treetops in a soft, diffuse blanket.

Such a blanket! Such a warm, lovely blanket. He tried to imagine curling up within it, warm to the soul, while his mother sang him to sleep the way she had done once, before the responsibilities of being Moireach of Arundel had increased. Their grand house was full almost every evening with equally grand visitors from as far away as Creiddylad and Eada. There were no visitors this evening, but Mother had been distant and distracted and even angry-seeming, so Wyth had come here to his window world.

He was glad he had been here to see such a grand show. It was almost like the fireworks of Solstice and it went on for a very long time.

He was still watching it as twilight darkened and lost its color, was pulled from the entrancing display when the tiny white dots that were sheep scattered in sudden chaos and something dark darted into the crystal pictures. He moved back to the flat pane and saw a horse dash along the wooded road to disappear out of sight around the flank of the great house.

He smiled. Father was home. He turned his back to the window and came to the top of the stairs as the front door opened and his father, cloaked and bundled despite the warm weather, stepped into the hall.

"Papa!" he cried. "Did you see the fire?"

His father looked up at him, white-faced, and said nothing. He was still staring voicelessly when his wife swooped into the hall like a great, colorful bird, and drew him away into the parlor. The doors closed behind them, but they did not seal away the sound of raised, yet muffled voices—the sound of anger, the sound of fear, the sound of weeping . . . of his father weeping. He had never heard his father weep. Never.

He sat down upon the stairs and listened to the frightening new sound while, behind him, the tiny window panes glittered with points of orange light.

Wyth Arundel awoke with a shudder and forced his eyes open. He hadn't had that dream for years. He hadn't wanted to have it because he feared it. Not for itself, but for its companion. If and when he slept again tonight, he would dream another dream that seemed always to pair itself with this one. A dream of a horrifying, stretched shadow swinging, pendulum-like, upon a slanted wall.

Wyth shuddered again and blinked rapidly, not daring to close his eyes for any length of time. He knew that if he did he would see his father hanging there, beneath the third-floor stair, his face white, his bulging, startled-looking eyes still full of an emotion his son hoped never to know.

Chapter 6

Beholding the worlds of creation, let the true Pilgrim attain renunciation and know this: The Spirit which is above creation cannot be attained by action.

In his hunger for divine wisdom, let the Pilgrim go reverently to a Teacher who lives the sacred words and whose soul has the peace of the Spirit.

To a Pilgrim who comes with mind and senses in peace, the Teacher gives the vision of the Spirit of truth and eternity.

—The Book of Pilgrimages (On Pilgrims)

The morning was hushed and wool-hood close. Mist drifted in puffs and tendrils, rising from the earth like waking angels and lifting ephemeral wings toward the Sun—a Sun whose own waking turned lead to gold.

Meredydd sat, cross-legged, on a grassy tussock, meditating on the alchemy inherent in light. Even scents grew more vivid, as if they escaped from dark recesses unlocked at sunrise. She breathed deeply, sorting out perfumes and mere smells—morn-blooming flowers, dewy vegetation, wet wood. Sweet, tangy, musky. This moment she would have gladly held forever—a moment with neither purpose nor passion, success nor failure; a moment with no inherent struggle, only peace.

"There is a village not far from here," said the Osraed Bevol.

Meredydd stirred, exhaling the fragrances of the wood. The first bird of morning sang somewhere high overhead.

"And in that village is a woman." The Osraed moved to sit nearby, choosing a fallen log over the dewy ground. "Some people call her Wicke, but they've done nothing to offend her in spite of it—or perhaps, because of it. She has, in her possession, several amulets."

Meredydd pricked up her ears, attention focused completely on Bevol's words. "Did you make me dream of the amulets, Master?"

"No. The dream was yours, I merely follow its prompting."

She didn't question that he knew the substance of the dream. "Tell me about these amulets, Master."

"There are three. Each of them has a focus, a particular power, which it may manifest when worn by a Pilgrim." He paused.

"Pardon, Osraed Bevol, but that is not how I understood the workings of an amulet."

"No? And how did you understand them, then?"

"An amulet is merely a magnifier, not a manifestor. It enhances powers or . . . qualities already possessed by the wearer. If the wearer does not know how to focus those qualities, the amulet is useless."

"Ah. Very good. Now, let me tell you about these magnifiers. One enables the wearer to restore faded health, return vigor, energy and youthfulness. It can aid in the healing of wounds, even soothe diseased minds. The second magnifies wisdom and knowledge, makes the crooked straight and the clouded clear. The third enables the wearer to use the Sight—a Sight far keener than any Past Tell. With this amulet, one could see the truth of any matter on which he or she meditated. For the spirit can know things it will not reveal to the conscious mind until focused properly. This amulet contributes to that focus."

Meredydd shifted uneasily. "And my task?"

"Bring me the most important amulet."

Meredydd turned her face to him and frowned. "The most *important* amulet? But important in what way?"

"This is all I am bidden to tell you. Bring me the amulet you think is most important."

"How will I know?"

Bevol smiled. "Anwyl, that is the test."

They walked slowly to the village, Bevol setting the pace. That was all right by Meredydd. It gave her time to ponder the significance of the amulets she was going to be offered. Healing, Wisdom, the Sight; which of these was the most important?

Healing brought obvious benefits both to the wearer and to his beneficiaries. To return to Bevol his vigor, to place in his hands the tool to magnify his already substantial powers . . . well, where he had healed tens, he could then heal hundreds. And if, indeed, it could also return his youth, perhaps it would lengthen his life—thereby lengthening her life at his side.

And wisdom—had there ever been a time when wisdom was not necessary, but in short supply? Yet Bevol certainly did not need something he already possessed in abundance. Perhaps she could eliminate that one.

And the Sight—

Meredydd wriggled inside as part of her lunged at it—to know for certain, once and for all time, if Rowan Arundel had been instrumental in the deaths of her mother and father. To know . . .

She tore herself from the thought. No! To know the truth of any situation, *that* was the purpose of the amulet. To be able to tell friend from enemy, good from evil, real from unreal. *That* was the focus. A tool for justice that was, and someone of the Osraed Be-

vol's influence could take such an amulet and make
Nairne a shrine of justice. People would come from
within and without Caraid-land for the dispensing of
real justice.

They stood on the outskirts of a village so tiny it
barely merited the title. It was little more than a market square outlined in white stones, a tiny Cirke and
a wayhouse.

The Osraed Bevol sighed deeply. "Ah! Here at last.
How loathe are these old bones to move. Especially
after they've been forced to sleep on the cold ground
all night. Now, anwyl, Skeet and I will visit the wayhouse while you seek out your first task."

Meredydd jerked her head about to look at him.
"But how will I find the woman who has the amulets,
Master? I don't know her name."

"Didn't you see her in your dream?

Meredydd's brow puckered. "Yes. I think so."

"Well, then, you've already met, haven't you?" He
patted her shoulder and moved off with Skeet under
his right elbow.

Meredydd followed them with her eyes, wondering
how it had escaped her notice that Osraed Bevol was
growing old. She had thought of him as young when
he took her in seven years past. His hair had been the
color of a copper kettle then, and the snow that now
streaked it had been a mere flurry.

She struggled to recall her dream. In a moment it
came to her, sharp, clear, in focus. A little cottage on
the southwest outskirts of town, off the path the villag-
ers trod, avoided by all except when an emergency
arose. Then there would be clandestine visits and
whispered pleas and secret compensation for secret
work. Meredydd moved forward on tentative feet,
amazed that her recollection held a depth of detail
and certainty she was sure had been lacking in the
original dream. And she *was* certain.

Once she cleared the village on its far side, she saw,

on her left, a fern-draped slope—short, sunny and completely familiar. She had never seen it before.

She hesitated a moment under the still chill shade of the broad-armed fir, then left the path and crossed the green slope to the sparser cover of grove of alder. The cottage was at the center of the grove. It was little more than a bundle of whitewashed twigs, really, with a thatched roof and wood-slat trim. A curl of aromatic smoke rose from the stone chimney, spreading itself into a blanket that covered roof and yard.

"Not grand," said a reedy voice from nowhere, "but it do me."

Meredydd didn't jump out of her skin, but might have. An iron-haired, silver-eyed woman stepped out from behind a crape myrtle, a bundle of straw perched on one muscular shoulder.

"I be Mam Lufu. Who be you, Pilgrim?"

Meredydd bowed her head, respectfully. "Daegeseage, Mam Lufu. I'm Meredydd-a-Lagan, a Pilgrim from Halig-liath."

The woman laughed. "So circum-respect! You'd be an Osraed-baby, sure enuft. Well, daeges-eage to you, Pilgrim Meredydd. Come in and tell me about your journey."

Entering Mam Lufu's cottage was like entering another world. The atmosphere was close and warm and copper-dim with firelight. The air within was as aromatic as the air without and redolent with the tangy perfume of incense and spices.

Rising from the crouch she'd been forced to adopt to enter the door, Meredydd stopped statue-still. Through the bundles and nets of herbs and vegetables and grasses that hung from and over the beams of the low conical ceiling, she could see an open area that the cottage exterior failed to even hint at.

"Bigger on the in than on the out, eh?" chuckled Mam Lufu. "That's what ye was thinkin', ain't?"

Meredydd nodded and followed her hostess into the nether room, ducking baskets and drying grasses and reeds that gave off the scent of faded spring marshes and rosemary. This part of the house was roughly round and possessed one deep window on its eastern wall, cut, misshapen, at an odd angle.

Of course, Meredydd realized, the room was hollowed out of the hillside, though that was almost impossible to tell from without.

"Things are sometimes not as they seem," said Mam Lufu and sat herself down in a rough rocking chair facing the window. "Now then, what'cher Pilgrim's purpose today, cailin?"

Meredydd looked at the woman curiously and spoke her thoughts before she could stop them from escaping. "You don't seem surprised to see a female Pilgrim."

"Nawp. Not surprised."

"Everyone else thinks it's a scandal or sacrilegious or just plain wrong."

"Everyone's entitled to some thinkin', I guess."

"Why aren't you surprised?"

" 'Spected it. S'time again."

"I don't understand."

"Hunnerd year ago, there's another one just like. Time again."

Meredydd perched in the window embrasure, the scent of moist earth rich in her nostrils. "Did you know her?" She asked the question without really thinking of what it implied. Mam Lufu looked to be about in her middle age, iron gray hair, aside. She was amazed when the woman nodded.

"She come to me. We passed by each other, you might say."

"On her Pilgrimage?"

"Aye. Long ago, that was."

"Did she come here for an amulet?"

"Amulet?"

"That's what I've been sent here for—an amulet. Was that what she came for—Taminy?"

"Everyone comes here for differ'nt things, child."

She rapped her chest with a loose fist. "Inner things. Spirit things."

"My Master, Osraed Bevol, told me she walked into the sea and drowned."

Mam Lufu gave her a sharp glance. "He said that, did he? That she walked into the sea? Well, s'true."

"I've heard that was her punishment for trying to be an Osraed when it was an unnatural desire for a woman."

"Ah? Who said that?"

"Osraed Ealad-hach . . . others."

"Well, a lot o' bodies say that."

"What do you say?"

Mam Lufu cocked a bright, silvery eye in her direction. "S'that importful, d'ye think?"

It was important to Meredydd, suddenly, and she said as much.

Mam Lufu leaned forward, her chair creaking in mild protest. "Ye're shiv'rin' in fear of the same fate, ain't ye? Well, don't. Every soul's fate's differ'nt. May be by only a hair's breadth, but so. I'll tell you the God's own truth: Taminy-a-Cuinn deserved her fate. And you'll deserve yours." She nodded her head emphatically. "Read the tales, child. Listen to the tales. Has Bevol ever told you the story of the Lover and the Wakemen?"

Meredydd shook her head, torn between wonder and terror at Lufu's assessment of Taminy-a-Cuinn.

"Make him tell you. Say, Lufu bids it. Now—" She popped to her feet, interview at an end, and strode toward a dark passage along the rear flank of the room. "Follow," she said, and Meredydd jumped to obey.

The corridor into which they passed was almost completely darkened and smelled pleasantly of earth-musk. It curved this way and that and Meredydd could feel rather than see the irregular doorways alongside. They had gone perhaps five or six yards when Mam

Lufu disappeared into one of the black-on-black holes in the uneven earthen walls.

Heart rabbit-beating in her chest, Meredydd hurried to catch up. By the time she reached the aperture, it was emitting a ruddy glow that warmed to gold as she entered.

The room was small and completely circular. It fit the environs of Mam Lufu's strange hovel perfectly and not at all. The floors were of polished oak and the walls of vertical slats of white fir alternating with a darker wood. Meredydd glanced back over her shoulder at the doorway. Somehow she had known it would no longer look like a hole carved out of a tunnel wall. It was a round-topped arch with a capstone and edging of jasper.

Mam Lufu moved across the diameter of the chamber to an altar of sorts. It hugged a curving section of wall and had a polished cedar top—a lid, Meredydd realized as Mam Lufu opened it. The two semi-crescent halves swung up and away, revealing that the inside was hollow. From the dark interior, the woman removed a large, flat box. She closed the twained lid and set the box down atop it.

"Come, child," she beckoned Meredydd. "Look."

Meredydd came. And looked. The top of the box was beautifully wrought with what she recognized as a Pilgrim's Rune in the form of a ship. Meredydd stretched forth a hand to caress the satiny wood, running astonished fingers from prow to sternpost. A curl of cloud crested beneath the keel where waves might have been; it seemed to undulate under her fingertips.

"Open it, child."

Meredydd glanced at Mam Lufu's intent face, then reluctantly, loathe to lose sight of that wonderful flying carrack, lifted the lid of the box.

The amulets were just as she had seen them in the dream Solstice Eve. But despite her ardent wish, none of the three glowed or shimmered or made her thrill when her eyes touched it. In fact, they looked very much the same—homely little lumps of some silver metal, each on a piece of colorful cord. Meredydd recognized the colors; there was the red of Power—that must be the Sight; the blue of Healing; the gold of Intelligence—that would be wisdom.

She studied them almost mindlessly in the mellow amber light that fell from somewhere overhead. Eyes half-focused, she was aware of Mam Lufu only dimly—as a presence rather than a person. The pull of the Sight amulet was strong, calling her to a knowledge she was no longer certain she wanted. She rejected that immediately, distrusting the attraction. Healing, then, or Wisdom. One practical, the other esoteric, both broad in their application.

Osraed Bevol had always taught her to tread the spiritual path with practical feet. Healing. Her hand reached, hovered over the amulet on the blue thong. Her eyes flicked sideways, trying to catch a glimpse of Mam Lufu's face, but the woman had disappeared and Meredydd couldn't be sure whether she had faded into the ether or backed away. There was no help there.

Wrong, Meredydd! she chastised herself. *This is your decision, not Mam Lufu's. The task is for you to decide which is the most important amulet, not guess which Mam Lufu or the Osraed Bevol thinks is most important.*

She stared at them hard, then—three nearly identical lumps of metal on three colorful cords. The Sight amulet tugged at her again, whispering of certain knowledge of secret acts, counseling revenge. She was dismayed to realize how important that still was to her.

She forced her attention to the Healing talisman. There lay true importance, and with no taint of personal gain to cloud the issue. Ah, but perhaps *that* was the test. Perhaps to own the Sight amulet while not using it for her own gratification was the point of the exercise.

Then, again, perhaps it was not.

In the split second that she caught herself wishing for it, realizing she needed it to make this decision, her hand closed over the amulet on the golden thong. There was no brilliant flash of light, no thunder, nothing to indicate that she had made the right choice. Only a flash of certitude—which swiftly faded.

She turned, finding Mam Lufu behind her, and held out the amulet, golden cord dangling between her fingers. "I choose Wisdom," she said.

Mam Lufu nodded and smiled and Meredydd suspected she would have nodded and smiled regardless of which shiny lump had been proferred to her.

"Take it to your master," she said. "And may God bless you."

Numbly, Meredydd followed the woman out to the dark corridor and back toward the main part of the hovel, clutching the amulet against her breast. *Is it the right one?* she longed to ask. *Did I make the wisest choice in choosing Wisdom?*

Instead, when they reached the crowded, thatched entry, Meredydd turned to Mam Lufu and asked, "Were you really alive when Taminy was a Pilgrim?"

Mam Lufu smiled, showing even, white teeth. "Aye."

"Are you Wicke?"

The woman laughed. "And what is that, Meredydd-a-Lagan? Is a woman Wicke 'cause she doesn't think as others do? Is she Wicke 'cause she tends other fires than her own, blesses other crops or births other babies? Does healing make one Wicke, or arriving from nowhere, or too long a life? Is a woman Wicke when she's known to all and understood by none? Are you Wicke, Meredydd-a-Lagan? Or are you Osraed-to-be? Or are you more or less or none or all?"

Meredydd could only stare and wish she had more time to spend with Mam Lufu, Wicke or not. But, Mam Lufu, still chuckling, patted her cheek with a calloused hand and turned to go.

"Thank you," said Meredydd, at last, and watched the woman disappear into her house of reeds and earth.

It was only as she mounted the slope of the meadow that Meredydd noticed the position of the Sun in the sky. Where it had been on this side, now it was on that. An entire morning had passed into late afternoon while she was with Mam Lufu, and now hurried toward evening. Meredydd hurried with it, down the grassy track toward the village.

Osraed Bevol was in the dining room of the way-house, sitting at a rough-hewn table beneath a fire-globe that cast its warm light in a circular pool about him. He smiled at her when she entered, caught and held her with his eyes even before she swam into his pool of light.

"I've had a busy day, Meredydd," he told her. "These folk see the Osraed so seldom, they take full advantage of one when he appears. We have a place for the night here. The house-keep was grateful for a small favor we did his family. Skeet is just seeing to our evening meal."

Meredydd nodded, barely hearing him. She held out her hand and let the amulet swing from her fingers before dropping it gently into her master's out-stretched palm. His eyes followed it, the expression in them changing not at all.

"Wisdom," he said. "And what made you choose Wisdom?"

"The need for it, Master."

"Ah."

That was it, then—just, "Ah?" She didn't know whether to laugh or cry. She didn't know whether she had succeeded or failed. She sat heavily in the chair opposite the Osraed, exhaustion of several kinds finally catching her up. Her eyes fell, unfocused, on the little amulet.

Osraed Bevol turned it in his gnarled fingers (When had they become so bent or his hands so pale and

veined? Had it been Healing she was to have brought
to him? Had she, in a moment, of personal uncertainty, cheated him of renewed life?), then held it out
to her.

"Here, put it on."

"What?" Meredydd stared stupidly at the golden
thong with its shiny, misshapen pendant. "What?"

"Put it on. It's for you."

"But I thought it was for you."

He shrugged. "I have chests full of amulets. This is
your first. Wear it. Let it remind you of this day, this
place."

"And Mam Lufu."

"And Mam Lufu."

"Who is she, Master? Is she Wicke?"

"Some people call her that." He smiled. "I'm sure
that's what Ealad-hach would call her."

"But is that what she is?"

"Well, anwyl, what if we were to agree that a Wicke
is any female who is talented and empowered in the
manner of the Osraed, but who is not Osraed? And
that having agreed upon that, we then agree that Mam
Lufu is such a female."

"Then she is Wicke."

"So it would seem."

"And isn't that evil?"

"Is it? How so? She is a part of your Pilgrimage
and that makes her an instrument of the Meri. How
can an instrument of the Meri be evil?"

Meredydd considered that. "Well, I don't see how,
but I know Ealad-hach would consider her to be evil."

"And?"

"And he's Osraed."

"Meaning?"

"Meaning he should know."

Osraed Bevol's mouth curled at the corners. "Or
should know better. Think, anwyl. I am also Osraed—
more recently than Ealad-hach, as it happens. Yet I
tell you Mam Lufu is not evil."

"Then one of you is wrong."

"Obviously."

"Then ... doesn't the Meri communicate Her Truth to you after you have become Osraed? I thought—"

"She communicates to some and not to others. It depends."

"On what, Master?"

He raised the hand holding the amulet and swung it before her. "On this, anwyl. On wisdom. On purity of heart. On clarity. Wear this and remember that it is possible for a man or a woman to be once enlightened and yet wander back into darkness."

Meredydd took the amulet in numb fingers and put it around her neck, slipping the pendant down inside the loose collar of her sous-shirt. She held her breath for a moment, then exhaled and blinked. "I don't feel any different."

"No?"

"No. I don't feel any wiser."

"How would you know?"

She considered that. "I'd know more, wouldn't I?"

"Wisdom and knowledge are two different things, anwyl. Like the two wings of the bird of the human intellect. Knowledge is a thing—inert, inactive. Wisdom is knowing what to *do* with that thing. Knowledge is acquired; wisdom is grown."

"Then I haven't grown any wisdom, have I?"

"You have enough to know you need more." He smiled.

She looked at him—dark eyes to light—and smiled in return. That was as close to success as she needed to come. Perhaps there had been no right choice, perhaps there had been only a right attitude. Perhaps she had at least that much.

"Master, Mam Lufu said I was to have you tell me the story of the Lover and the Wakemen."

"Did she? And what made her suggest this, do you think?"

"We were talking about Taminy-a-Cuinn. About her fate . . . and mine. Mam Lufu said Taminy deserved her fate and that I would deserve mine. Then, she said you must tell me the tale of the Lover and the Wakemen."

"Then I'll tell it." He gazed for a moment at the time-polished wood of the tabletop between them as if the tale was being enacted there. Meredydd found her eyes following his, trying to see scenes in the grain of the worn wood.

"There was," he began, "a young man of Creiddylad whose name has long been forgotten. He was in love with the daughter of a wealthy mercer. He had first caught a glimpse of her in the crowd at market, and had spoken to her later at Solstice Festival and had fallen quite in love. Well, he discovered she had moved from Creiddylad and had returned to her ancestral home in a city far up the coast. So he followed her. But all he knew was her given name—he'd never asked after her family—and when he reached the city where she lived, he found he had no idea at all where to begin his search.

"The young man got a room at an inn near where there were the grand homes of many mercers and cleirachs and scholars. He searched for his Beloved by day, every day, but he never saw her. He searched for her by night, but never glimpsed her face. At last, in despair, after endless nights of sleeplessness, the young man gave up and began wandering aimlessly about the darkened city. Well, at last the wakemen, patrolling the night streets, saw him, and thinking by his disheveled appearance that he must be a thief, they began to pursue him."

"What did he do?" asked Meredydd, completely engrossed in the tale.

"Well, he ran. What would you do if you were being chased through the cold, dark streets of a strange city by big, armed men?"

Meredydd smiled. "Run."

"No doubt. And that is what the young man did. He ran and they followed, shouting at him to stop, calling him a thief and, at last, firing on him with bow and shot. He ran until he was exhausted. No, he ran until he was past exhaustion. And as he ran he thought, 'Surely these wakemen are daemons from some abyss pursuing me for my immortal soul. They will catch me and I shall die without ever seeing my Beloved again.' And he bemoaned his fate most pitifully.

"Well at last, he entered a blind alley, bordered by tall walls. And when he reached its end, he realized that he was trapped and that the only way he could escape the wakemen was to climb the huge, high wall before him. Crying and terrified, the young man climbed the wall, painfully, arduously—for his very life now depended upon it. He climbed all the way to the top of that wall, but when he got to the top, he slipped and fell to the ground on the opposite side."

"And?" asked Meredydd, when he paused to look at her.

"The young man saw that he was in a garden and in that garden was a light moving across the grass. He went toward the light and when he reached the place where the light was born, he saw his own dear Beloved holding a lamp and searching for a ring that he had given her—a ring she had lost and thought never to see again." Osraed Bevol sat back in the rough chair and cocked his head to one side. "What do you think our young friend thought of those wakemen then, anwyl? Do you think he would still call them abysmal daemons?"

"If he could have seen the end of his quest, or she the result of her loss—" Meredydd began.

"Ah," said Bevol, "but we never can, can we?" He broke his eyes from hers, then, and waved at someone across the room. "Ah, good. Here's Skeet with our dinner." He glanced back at her and patted her hand where it lay on the table. "The end, anwyl. The goal. That is what any quest is about, is it not?"

She could only nod and rub the little lump of metal she wore close to her heart.

He was in the throne room. The throne room of Cyne Liusadhe. Lofty, it was. Mighty. So high of ceiling that the nether corners were lost to sight and the tops of the great arches were draped in night even in broadest daylight.

Before the throne of Cyne Liusadhe stood eleven women. The oldest was eighty; the youngest was fourteen. Different they were, in form and face, but alike in defiance. Heads up, eyes focused on the Cyne as if they feared him not at all.

Brazen, he thought, looking down on them from somewhere and nowhere. Horrid, brazen creatures, black as the darkness that spawned them. Wicked as the vanity which urged them to pretend to greatness, which led them to parade before all their evil talents.

Their sentence was being pronounced now, by the Cyne himself. "Wicke," he said. "Ye are all Wicke—Dark Sisters. We abhor you, yet we are merciful. Ye shall not die. Ye shall be banished only. Leave here, Dark Sisters, and never return. Creiddylad is death to you, for if ye return to it then ye *shall* suffer death. Indeed, to your families, ye are dead already."

Generous was Liusadhe, and the unborn Osraed, from his ethereal vantage point, nearly wept at the knowledge of what that generosity would mean.

The women were led away to a place outside the city where their guards turned them loose upon the road. *Oh, that you would have killed them*, he thought, and watched them as they linked hands and bowed their heads and formed a circle there. They began to pray. *Blasphemers!* Their bodies swayed in time to some unheard rhythm, their feet shuffled upon the sandy roadbed.

Ah, if only he had hands and might close his ears!

But he had no hands. He had no body. And so, he listened to their prayers and their duans and made no sense of their words. It was forgiveness they asked for, not for themselves—oh no, their wickedness was too complete for that. They begged forgiveness for the Cyne in his palace, for the Osraed in their Holy Fortress, for the people who had served them up for exile.

Dear God! How did they dare? But they did dare and stood and swayed upon the road until it was near dark. Only then did they cease their profanity and begin to move away.

They had gone only a few yards when one turned back, hearing the approach of horses, and pointed. Perhaps, he thought, the soldiers would return to render them forever silent, forever impotent. But no, they were smiling, laughing, pointing, as out of the darkness came wagons and horses and men and children.

He could see it clearly now, what their evil ministrations had wrought. The ones they had left behind, the ones who had been ordered to think of them as dead, these creatures had, with their hideous powers, drawn from the safety of Creiddylad into the night.

Now he did weep. He could even hear his own voice, a thin wail in his ears, as he watched the women embrace their men and children, climb aboard their wagons and disappear into the sea mists. Soon those mists became too thick to penetrate and he drifted for a time, his sorrow a blunted ache in his nonexistent breast.

Then, at the edge of his senses, he heard it, the lapping of water upon the sand. The whisper of waves. And he saw a lone figure detach itself from the mists and move out upon a shore he could but dimly perceive. It was a girl. One of the eleven, he realized. The youngest of them. She had hair as black as a raven's wing and eyes the color of a cloud's belly. And she stood upon the shore as boldly and as brazenly as she had stood before the Cyne, her queer silver eyes fixed upon the waves as they had been fixed upon the royal countenance.

His non-eyes blinked and the hair was burnished chestnut and the eyes were a clear brown and he understood, in that moment, that he was witness to a timeless sacrilege. The Wicke, smug smile on her pretty face, waited to attain the unattainable. It was the Meri she had waited for then; it was the Meri she would wait for only days from now. Did she know what her sacrifice would bring upon Caraid-land?

He stared full into those dreadful eyes—silver again—and imagined that they could see him, though there was nothing of him to see. She must know, the young Wicke, for those eyes laughed wickedly and those lips parted in a smile.

The shriek that woke him was his own, and he sat straight up in his big, warm bed, suddenly chilled to the marrow. Sea-cold sweat stood out all over his body and he clutched at himself, trying to rub the terror away.

"Ealad?" His wife's voice came to him, gentle and warming, and her hand lighted upon his damp back. "Whatever is wrong, dear man? Have you had a dream?"

"I have had a nightmare," he whispered and reached a hand out to feel the solid flesh of her good, strong arms. "Ah, Bevol," he breathed, "you don't know what you are doing."

Chapter 7

*The Spirit of the Universe is seen in a pure soul as
in a bright and shining mirror.*

It is seen in the world of Heaven as clear as light.

*But in this Land of Shades, It is seen only as a
memory of dreams, as a reflection in trembling waters.*

—The Corah, Book I, Verses 25–27

She slept in a bed that night—or at least it passed
for one. The mattress was of fresh straw covered with
a thick woolen blanket. A wooden box-frame held the
straw staunchly in place. It did not hold Meredydd's
dreams. Those were already outside in morning sunlight that had yet to arrive, listening to the words of
her Master, Bevol.

"I am too old," he said. "Too tired. I cannot continue. You must take Pov-Skeet and go on without
me."

She must have protested. She knew she must. Protested that Skeet instead of Osraed Bevol would stand
as her Weard, oversee her quest for the Meri's Kiss.
She must have quaked with fear and uncertainty at
that, for she had not been without Osraed Bevol since
he lifted her out of the mud seven years before. He

117

had become both her mother and her father, friend and counselor, teacher and mentor.

But she heard herself say nothing—the crush of emotions remained bottled in that strange, dream-ether that dimmed senses or heightened them at a whim. She listened—the Osraed was speaking again:

"I have a riddle for you," he said. "A riddle."

She waited, poised, tense.

"I have a riddle," he said again . . . and again, then faded into her dream. She saw his lips move, but could no longer hear what he was saying. She stared at those lips. "A riddle," they said.

She woke suddenly, tumbled out of her bed of straw and dressed herself, hurrying. She had to force herself to perform her morning meditations, then, unable to concentrate, recited the Table of Medicinals and Herbs to calm herself and gain composure. With some semblance of that, she tried the meditation again with more success. Still, as she descended the crooked stairs to the ground floor of the wayhouse, she was already filling with dread, already cringing in anticipation at what Bevol would say to her this morning.

She pulled the Wisdom amulet out of the collar of her shirt and stared at it. It looked no different from yesterday, except for perhaps being a bit more shiny from prolonged contact with her skin. But she needed wisdom and wondered how the amulet could help her focus what little she had . . . if, indeed, she had any. She remembered how Bevol had taught her to focus her energies through a poultice of herbs while performing a Healweave. Perhaps this worked in a similar way. Or perhaps it was more like a rune crystal and you had to sing it a duan and focus the inyx *in* it instead of *through* it.

It was odd, she thought, how everyone thought of Osraed-hood as having to do entirely with Runeweaving and amulets and magic potions (especially new Prentices) but here she was, two days into her Pilgrimage, knocking upon the very gatepost of Osraed-hood, and she knew less about that than she did Dream Tell and Medicinals and the many ways of determining what another was thinking by bodyspeak and eyetell. Bevol had concentrated her education on prayer and meditation and growing and selecting herbs that healed. He emphasized the power inherent in honesty, fidelity, charity and wisdom and spent little time discussing the totems and tokens of his station, myriad though they were. She had used crystals, of course, but this—

She had been worrying the little midge of silver in searching fingers. Now the worry became a caress. A totem. A rune. A *thing*. Wisdom lay in how one *used* a thing. She tucked the amulet into her shirt and went down to the dining room.

The house-keep's wife was there, working behind the long table where food and drink were served. A little girl played on the floor at one end of the table, galloping a small, carved wooden horse along the rutted wood-grain trails. Meredydd smiled at them.

"Daeges-eage, Moireach. Is the Osraed Bevol out?"

"Not as yet, mistress." She smiled shyly in return and wiped her hands on her apron. "I'm layin' on breakfast now, though." She studied Meredydd for a moment, then asked, "You his daughter?"

"No. Well, that is, he's raised me as a daughter. My parents are dead. I'm his Prentice."

The woman's eyes grew round as coins. "But ye're cailin! Oh, beg pardon, I meant—well, I didn't think—"

"Neither did I," said Meredydd, "but Osraed Bevol brought me up and taught me and took me to Haligliath to study. I'm very grateful to him."

The woman's smile was back. "Oh, and so'm I. Grateful y'all come here." She glanced at her daughter fondly. "Yer Osraed Bevol's a saint, Prentice. I thought we'd be buryin' our little Ambre 'fore the week was out, but now—well, ye can see."

Aware of the scrutiny from above, the little girl suspended play and favored Meredydd with a gap-toothed grin.

"What was wrong with her?"

"She fell two day back. Off the fence 'round goat y'rd. Hit her head and went into this awful sleep. My husband was sure it was some Runeweave that old Wicke-woman threw—a magical sleep-like. But Diarmaid, tha's my husband, he'd not go to Mam Lufu t'ask, for he figured she's the cause of it all. But your Master, he looked down into Ambre's eyes and listened t'her heart and says it's just the 'fects of falling and hittin' 'er head. Con-somethin'. An' he had us leave the room an' he sat with her. I could hear him prayin' and talkin' to the Meri an singin' duans. And when he come out she was just sleepin'. Quiet-like, natural-like. Not . . . charmed, y'know."

Meredydd marveled, wondering if she'd ever know how to do something that miraculous. She had healed wounds, diagnosed ailments and treated them under Bevol's careful supervision. She knew the correct herbs to administer for the colic, the croup and the mild pox. She'd drawn aches out of bodies and heads, but never done so much as restoring a comatose child to consciousness. She found herself fingering the small lump beneath the fabric of her shirt and tunic.

"There was one other, wasn't there?" asked the woman.

"Pardon?" said Meredydd.

"Girl Prentice. I've heerd tales from Grampus, I think. Oh, it'd be ages back, then. Wrought terrible things, Grampus said."

Meredydd's throat tightened and her heart hung, cold and still, in her chest. "What terrible things?" she asked, without really wanting to know.

"They say the sea boiled," said the house-keep's wife, giving complete conviction to something she'd struggled to recall only moments before. "And the winds blew havoc o'er the land and dead fish and men floated ashore. And no new Osraed came out of Halig-liath for many a year. Osraed said it were proof the Meri'd changed."

"Changed?"

"Well, She must have done. To stir up such grief. Something must have angered Her powerful to put Her off being so loving and gentle. *They* say She changed." She nodded, certain that "they" must be right. "It happens from time to time," she added. "But then, you'd know that, bein' Prentice."

"Yes," said Meredydd automatically, "once every century, my Master says." And was it a coincidence that Taminy-a-Cuinn had gone on Pilgrimage the year the Meri had last changed? Osraed Ealad-hach didn't think so, of that she was sure. Was he right? Had the Meri's anger been directed at the sheer heresy of a female Pilgrim? Had Taminy walked into the sea or had she been dragged?

A chill of cold deeper than any she had ever known sliced through Meredydd's soul. She pressed her hand flat against the amulet and excused herself, seeking the warmth of the summer morning. She smothered the suspicion in prayers, immersed the fear in contemplation.

She was still sitting under the wayhouse's battered wooden awning, her worn prayer book in her hand, when Skeet came out in search of her.

"Maister's out, Mistress Meredydd," he told her, his dark eyes glittering. He seemed always on the edge of smiling, and she always on the verge of asking why. This morning she did.

"Skeet, you have smiled knowingly and secretly and mysteriously since I've known you. Why are you smiling?"

"Why, 'cause I'm knowing and secret and mysterious."

"And what do you know?"

"That I know naught."

"And what's your secret?"

"Something only I know."

"And what's your mystery?"

"That I know a secret and yet know naught."

"Meaning, you have no secret."

"Or meaning I've a secret, but I've not the wisdom to understand what it is." He held open the thick wooden door of the house and ushered Meredydd inside.

"You're posing me," she accused him.

"Everyone has a secret and every secret poses a riddle."

It was Osraed Bevol's riddle that Meredydd wanted to hear, but he made her wait through breakfast, uttering no word of her Pilgrimage until he had sat back with his tea and closed his eyes.

"I am tired," he said. "Too tired to continue on this journey with you."

She said nothing.

"You must take Pov as your Weard and continue without me."

Still, she said nothing.

"You must next find . . ." He opened his eyes and looked at her. "What must you find, Prentice Meredydd?"

"The Gwenwyvar." She said the name, only just realizing that she knew it and that it was connected somehow with the place she had dreamed of and forgotten.

"The Gwenwyvar," said Bevol nodding. "The White Wave. She is a being as pure as air . . . as pure as thought. She will guide you. Now, how will you find her?"

"You have a riddle for me. I dreamed last night that you had a riddle for me, but . . . I'm ashamed, Master. I've forgotten what it was." She felt the clammy hand of failure lay itself over her again.

"How could you forget, anwyl, what you never knew?" asked Bevol, eyes failing to mask his amusement. "Listen to me. Near the village is that which runs, but which neither rests nor sleeps. Find it. It will take you to a place where there are many white houses, each with a single pillar, and where children dance while their mother dances not. There, maidens rise from water without wetting their white gowns. In this place you will find the Gwenwyvar."

"When will I see you again, Master?"

"When you have completed your Pilgrimage and come home to me."

"Then I will come home?"

"You will always come home, anwyl. Everyone comes home eventually. And when you do, I will be waiting for you. Now, when you are ready, go. Pack food enough for several days—you see to that, Pov."

The boy nodded, already rising from his chair. Bevol turned his attention back to Meredydd.

"Listen to me carefully, Meredydd. The goal is the purpose of Pilgrimage. Let nothing distract you from your goal."

She pondered that exhortation as she and Skeet headed out of the village later that morning. She had not cried at their leave-taking, much as she wanted to. She comforted herself that Bevol would be waiting for her at home and that Skeet was beside her on the trail as their Master's surrogate. She was not, then, without family on her journey.

As they passed by the sloping meadow just beyond the village's sparse jumble of buildings, Meredydd wondered what Mam Lufu would do if she went to her for help. She combed the stand of alder and fir with her eyes, but the big/little cave/hut was completely obscured. She wondered whimsically if it moved about the countryside, appearing here and there, wherever people needed healing or comforting or had crops to be blessed.

She drew the amulet out of her shirt neck and held it in the palm of her hand. Wisdom. Wisdom for the riddle. She looked high and low. Followed every flash of movement with her eyes, seeking something that ran, but neither rested nor slept. She saw nothing that merited that description, no bird, no animal.

A sound tugged at the fringes of sensation, tumbling, gurgling, trilling atonally. It was the Bebhinn, of course, the Melodious Lady, singing her way wildly toward the Western Sea.

Meredydd stopped stone still in the middle of the path. That was it! That which ran and neither rested nor slept. She ran herself, following the liquid duan, vaguely aware of Skeet behind her, his feet near silent on the pine needle carpet of the trail. She rounded a huge rock, ducked beneath a pine bough and stopped. Skeet nearly collided with her from behind.

"The Bebhinn-tyne!" she said and laughed, glancing at her younger companion. "That which runs—"

"But ne'er rests nor sleeps," he finished, and nodded. "Aye, and babbles ceaselessly, as well." His eyes sought her face. "And now?"

"Now we follow it downstream, toward the Sea." *And look for a village with many houses on white pillars in which a mother, who does not dance, watches her children, who dance.* It would have to be a village, she supposed. But no, that was too obvious, wasn't it? The houses wouldn't really be houses, they'd be something else. Something that you might find along a river.

She took a deep breath of the river air and started along the bank, feeling much better with one piece of the puzzle safely tucked away. She began thinking of the maidens rising from the water and chuckled at herself. Here, she'd been half-visualizing a little village full of white houses and empty bath tubs full of maidens in white dresses. If the place was along a river, the maidens' water would most likely be a pool.

The Sun was high in the sky when the Bebhinn's narrow stream dropped suddenly downward several feet, disappearing over a crown of mossy rocks. Meredydd hurried forward along the gently sloping bank, feet slipping in the grass and detritus from overhanging trees.

She reached the descent and uttered an exclamation

of triumph. Below was a small pool not much bigger than the main room of Mam Lufu's hovel. At its nether end, the water continued on its way, laughingly escaping the blunt teeth of scattered rocks. She and Skeet slid down the shallow embankment onto the moist sandy shore of the pool. Then she paused to look around her, frowning, her exhilaration cooling to anxious uncertainty.

"I see no houses," said Skeet, echoing the movement of her head.

Meredydd lifted a hand to shield her eyes from the midday Sun and scanned the trees. "They won't be houses, really, Skeet. Not *people's* houses, anyway. They might be bird's houses or—or bees, or . . . anything."

Her eyes sought weaver nests. Those could be described as houses with a single pillar—if you granted the pillar could be upside-down. But wait, weren't *trees* houses? Wasn't the trunk a pillar? But these trees weren't white. They were dark-skinned oak and pine. Meredydd chewed her lip. And where was the still mother with her dancing children? Nothing in this place was moving at all.

"This be the place, Meredydd?" asked Skeet from behind her.

"No, Skeet. I don't think it is."

He nodded. "But it looks a fine place for dinner. Shall we stop and eat?"

She wanted desperately to go on—to walk until she either found the Place of the Gwenwyvar, or dropped from exhaustion. But there was Skeet to consider. She agreed, reluctantly, and they dropped, cross-legged, where they stood and dug into their packs.

Half an hour later, they refilled their water bags and went on, ever following that which ran and sang and neither slept nor ceased babbling.

Meredydd's mind traveled also, back the way they had come to the village where they had left Osraed Bevol. She wondered, now, if the village had ever ex-

isted at all, or if it had been some masterful Runeweave on her Master's part—a place which appeared
only when Pilgrims passed through, which existed only
for their edification. And Mam Lufu—had she been
real? Had she really known Taminy-a-Cuinn—a char-
acter Meredydd knew not whether to accept as hero-
ine or heretic, martyr or monster, victim or justly
punished errant?

It was suddenly critically important that she resolve
this dilemma, for it created another, larger one. If
Taminy-a-Cuinn had been a heretic or worse for daring to seek a station traditionally accorded only to
men, if she had died horribly as a result of that heresy
and brought retribution on all of Caraid-land, why
then—*why*—was Osraed Bevol leading Meredydd-a-
Lagan into the same sacrilege?

Her feet stumbled on the path, making Skeet glance
over at her in momentary concern. She didn't look at
him, but only shook her head, trying to distract her
thoughts from the direction they were taking. Shame
tumbled through her that she could even have wondered, however briefly, about the purpose of her goal.
Bevol loved her, that was the only assurance she need
have. And these thoughts—she wanted them gone,
purged, cleansed from her heart, her mind.

She felt desperate and dirty, and she felt Skeet's
eyes on her still. Foolishly, she glanced over to meet
them. There was a joyless collision and Meredydd's
gaze careened away. She was a betrayer—faithless,
ungrateful.

She concentrated on directing her feet onward
steadily, murmuring prayers, searching for signs she
surely must be unworthy to see and incapable of
comprehending.

It grew both later and cooler as they traveled along
the Bebhinn and, as evening approached, a sly wind
snuck about them, blowing damp, chill breath up
sleeves and down collars. Meredydd struggled her
cloak out of her pack and wrapped it about her shoul-

ders. Her eyes narrowed against the gusts, watching
the boughs and branches of trees sway this way and
that, she did not see the ground drop away before
her. With a loud shriek, she tumbled over the root-
studded embankment and into a grassy glen.

Skeet was after her immediately, helping her to her
feet and checking her solicitously for injuries. Glancing
over his shoulder, Meredydd exclaimed and pointed.

"Look, Skeet! Another pool!"

He turned, following her gaze, and nodded. "Aye,
mistress. Another pool. But I yet see no houses."

Meredydd clamped her jaw in frustration. "It's getting too dark to see." She squinted at the water. No
maidens appeared. And the trees here were all time-
gnarled oaks, nodding like ancient sages in the wind.
She shivered, as much from disappointment as from
cold. "Let's make camp," she said, and began to seek
a protected hollow for them to curl up in.

There were no dreams that night. No comforting
visions of Osraed Bevol, no affirmations of direction,
no assurances of purpose. Meredydd woke just after
dawn, stiff, cold and with her hand clamped so tightly
around her amulet, her fingers hurt when she opened
them.

She lay for a moment, taking in the half-lit glen, its
features tipped and tinted in the barest flush of rose-
ate amber. The grass was darkly green and damp with
diamond dew, and mushrooms lay scattered like
chicken eggs among the tender spikes. There were
sounds too, of the waking forest: the pips and trills of
morning birds, the chitter of squirrels and 'munks and,
over all, the song of wind-sough and twig-talk as
branches and boughs brushed.

It was peaceful here, beautiful, magical. Meredydd
longed to stay—to not have to travel onward and onward toward a goal that must surely be lost to her
already after yesterday's treacherous doubts. Leaning
on one elbow, she watched as the Sun breached the
trees and poured warm light onto the pond. Watched

as mist rose sinuously from the wind-rippled surface, sailing up on invisible wings toward a tryst with its glorious Beloved.

She sat up. Maidens rising from the water! Her eyes raked through the trees. Live oak, some pine—no white-barked birch or alder. Then where—

She scrambled to her feet and moved to the moist ground beneath one particularly grand oak. It was littered with the white caps of myriad mushrooms. She plucked one from the ground and turned it over. A fat, white stem rose from the delicately ribbed underside. A white house on a single pillar. She glanced at the ground about her feet. An entire *village* of them. But where was the mother whose children danced? The thought that this might not be the place crossed Meredydd's celebrating mind. Her regard of the glen grew fiercer. *It* must *be here. Somewhere in this glen, by this pool.*

She turned around once; then again. Movement— the entire glade was in movement. Dear God, *everything* danced for the piper wind. Everything but rocks. But rocks had no children.

She put her hands to her head. Too hard. She was trying too hard. She calmed herself with an effort. *All right*, she thought. *The bushes dance, the trees dance, the—*

"But not the tree *trunk*!" she said aloud and stared hard at the old oak, daring its golden pillar to contradict her. It did not, but its branches nodded sagely in affirmation. The branches of the tree danced, the tree itself did not.

Meredydd turned to wake Skeet and tell him, but he was already sitting upright, watching her with his dark, miss-nothing eyes.

"Is this the place, Meredydd?" he asked her.

"Yes, Skeet," she said, smiling beatifically. "I think this is the place."

"Ah," he said. "Then we'll bide awhile. Breakfast, mistress?"

"Breakfast? Skeet, we have to wait for the Gwenwyvar."

"Aye, but why go hungry a-meantime?" He grinned at her saucily and began to dig about in the packs.

Meredydd turned back to the pool. Well, this was her Pilgrimage, after all. Skeet certainly had no need to wait with her for the Gwenwyvar to appear. She cast about for the best vantage point and settled quickly on a great rock that sat half in the water. She climbed across two smaller boulders to reach it and settled on top to await the Gwenwyvar.

The mist thickened around her and she shivered in anticipation, though it was already warming. But her anticipation was not rewarded. The Sun rose, the misty veil burned away, and no Gwenwyvar, no thing, no one, appeared.

Skeet brought her breakfast out to the rock. She ate it and waited. As the Sun rose to noon, he brought her some berries for dinner. Still she waited. She drank water from the pool with cupped hands, she stared into the cold, clear emerald depths, counted the stones lying about the foot of her perch, counted the fish swimming just below the surface. No one came.

She left the rock only once to relieve herself of the water she had drunk. She didn't speak, but returned to her post and sat, face pink from the Sun. Skeet, meanwhile, watched, foraged and watched some more. Then, as the Sun slipped away again, he gathered wood for their evening fire. He had whittled himself a little spear and skillfully used it to provide them with a supper of roasted fish.

He hunkered down on the shore then, close to the water, and watched her pick at the spitted fish while he quickly dispatched his own. The Sun glided behind the trees and both sat as frozen, the firelight scampering across the ground between them and out onto the water, where it sparkled in tiny points of radiance.

"What are you thinking, Meredydd?" asked Skeet quietly.

"I am thinking nothing. I am only waiting."

"Will you stay on that rock the night?"

"If need be." She picked at the fish, putting a tiny morsel of it into her mouth. She barely tasted it.

"How long will ye wait?"

"Until the Gwenwyvar comes."

"And what if the Gwenwyvar ne'er comes?"

"She will come. Osraed Bevol said she will come."

"What if this isn't the right place?"

Meredydd turned her head, her gaze sweeping the glen with its guardian trees, turning just now to watchful, waving giants in the dark. Firelight danced up their flanks and over the water and the wind blew the flame-jewels across the pool, scattering them into a thousand directions.

"This is the right place."

Skeet nodded and settled himself back against his pack. "So certain are you," he said.

"So certain am I," she agreed and realized, almost with surprise, that she *was* certain. This was the place. The Pool of the Gwenwyvar. The Gwenwyvar would come.

She finished the piece of fish and laid the bones on the piece of bark Skeet had given her for a plate. She washed her hands in the pool, dried them on the foreskirt of her tunic, and rose to take the remains to shore where Skeet would bury them. She had just started to slide down from her rock when Skeet rose and pointed at the center of the pool.

"Look, Meredydd," he said.

She turned, following the thrust of his arm, and saw what looked like an accumulation of mist just over the heart of the pool. She slid back to the crown of rock without realizing she had moved, the bark with its fishbones forgotten in her hand, her eyes fixed on the spot.

The tendril of mist curled and coiled, looking first

like a snake, then like a white bird, then like someone in flowing white robes. The mass grew, turning, spiraling, sculpting itself, above the black, jeweled surface of the water, into a thing with features and form—the features and form of a woman with long white hair that billowed in the night wind and spilled into the water.

Meredydd's eyes burned from watching and she blinked them, straining to see the thing hovering before her. A moon was rising now, washing its pale, lustrous light over the glade, turning the figure's hair and robes to silver, touching every blade of grass, every twist of twig, every crown of rock. The light of Skeet's fire rose to meet it, melted into it, turning the pool into a glittering glory of gold and silver, topaz and diamond. And in the center of the pool, the misty being seemed to take on more solid form.

Me-re-dydd . . .

Her name. Had it spoken her name? Or had Skeet, fearful, whispered it?

Me-re-dydd.

"Here I am," she said and waited.

Let nothing distract you from your goal.

"No. I won't."

The path. Keep to the path. The path of Meredydd. The path of Taminy.

Meredydd felt a chill that was not part of the watery glen.

"What path, mistress?"

The path of Meredydd is the path to the Sea. This path, here.

This path? Meredydd glanced around. "But, which path, mistress?"

This path, here. The Gwenwyvar's head bobbed.

Meredydd looked at the pool, ablaze now with the glory of the moon, followed its rippling trail to where the stream poured out and continued on its way toward the Sea, a silver ribbon in the velvet dark. A ribbon of light—the Path of Taminy.

She nodded. "Yes. I understand. I must follow the Bebhinn to the Sea. And then what must I do?"

Wait.

Meredydd licked parched lips. "Wait? For the Meri?"

Wait for your destiny.

"Will I see her? Will I see the Meri?"

Wait. . . . You are good at waiting.

There was a twinkle of wry humor in that, and Meredydd marveled at it. What sort of creature was this Gwenwyvar?

"That's all, just wait?"

Ah, but first . . . a task.

"Yes, mistress? What task must I do?"

A jewel. A jewel of great value, of great virtue. You must find it.

"And where shall I look for this jewel, mistress?"

A village due north. A dark place. A place of veils. Go there and find the jewel and bring it to me.

"But where shall I find it? Where in the village shall I look?"

That is the test.

Meredydd licked her dry lips. "Yes, mistress."

One thing more. . . . You must leave your companion to seek the jewel. This is your test, alone. He cannot attend.

Meredydd felt a thrill of fear. "Leave Skeet? Oh, mistress, must I?"

There was no answer, only the moon's beams slanting obliquely through the trees while a cloud threatened to obscure it altogether. Already the white form was becoming more nebulous, more fickle. Locks of ghostly hair detached and floated away on the breeze along with frays of gossamer gown.

"Oh, wait!" Meredydd scrambled to her knees. "Please don't go! Are you—are you really the Gwenwyvar—the White Wave?"

I . . . am . . .

"Please, what sort of spirit are you? Are you of the Eibhilin?"

Your goal. Let nothing distract you from your goal.

A gust of wind swooped down from the sky, tearing the Gwenwyvar's fragile form to vapor, dismembering and dispersing it utterly. Far-off thunder growled and the moon hid her face behind a cloud, leaking silver onto its uneven hem.

Chapter 8

*The soul of the Osraed must be a steady lamp which
burns in a shelter that denies even the strongest winds.*
> —Book of Pilgrimages (On the Osraed)

Due north. She faced that way now, the rising sun
at her right hand, the forest spread before her in a
pristine tangle of tree and shrub. She shivered, though
it was not really very cold, and glanced back over her
shoulder.

Across the pool, Skeet stood and regarded her un-
blinkingly, his hands thrust deep into the oversized
pockets of his jacket, his expression studious.

Yes, Skeet, she thought absently, *this is what Prenticeship is about. Obedience. Following the promptings
of the Spirit.*

She had not, she realized, as she took her first step
under the verdant canopy, even bothered to ask how
many miles north she was expected to travel. She was
momentarily perturbed at herself for being so careless,
then knew an absurd pleasure at her own ineptitude.
Surely this meant that she was improving in that es-
sential quality of obedience. The Gwenwyvar had told
her to jump and she had not even asked, "How far?"

134

She turned as she ducked down behind a massive, gold-flanked oak and waved at Skeet, a gay smile on her lips, her hand caressing the amulet at her neck. Perhaps, at last, she was getting somewhere.

Keeping the Sun at her right, she walked—at first pondering her task, then, realizing the danger of pre-conceptions, clearing her mind of all but the sights and sounds of the forest around her. It did no good to ask herself where in a woodland village one might be expected to find a jewel of great value when she had no idea of what the village, itself, would be like. For all she knew, it could be patently obvious where the jewel was; the difficulty of her task might be in how she went about getting her hands upon it.

She had traveled for what seemed like hours when the ground, which had been gently rolling, suddenly sloped away downward into what appeared to be a deep wooded depression. Mist rose from it, gold-tinged by the Sun, and dissipated into the blue-gray stipple of the sky. She peeked through the trailing limbs of fir and thought she spied the unnatural angle of a roof-peak below.

Just the sort of place a mystic village might be expected to inhabit, she thought wryly, and stepped carefully onto the woody hillside. She began to imagine what she would find when she got to the bottom of the deep vale: A scattering of poor houses, a wayside roadhouse. Perhaps the Osraed or the Gwenwyvar or whomever was actually in control of her Pilgrim Walk had just relocated Mam Lufu's nameless village to this spot, where she was expected to find it again and execute, with whatever degree of success, her third task.

She moved cautiously down through a thick band of mist and felt, all at once, as if she was swimming in a lake of diffuse, particulate water. Indeed, when the ground beneath her feet leveled off once again and cleared to reveal a soggy carpet of oily-looking dead leaves, the layer of fog floated above her, so thick the Sun was at a loss to penetrate it. She reached up a hand. It disappeared into the chill cloud just above her head. She snatched it back again, thrust it under her arm and glanced quickly about, still half-expecting to see the familiar wayhouse, the white stone circle, the falling-down corral of the jumbled market square.

For that reason alone, the true state of the village stunned her. It was not the same as the place where Mam Lufu lived. Oh, it was poor and sodden, but it was also mean and dark and filthy, and there was about it a sense of decay. The absence of sunlight contributed to that effect, Meredydd realized, and she felt that absence keenly, shivering though her senses told her it was merely cool, not chill.

Damp clung to her face and hands as she moved forward. The carpet of leaves gave way to grass-choked mud, rutted by wagon wheels. There were buildings ahead; she could see their lower regions—flaking mudpack, falling stone, rotting wood. Except for the obvious passing of wagons and the depressions left by horse hooves and booted feet, she would have thought the place derelict. It was eerily quiet; there was no birdsong, no wind sough, only her own feet uttering squishy little whispers as she moved forward toward the nearest building, her head bent and tilted—listening, peering ahead, holding her breath.

He appeared with no warning, his face thrust close to hers, his near toothless mouth leering horribly, his eyes glistening and bloodshot. "Cailin!" he reeked at her and brought a claw-like hand to her shoulder.

The shriek that shot from her throat met the chill air as little more than a wild hiccup. The twisted face with its grease-buffed skin grinned, the mouth split. He laughed.

Meredydd recoiled from the rank odor of his breath and wrenched her shoulder from his talon grasp. Her heel slipped into a rut and she all but toppled over—would have if the warped creature hadn't caught her at the last minute.

"Ye'd best watch yer step out here, girlie. Ye might muddy up yer nice clothes."

"I—I . . ." she stammered. "T-thank you."

"Ah? *Thank* me, she say. Well, well, cailin, if ye really wish to thank me *proper* . . ." The leer wrested itself into something a babe in arms would have found disturbing.

"Pardon, kind sir," Meredydd chattered, glancing anywhere but at his face, "but what place is this?"

He pursed his lips then grinned again. "I calls it Dark'ole. Somethin' ye fall into and canna get out. Blaec-del, tha's the proper name. Blaec-del Cirke."

Meredydd blinked. "Cirke? Is there a—a Cirke, then?" Perhaps she could enlist the aid of the Cirke-master.

"Aye. There is tha'." The misshapen head twitched in a northerly direction. "T'other end of town. An what might you be, then, girlie—a White Sister on yer way to take the vow?"

Her heart hammering against her ribs, Meredydd lied. Well, it was a very small lie, really, because she was more or less taking a vow. "Yes," she said breathlessly. "I wish to see about . . . going into the Cirke."

"Well, well. Then I'd say it were a rare fortune tha' Old Mors come across ye first. I'd surely hate to see a young joy like yerself take up the piety not knowin' what was bein' missed." His hand was back at her shoulder again, tugging at her. "I got me rooms over livery, sister. Come up hither while yer still a *lay-woman* an' I'll give ye somethin' to take to th' altar." He wheezed gleefully at his pun, his talons tightening, pulling more strongly at Meredydd's shoulder.

She resisted, but found "Old Mors" was much stronger than his spindly, twist frame implied. He was drawing her to the right-hand side of the road where she could make out the gaping, crooked maw of a stable. "Please, sir," she begged, "let me go. The— the Cirke-master is expecting me. He'll wonder where I've gone."

"He'll wonder naught, sassy cailin. Ye didn't e'en know there were a Cirke in this 'ole. So, now, come get evil with Old Mors an' give the Cirke-master somethin' to repent ye of."

Terrified, Meredydd lost her temper. "I don't *want* to get evil with you!" she shouted. "Get your hands off! Now!"

"Woo-hoo-hoo!" Old Mors cackled at her. "Fearsome! I'll like this, I'm thinkin'. Hands off! Hands off!" he mimicked.

"You'll like naught, sir," said Meredydd angrily, trying to strike a defiant pose. "I lied. I'm no Cirke-bound White Sister. I'm another order of Sister altogether. And if you treasure your soul you'll unpaw me."

"Or what? Or what?" he cackled. They had reached the stable door and Meredydd could see the animals within. The lecher glanced back over his shoulder, following her gaze. "Turn me into a horse? Eh? Aye, go ahead, Dark Sister. Make me a stallion. I'll still take me a young mare." He got both hands up now— one on her throat, one at her waist—and dragged her forward into the dust-shrouded stable.

"I'll give you a mare," she hissed and stamped, with every ounce of her strength, onto his foot. On the solid ground within the stable the heel of her boot was especially effective. He yawped and wheezed, letting go with one hand and hopping painfully about while Meredydd struggled to get away from him. She had almost managed it when he recovered and lunged at her again.

A loud *chuff!* at her shoulder made her jump to one side as a huge, black shape, radiating heat and smelling of sweat-matted horse hair and leather, forced its way right into Old Mors's face, bowling him completely over. Meredydd turned and fled.

"Hey, y' old sot!" cried the horse's rider. "Quit yer tommin' and take care of my mare. Gawd, but ye're a disgrace. Glommin' onto children, now, is it? Leave somethin' about for the boys to wed, will ye?"

Whatever else the rider might have said was lost in the pounding of Meredydd's heart and in the wild confusion of a street that seemed suddenly to have come to life. She heard voices raised in raucous laughter; discordant music played on an out-of-tune stringed instrument; the slurping, sucking sound of people moving through the all-encompassing muck; the creak and pop of wagon wheels and springs.

In the misty pandemonium, Meredydd remembered only that the Cirke was at the north end of town. She turned that way and ran, hugging the right-hand side of the rutted street.

The Cirke dominated the center of the village. It was not half so big as the sanctuary at Nairne, but compared to the rest of the buildings of Blaec-del, it was quite grand. Even the fog stood off it, as if in awe or respect, and Meredydd could see right up the bell tower to the bottom ledge of its peaked roof.

Without hesitating, she skinned up the flight of stone steps and through the heavy plank doors. They creaked closed behind her, lending a welcome support for her quivering backbone. The sanctuary breathed tranquillity over her; the guttering candles, torches and altar braziers whispering holiness and safety. Shadow Eibhilin danced for her along the walls, their songs silent. She reached again for her amulet. Trapping it securely between her fingers, she stood away from the door and moved down the narrow center aisle, glancing from side to side.

The floors were foot-worn, aged stone; the wooden benches were faded and glossy with much restive sitting. The altar was plain, unadorned but for simple brass braziers and a hip-high chunk of granite whose thick scattering of mica glittered like jewels in the half-light.

Jewels! Meredydd glided up to the altar stone and laid her hands upon it gingerly. Was it a chunk of the

Cirke's altar stone that she was to appropriate? That
could be construed as a jewel of great value . . . or
was that virtue? Well, perhaps here the two were
synonymous.

She glanced around, wondering what she might use
to chip off a bit of the stone, then caught herself and
grimaced. No mission of Pilgrimage gave her the right
to desecrate a sanctuary. She would ask for a piece of
the altar stone if it came to it, but first, she'd like to
hear a bit of its history. That might help her determine
if it was the jewel she sought.

With that in mind, she turned and glanced about
the sanctuary again. "Hello?" she called, and waited,
listening. "Hello, Cirke-master?"

There was no answer. There was, however, a simple
door at the far left-hand side of the altar. She made
her way to it and knocked. There was still no answer.
She laid her hand upon the iron latch and pressed
downward. It gave with a protesting shriek and the
door ghosted open. It was darker beyond and Meredydd was reluctant to put her head through the crack,
but she did. There was a short, narrow flight of stairs
slanting away toward the back of the sanctuary. Below
she could see the floor of what was probably an access
to the Cirke-master's private quarters.

After a moment of indecision, she called again,
more loudly this time. "Hall-ooo!"

Nothing. She was about to step out onto the landing
when she heard a scuffing sound behind her in the
sanctuary. She turned quickly, praying she would not
see that horrible Old Mors coming to teach her things
she had no desire to learn from him.

It was not. The person who had come up the narrow
aisle was a child. Her long hair was in ropy coils and
her clothes were stained and tattered. Silently she
moved down the aisle, directly into the patch of faded
sunlight that fell from a tall window above the entry.
The patch turned her sad tunic into a coat of many
colors and her pale hair into a glorious rainbow mane.

Smiling, Meredydd glanced up over the doorway. The stained glass window depicted the customary rendering of the Star of the Sea floating serenely above waves of white and azure and green. She glanced back at the little girl, amused and gratified to see that she was not the only cailin who found she could be a myriad other things while standing in a pool of colorful light. She moved, her boots scuffing the floor, and the child froze and whirled, obviously ready to bolt.

"Oh, please!" she said, putting out a hand. "Please don't run off. You look so lovely there in the rainbow." She took a few steps nearer. "I like to play that game too—pretending I'm some wonderful Eibhilin creature."

The girl smiled, tentatively. "You do? Really?"

Meredydd nodded, moving to stand before the child. "In my home Cirke at Nairne. Your window is quite pretty too."

"Aye, it is lovely, in't it?" She beamed up at it and it beamed back in a spray of color.

Meredydd followed her gaze, then frowned. "Oh, there's a hole in it. Right in the center of the star. How did that happen? Surely someone didn't throw a rock at it."

"Oh, aye. I suppose that must be it, although . . ." She glanced furtively about and lowered her voice. "I've heerd Tell the Cirke-master may've nipped it for his own reasons."

"Nipped it?"

"Aye. It were a crystal, see. A big, old egg-size crystal. Just like that one." She turned, putting her smudged little face into shadow, and pointed at the wall above the altar.

By the Kiss! thought Meredydd, *how could one Prentice be so completely oblivious?*

There was, indeed, a second stained glass window high above the altar. It was nearly identical to the first, right down to the crude stellar depiction of the Meri. But at the center of the star—analogous to the heart of that Divine Creature—was set a large, dust-dulled chunk of lead crystal the size of a child's fist. Some egg.

There was a nervous fluttering in her Prentice heart of hearts. This could be it! The Gwenwyvar's jewel. But, dear God, if this was it, how could she ever be expected to remove it and bring it back? Or was that a metaphor, just as the star, hovering over its glazen sea, was a metaphor for the Meri? Perhaps there was some spiritual way in which she was expected to bring the jewel back to the Gwenwyvar's pool.

Well, all right. If it was the Meri's heart or spirit or essence that was meant . . . Meredydd grimaced. But what if it was not the window crystal? What if it was the altar stone that now, with the cloud of vari-colored light creeping down its granite flank, sparkled like the Cyne's treasury? And in either case, was she to take a bit of one or the other to the Gwenwyvar physically or metaphysically? Automatically, her hand reached for her amulet.

"What's the matter, mistress?" asked the little girl.

Meredydd brought her mind back to the present and her eyes back to the child's face. It might have been a pretty face, she thought, if it were not for what were obviously bruises and abrasions on the pale, smudged cheeks.

"Is the Cirke-master about?"

At the mention of that person, the little urchin cringed, her mouth twisting. She uttered a nervous giggle. "Oh, I hopes not, mistress, or I'll be out of here. I upsets him."

"Upset him? How?"

The child's head moved in an oddly adult gesture. "I'm sure only the First One knows tha', mistress."

"You see," Meredydd said, deciding to confide a bit in the child. "I'm searching for something and it's supposed to be in this village. Have you ever heard of the Gwenwyvar?"

"Oh, aye. Least I've heerd the Tell of her. Are *you* her?"

Meredydd laughed, delighted. Only a child would expect the Eibhilin to visit them on their own turf, come to them in their own form. "No, silly! Of course not! The Gwenwyvar is an Eibhilin spirit. Do I look like a Being of Light?"

"Yes, mistress. Just now you do."

Meredydd realized she was standing smack in the middle of the window splash and laughed again, stepping aside. "There, see? I'm just like you. A girl. Just a girl searching for a jewel."

"Why?"

"Oh. I didn't say, did I? Because the Gwenwyvar told me to fetch it for her."

The little girl glanced back up at the window above the altar. "And you think tha's it, mistress? Tha' old hunk of rock?"

"Well, it may be an old hunk of rock, but it represents the Meri's heart. Wouldn't that make it a jewel?" She pondered the empty spot in the entry window. "Do you suppose the Cirke-master really took it?"

The urchin blushed right up to the roots of her pale hair. "Oh, do forgive me for even sayin' tha', mistress. It were a mere magpie-tation of what I heerd. I've no right to go on about the cleirach. It weren't a proper Tell at all."

Meredydd was immediately sympathetic to the child's sense of shame. Getting caught backbiting was probably one of the least pleasant situations to find oneself in. "Please," she said, "you really said nothing so terrible. Tell me—well, first of all tell me your name."

The pale head bobbed. "Oh, it's Gwynet, mistress. 'Blessed,' tha' means."

"Yes, I know. It's a lovely name. Mine's Meredydd."

Gwynet's eyes grew quite round. They were as pale and colorless as her hair. "Ooh, now tha's a name as fair radiances magic. You ought to be marked for the Meri with a name like tha'."

Meredydd blushed. "I pray that's true, anyway.

I'm . . ." She studied Gwynet's earnest face for a moment. "I'm a Prentice, Gwynet. A Prentice on her Pilgrimage from Halig-liath. Have you heard—"

The girl's head bobbed up and down with great animation. "Oh, surely, mistress. So, *tha's* the purpose of your seekin', then. I'm all of honor, mistress. And if I can help—"

Before Meredydd could say that she'd be most glad of anyone's help, the side door of the sanctuary opened and a portly little man in the robes of a Cirke-master entered the room. He'd barely stepped through the door when his eyes were riveted on Gwynet and his mouth drawn into what was almost a snarl.

"Vile animal!" he spat at her. "Get your heathen carcass out of my Cirke! This is a house of God, damn you. Be gone!" And arms flapping wildly, he drove the child from the nave. She went swiftly and silently, with only a backward glance at Meredydd before she slipped between the front doors.

The Cirke-master turned on Meredydd, then, and gave her an arrogant, suspicious sweep of the eyes. They were small eyes, narrow and sooty with the gleam of anthracite coal. They pinned her in the panel of light and held her there for inspection.

"And who are you?" he asked. "I've never seen you before . . . have I?"

"No, sir. You haven't. I'm Meredydd-a-Lagan from down-country. I was passing through Blaec-del and thought to visit the Cirke for my meditations." She returned his suspicion with a dose of her own, meaning to ask him about his treatment of Gwynet. She thought better of it. First she'd plumb him for some information. She tried to make her voice and expression as ingenuous as possible. "Your Cirke feels like a place with great history. I'd love to hear the Tell of it, if you've time."

The man's face relaxed a bit and he nodded. "Aye, it's got a great history, all right. But none of it particularly pleasant." He gestured around the sanctuary with

his head. "The Cirke here, was built on a burial
mound. That's the local story, anyway. Two hundred
years ago, more or less, when Liusadhe chased the
Wicke out of Creiddylad, the folks here figured what
was good for the Cyne was good for the common.
They rounded up their local girls and proved them.
Finding three of them wanting, they buried them."
He stomped his foot. "Right here. Right beneath this
floor." He smiled almost fondly at the worn stones.
"Built the Cirke on top of them. Keeps them down,
you know. Keeps them from coming back."

"That's . . . horrible," Meredydd said, staring at his
feet.

The cleirach fixed her with a speculative look. "Aye.
But this place is still cursed, for all there's a House
of God holding those damned creatures below. Place
is evil. People are evil. Cursed."

Meredydd was all but hypnotized by the chanting,
musical quality of the man's voice, by the way the light
played about his face, making shadows crawl and ca-
vort across its lumpy contours. She swallowed. "That—
that altar stone—is it from around here, sir? It's a fine
piece of work." She pattered quickly to the stone's
smooth flank and ran a hand over the Star of the Sea
worked crudely into the face.

The Cirke-master shrugged. "Brought it up out of
the Bebhinn. Nothing special about the rock except
for the amount of blood on it."

She must have goggled, for he smiled and moved
over to lay a hand on the granite block. "Oh, yes.
Nothing so mysterious or exciting as our pagan ladies.
No. Merely some casualties along the road from the
quarry. They say three men were crushed beneath it."

Meredydd winced; the hand stroking the stone
stilled and moved to grasp at Wisdom. She straightened, rubbing the silver lump as if to sponge away the
ancient blood. "How sad. I'm sure God would rather
have had the three men than the fine stone."

The cleirach studied her. "I'd not be so certain of

that. I doubt they belonged properly to God. But then, you'd have to live around here to understand that, and you don't, do you?"

"No, sir. No, I don't. I'm from Nairne."

"Far from home for a young cailin, aren't you?"

"I have family hereabouts," she said, thinking of Skeet waiting for her at the Gwenwyvar's pool. It wasn't *really* a lie. "The windows are beautiful, too. Did a local craftsmen do them?"

"Not exactly. If you can believe the local legends, it was a crafts*woman*. Sister of the blaec-smythe, they say. Mixed her own glass, her own colors—a true gem among women. Actually, I find it hard to credit. Seems to me if she was that rare a talent, she'd've been buried with the other Wicke."

He was studying her again, his eyes narrowed to mere slits. *Who are you?* they asked. *What are you doing in my Cirke, asking me these questions?*

Discomfitted, Meredydd made a half-turn and an uncertain gesture at the entry window. "I notice the crystal is missing from that one. What happened to it?" When she turned back again, she found the Cirke-master had stepped down from the altar's raised slab and was so close, she could feel his suspicion, prickly, against her face.

"You ask very many questions for a little girl. Who are you? What do you really want here?"

"I'm not a little girl, sir. I am fifteen." And a Prentice, she'd been going to say, but decided against it. Instead, she drew herself to her full height and felt her initial sense of threat subside. The Cirke-master was very little taller than she was and did not appear to be in great health. If worse came to worst, she could easily slip away and outrun him. "I was passing through your village and happened to see the Cirke. I thought it might be just the place to rest and renew myself. And it's natural of me to ask questions. I'm a very curious person."

She was strolling up the aisle away from him during

this little discourse, keeping him intentionally at a distance. Anyone who spoke so blithely of women lying buried beneath his feet unnerved her a little, no matter how small in stature he was.

"More than curious, I'd say," he told her. "Bold . . . brazen, more like it. Do your folks know you're out wandering the countryside?"

"My folks are dead, sir. Which is one of the reasons I *am* out wandering. I'm seeking a new . . . situation." There. She'd done it without lying. Just rearranged the facts a bit. . . .

The man's brows—neat little black crescents—rose over his eyes. "Indeed? Well, perhaps a situation could be found for you here in Blaec-del. Do you cook, sew?"

"Well, sir. I don't cook well, sir. And my sewing is poor, at best. But I've a way with medicinals . . . herbs and such. If you've a Healer in town, I could be of assistance."

His sharp little eyes flew at her, battering her face. Fleeing them, she glanced, again, at the entry window with its neat little hole. Perhaps the crystal had been of Runeweave quality. If that were the case—

But the Cirke-master had caught the movement of her eyes. Suddenly agitated, he sprang after her up the aisle. "You seem most interested in that missing crystal, cailin. Do you think it special? Do you think you could . . . weave a rune with it?"

He'd caught her by surprise and she let it show. "What do know of crystals and Runeweave?" she asked.

"Ah! Ah! What do *you*, cailin? What do *you* know?" He fairly pranced in the aisle now, and dew stood out on his round forehead, glistening like the mica in his altar stone. "A Healer, is it? You have those talents, do you? And do you use the crystals then?"

"Well, yes, sir. I was apprenticed to—"

"I find that most interesting. Yes, *most* interesting. Did you know, cailin, that there is, among the myriad legends of this wretched place, one that speaks of the resurrection of the Wicke? Oh, aye," he went on. "And at the hands of one of their own. It's a most interesting legend. I don't believe it, of course." His eyes glowed, belying that. "An inauspicious female shall redeem the souls of the Wicke of Blaec-del Cirke and free them. Absurd, of course, since how can anyone redeem what those fiends never had—souls, I mean. Wicke don't have souls . . . do they?"

He was in her face again, mesmerizing her with his dulcet, singy voice. "Do they?" he repeated, and raised his hand suddenly to her cheek.

She yipped and jumped aside, seeing, as she did, that he held a star-shaped amulet in his hand. Worked from a metal plate, it covered his whole palm.

"Ah-ha! See there! You fear it! The sign of the Meri. You shrink from it!"

Recovering herself, Meredydd tried to resume some semblance of composure. She smoothed the front of her tunic, running her hand over the amulet there. "Nonsense," she said. "You startled me, that's all. Jumping at me like that."

"No, you're afraid." He held the star before his face. "Yes, you're the one, aren't you? The Dark Sister come to rescue her soulless cronies. Well, it won't happen. *I'll* see to it." He stepped toward her, the star clutched in his hand, and Meredydd did the only thing she could think of. She grabbed the talisman right out of his fingers.

"There," she said to his shocked face. "You see? I'm not at all afraid of it. The Meri is the last thing in the world I'd be afraid of. I—" Her eyes fell on the thing in her hand then, and she saw it clearly for the first time. In the center of the silver, stellate plate was a crystal the size of a large egg, which was almost certainly the one missing from the sanctuary window.

Before she could decide what to make of that, the little cleirach had wrested the talisman back again and concealed it beneath his robes. "Get out of my sanctuary," he hissed, "or your situation shall be the same as your Dark Sisters—buried alive beneath this Cirke. I give you fair warning, Wicke. This talisman possesses powers far greater than the one you wear. And I will bring them to bear if you do not get out of Blaec-del. You shall not free your sisters, nemesis. You shall not!"

He raised his hand again, this time apparently meaning to strike her where she stood. The light of fanaticism inflamed his eyes and Meredydd, knowing there was no balm made that would soothe that, turned and fled the Cirke.

Intellectually, she knew the Sun was higher in the sky and she had to allow that the mist seemed to have lightened visibly, but for all that the little village of Blaec-del Cirke looked more dark and dismal than it had when she'd first stumbled upon it. Her eyes swept the swaddled street for any sign of Old Mors, but she didn't see him. She needed a place to sit and think. A place to decide how she was going to go about retrieving the crystal talisman from that horrid Cirke-master.

A man of God, indeed. How dare he even mention himself and God in the same breath? And to speak so cold-bloodedly about burying people alive. . . .

Meredydd twitched and rubbed her arms, darting away from the Cirke toward a shambling line of buildings along the street, afraid if she tarried much longer before the sanctuary, she'd be able to hear the two-hundred-year-old screams of Blaec-del's victims.

At the corner of the first building she met, she beheld steps leading up to a wooden walkway. It seemed to stretch the length of the building and even to continue on to the next, showing that at least some of the denizens of Blaec-del preferred not to wallow in the mud. She mounted the steps and moved along the façade. It was a shop of some sort, she realized, and as she neared the doorway, she saw two men go inside. Screwing up her courage, she followed them.

Inside, there was the smell of leather and sweat, of

oil and tallow and smokeweed. The source of the latter
was easy enough to see. A wizened person who could
be either male or female sat before a little black parlor
stove puffing on a horn pipe, while along a nearby
counter, several customers jostled each other for the
mercer's slow attention.

The shop seemed to sell a little of everything: food-
stuffs, leather, small gardening implements, animal
traps, lamp oil. Lumpy candles hung from their wicks
all along the fat, low beams that supported the dingy
ceiling; long strips of jerky were draped over a piece
of twine stretched over the counter; wooden dippers
hung everywhere. It made Meredydd realize that she
was tremendously thirsty. She could tell by looking
that the only drink in this place was the homemade
brew being foisted upon the mercer by one of his
patrons.

"S' good stuff," complained the brewer, shaking a
small-mouthed jug at the shopkeep. "Fresh as the
mornin' dew and ten times as frisky."

"Good stuff, is it? Care to explain then, how such
good stuff gutted old Tuathal? Man's sick to death. To
death, I tell you. Spittin' up blood this mornin', his
wife says."

"No fault of mine if he'll drink this stuff on empty
stomach. I tell him 'twere not for breakin' fast. Come,
Ruhf, don't be shunnin' me, now. Ye're my salvashin'."

The mercer laughed. "Hadder ain't buyin'?"

The brewer scowled and pecked at the filth that lay
across his knuckles. "Didn't 'spect her to what with
her thinkin' my stuff done foul to one of 'er payin'
customers."

"Well, if she ain't buyin' . . ."

"Damn you to hell, Ruhf! Ye're a fine one t'talk!
Every man here knows ye're the horse what had her
filly. Why, if enough of us were to give Hadder *that*
Tell—"

The mercer, Ruhf, had the surly brewer by the scarf
around his throat before Meredydd could even squeak

in surprise. He hauled the other man half over the counter while the other customers looked on with a singular lack of distress. "If ye breathe a whisper of tha' to the old hag, I'll treat you the same as I treated the girl. Why d'you think she's said naught of who done her? She knows me fair well, now. Knows what I'm likely to do, angry."

"Hadder'd ne'er believe her if she spilt it now, anyway," said one of the other men casually. "Not after she made up that grand Tell about the magic buck leavin' its spore on her belly." He wheezed and slapped at his leg. "Gawd-the-Spirit!" he guffawed. "Magic buck!"

"Only Hadder'd believe something that wild," chuckled Ruhf, loosing his hold on the brewer's kerchief. "Half Wicke, herself, I think."

The brewer coughed and pointed across the counter. "It were your belt buckle."

Ruhf's grip tightened again. "Which she'll never take note of. Will she?"

The brewer coughed again. "Maybe if you were to buy some still—"

"Buy it?" roared the mercer. "I'll make you *drink* it!" And, with his free hand he snagged a jug of the brew from the counter and popped the cork out with his teeth.

The brewer squealed, the other men roared with laughter and Ruhf hollered obscenities at the top of his lungs, all the while trying to force the suspect liquid down his adversary's throat. Meredydd stood transfixed, completely unwilling to believe that any of these people were any more than a figment of her Pilgrim's imagination.

I'm in an aislinn world, she thought. *I've fallen asleep somewhere in the wood and I dream.*

She started to back toward the door, praying no one would notice her amid the howling chaos in the room. But she would trip over an uneven floorboard and the old person smoking by the cold stove would glance up with rheumy eyes. The eyes pierced her and the gums clamped hard over their pipestem.

"Who're you? Who're you?" The voice was as shrill as breaking glass, as strident as a hawk's hunting keen. The entire universe could hear it. Every star, every sun, every being that ever lived on every planet.

Five pairs of eyes speared her where she stood, back to a rough support beam. One man wondered if she'd heard everything said and if so, she knew who to tell about it.

"Who're you, cailin?" asked the mercer. "What ye want here?"

"Please, sir. A drink. I was just looking for someplace to get a drink. A wayhouse?" She gestured at the street with one hand, saw it was shaking and pulled it down to her side.

"Ye were listening," accused the old one by the stove. "Ye were pryin'."

"That true, girl?" asked the mercer. "You hear aught?"

Lie, Meredydd. Lie! whispered a fierce voice in her rabbiting heart.

But her hesitation was enough to damn her. Ruhf let go the brewer and came around the counter. "What'd ye hear, girl? What'd ye hear?"

He had huge hands; fists like flesh and bone mallets. He was as broad as a century oak and around his thick waist was a studded belt with a clasp shaped like a cloven, upside-down heart ... or a buck's hoof.

"I said, what'd ye hear?" Her hair in his fists, he yanked her nearly off her feet.

Blood pounded in her ears, forcing fear down into her heart. "Magic buck!" she cried. "I heard magic buck! That's all, sir! Please!"

The mercer brought his face on a level with her own. Bloodshot blue eyes ferreted for the truth. His fingers twisted her hair, making her tremble with pain. "And do ye believe in this magic buck, cailin?"

"I do. Yes. There's powerful magic in these forests, sir. I do believe."

"Ah, ye say that now, but what'll ye tell Hadder, if she asks?"

"I don't know any Hadder!" Meredydd gasped as he yanked again at her hair. "I'm not from Blaec-del!"

"She's right there," said one of the other men. "I've ne'er seen her. And I'd be sure to recall such a fine pretty. You married, girl?"

"No, sir."

He grinned. "My son'll be interested to hear tha'. Come to think, *I'm* interested to hear tha'."

Ruhf guffawed. "And what difference to ye? You'll poke anything movin' on two legs, if it swishes its skirts at ye."

"Aye," muttered the brewer, seemingly relieved the attention was no longer on him. "I ne'er heerd ye ask the girls at Hadder's if they're married or not."

Meredydd cleared her throat, managing to coax it into producing a semblance of speech. "I'm just passing through, sirs. Please, sirs, a drink is all I want."

Ruhf leered and all Meredydd's hope of slipping quietly away dissolved out from beneath her feet. "Drink is it?" He glanced back over his hammy shoulder. "Okes, bring me a jug of that swill."

Terrified and chafing at her own cowardice, Meredydd's eyes scoured the room for some source of help. It would certainly not come from any of the other men. They watched her the way a pack of dogs watches a limping grouse, intent on her pain, relishing it.

"Don't do this, sir," she said, keeping her voice even.

"And why not?"

"You will surely regret it." *Oh, won't something fall on him? Won't someone distract him?*

He laughed and glanced back at his cronies. "A threat! The little cailin utters a threat!" He straightened completely then, his crown catching the handle of a wooden dipper that hung from the beam over head. It dropped, bringing with it two more dippers and a metal lantern. They pounced, as if alive, upon his head and shoulders. He let go of Meredydd's hair.

She leapt back a good three feet and started to turn, but his hands were fast as well as large. He reached out and grasped her shoulder, yanking her off balance. She found herself suddenly facing the door of the shop and wishing, praying, that she was just now sailing through it to safety. She even gave a half-hearted leap in that direction but just as suddenly, found herself staring at Ruhf's immense chest.

"Ruhf Airdsgainne, what are ye doin'? Where's my Okes? Ah! There!"

Rudely deposited on the rough floorboards, Meredydd could only skitter aside and stare at the personage in the doorway. She nearly filled it with her bulk and her skirts and her awesome height. If this was Okes's wife, she was more than his match in stature. She was almost, in fact, as big as Ruhf. Entering it, she impressed herself upon the room, making it seem suddenly much smaller and more cramped.

"Who's this then?" she asked, glancing down at Meredydd.

"Just a girl seekin' the wayhouse," said Ruhf. He looked at Meredydd. "It's up the street. This side." He bent to pick up the stuff that had fallen from the beams, muttering about "useless girls."

Okes's lady collared her husband and ushered him out. Meredydd made to slip away on their heels.

"Damn," she heard the mercer snarl. "Where's that good for naught child when she's wanted. Gwynet! Gwynet, come clean up!"

Meredydd paused in the doorway, frozen by the horrific idea that this man was in some way related to the gentle, skittish little girl. As if he sensed her gaze on him, Ruhf rose and faced her, eyes spewing hatred across the dusty, rough-hewn floor. "Get out of here, you little bitch, or you'll know more of magic bucks than Hadder's lame-brained get."

She got out—fear pouring cold and electric through body and soul. She ran up the rattly walkway, her eyes scraping along the buildings searching for any sign that one of these horrid, gray shacks was the wayhouse.

It was four doorways up, a little better kept than the other shops in Blaec-del and somewhat more tidy. She tucked into the doorway and found herself in a dark, low-beamed cavern of a place with a huge ember-filled hearth at the far end and a service bar near the door. There were people here, sitting at rough little tables about the room. The only light in the place came from the hearth coals and candles, and from dirty sunlight, falling exhausted from high narrow windows in the second floor gallery.

No one had seen her come in or, if they did, they didn't seem to care. She scuttled over to the hearth and huddled there, curling herself into as small a ball of flesh and hair and cloth as she could. She felt whipped and raw inside; ready and willing to lie down and give up and weep until she ran out of tears. Clutching the Wisdom amulet in both hands, she closed her eyes and gave in to silent despair.

Chapter 9

The goal of the Osraed must be to open the hearts,
fill the stomachs,
calm the minds,
brace the bones,
and so clarify the thoughts and meet the needs
that no sly meddler could touch
those he has touched.
                    —Book of the Meri, Chapter 9, Verse 72

Meredydd woke with a start, unknowing how long she had slept. She did not feel particularly cramped and the embers in the big hearth looked about the same; she thought she must have merely napped. Reluctantly, she uncurled herself and raised her head. She was still in the wayhouse and the little village of Blaec-del was very likely still outside its doors.

Yawning silently, she began watching the room. There were few people in it, and most of them were involved in eating breakfast or drinking hot beverages. Behind the bar worked a sturdy, crane-like woman who, though her clothes were poor, exuded an aura of cultivation. She held her head high, even while cleaning up after her more careless patrons.

At the end of the bar opposite the door was a staircase on which sat a girl about Meredydd's age. She was huddled in a misery which seemed no less abject than Meredydd's own, and rocked continuously back and forth, back and forth. While Meredydd watched, the woman behind the bar called to the girl sharply and she rose, moving awkwardly to the woman's bidding. Even in the half-light, Meredydd could tell she was pregnant.

The woman continued to speak to the cailin harshly, gesturing with both hands. The words were lost in the field of chatter and mumbles that lay between them, but the gestures were clear enough to Meredydd. The girl was lazy, they said, had left something undone, had not listened, had not obeyed.

Her sympathy was immediate. She doubted this poor creature could have managed a disobedience comparable to her own and no one deserved to be derided before a room half-full of people. Not, Meredydd had to allow, that anyone was paying the least bit of attention. That implied the scene was not an unfamiliar one.

The front door opened a crack just then, and a small, shapeless figure appeared for an instant before the room was plunged once more into shifting gloom. Meredydd sat up straighter and strained her eyes in the direction of the door. In seconds she was looking into a pale, grimy face that wore an incongruous grin.

"Hello, mistress," said Gwynet and plopped down next to her on the hearth. "I thought you might be here after what happened—" She jerked her head toward the mercantile.

"How did you know about that?" Meredydd asked, puzzled.

"I was about. I'm always about. Kind of have to be. Ruhf always needs somethin' done."

"Ruhf ... he's not—not your father, is he?"

The little girl let out a trill of laughter. "Oh, no,

mistress! Whatever'd make ye think tha'? My folks're dead. Ruhf, he just . . . looks after me."

"He's your guardian, then."

"He gives me a place to sleep when I'm not on outs with him. Otherwise it's the stable." She grinned as if she had not just said something that twisted Meredydd's heart. "Hay makes me sneeze, so it's best I stay in wi' Ruhf."

"Aren't you afraid of him?"

Gwynet cocked her head to one side and seemed to consider the question. "I s'pose ye could say he's sparked some fear in me now and again. But if I stay clear while he's in one of his dangerous moods, well— I'm safe enough."

Meredydd raised a hand to the girl's cheek. "Did Ruhf give you those bruises, Gwynet?"

The blush was visible even beneath the smudges of soot and grime. Gwynet covered the other cheek with her own hand. "I can't rightly recall, mistress," she said. "It means naught."

Meredydd opened her mouth to say that it meant a great deal, when a sharp voice called over the welter of conversation in the room.

"Gwynet! Gwynet, where are you? I heard that laugh of yours. Get over here!"

"Yes, mistress. Right here." Gwynet popped obediently to her feet and moved toward the bar. Meredydd followed her.

The house-mistress was glowering into the semi-dark room, her eyes lighting unpleasantly when they fell upon Gwynet. "Here you are, girl. My stupid daughter's having her sickness again. Take her upstairs and see to her. Then take up her chores." She glared at the pregnant girl, who was now cowering beside her just behind the bar. "*Someone's* got to do them."

Gwynet's head bobbed. "Yes, mistress. At once, mistress." She moved swiftly to the older girl's side and helped her to her feet.

Even in this dark hole, Meredydd could tell the girl

was pallid and sweating. Her eyes were like two
bruised jets set in her pasty face; they were devoid of
any defiance and held a hopelessness that Meredydd
found hard to bear. Instinctively, she found herself
moving to help Gwynet with her huddled charge.

"Who are you?"

Meredydd swung about and found herself face to
face with the girl's mother. "I'm Meredydd, Moireach.
I'm . . . a friend of Gwynet."

"A friend, is it? And of Gwynet? And how does such
a filthy little urchin collect friends? Where're you
from, girl?"

"From Nairne, mistress," answered Meredydd without thinking.

"And how do you come to be in this hole, Meredydd from Nairne?"

"I was . . . just passing by and came in to—to get
a bite of food and visit the Cirke."

The woman laughed. "Did you hear that?" she said
to the room in general. "This little lady wants to visit
our Cirke. Well, I doubt it'll be a pleasant visit, little
lady. Our Cirke-master has a way about him that visitors seem to find odd. He's a strange one, our Cirke-
master."

Meredydd nodded. "I've met him, thank you. I
found him . . . most interesting on the history of
Blaec-del Cirke."

"Oh, aye." The woman nodded. "Him and his
Wicke stories."

"Aren't they true, then? The story of the Wicke
buried under the Cirke, and the altar stone and the
windows?"

The woman eyed her speculatively. "Oh, they're
true enough, I suppose, as true as any two-hundred-
year-old legends might be. But that fool really believes
that some Wicke is going to challenge him in his own
Cirke. Free the souls of the dead Sisters . . . Tell me,
girl. You didn't come to Blaec-del to hear tales of
Wicke and live burials."

"No, Moireach. I came here to . . . to find a new situation. You see, my parents are dead and I've no home to return to and—"

"Oh, dear God, another weepy Tell!" The woman rolled her eyes and moaned. "This place is full of tales of orphans and death and homeless urchins. You're just one more story, here, cailin. But look here, do you cook, sew?"

Meredydd nearly smiled. It seemed that question had been put to her once today already. "No, Moireach. I do neither. I've a way with herbs, is all."

The woman's brows rose. "Healing? That's not something you'll get to do around here. Only men and Wicke heal. They'll take healing from the one and bury the other alive."

Meredydd tried hard to pierce the darkness—to receive a clearer view of the other's face. "You're not from here either, are you, Moireach?"

"No, I'm not. I married myself to this God-lost place. Fool." The disparaging comment was clearly directed at herself. She grimaced and shook her head. "So, it's a situation you want is it? Well, I'm short of girls right now. One's more pregnant than even Flann, here, and another left just last week with some sheepherder. Since you can't cook and you can't sew and you can't heal, you might just want to think about setting yourself up here." She jerked her head toward the stairs. "The men hereabouts are a crude lot, but except for a few, they'll leave you in once piece."

Her smile was one that made Meredydd's blood run absolutely cold. She was innocent, but not enough to mistake what sort of "situation" the woman was offering.

"Ay, Hadder!" A man leaned against the bar several feet away and set his mug down on the pitted wooden surface with a sharp crack. " 'Nother ale."

The woman nodded briskly then gestured up the stairs with one hand. "Get her to her room before she's sick all over my lodge. Stupid girl," she added, and went to serve her customer.

So, Meredydd thought, as she and Gwynet helped the unfortunate Flann up the stairs to her bare little room, that was the fearsome Hadder. It was not surprising Ruhf Airdsgainne trembled a bit at the thought of her wrath.

When she and Gwynet helped the mute girl out of her dirty gown, Meredydd's empty stomach curled in on itself. The girl's distended belly still bore the marks of what could be taken for any number of things: buck's hooves and upside-down cloven hearts among them. The scene in the mercantile came back as clearly as an aislinn vision, rocking Meredydd in a sea of sudden nausea.

Chilled completely, she sat back on the edge of Flann's bed and watched Gwynet gently minister to the older girl, cleansing her sweat-soaked body and easing her into a ragged but clean gown. Through all, the child kept up a running monologue in a sweet, musical voice—soothing the ears, quieting the mind. Flann ceased shivering and even seemed to regain a little color.

"I know an herbal medicine for this," Meredydd said after a while.

Flann's eyes moved sullenly to her face, but she said nothing. Gwynet, on the other hand, smiled broadly. "Oh, do you, mistress? Is it easy to get?"

"Well, yes, if the herbs are available—and they should be around here. It's a really simple thing—some grasses and leaves. Do you know where there's some chamomile and mint?"

Gwynet nodded. "Surely. We'll get some as soon as I've got my chores done." She glanced at Flann. "Is that good, Flann? Can ye wait?"

The older girl finally spoke. "Must I? Please, if ye can take away this pain—" She wrapped her arms around her stomach and leaned forward. "It's awful, really it is." Her eyes, pleading, had more life in them than Meredydd had yet seen.

"I'll help you with your chores, Gwynet. That way they'll be done more quickly."

"Please!" moaned Flann. "Please don't make me wait."

Gwynet put a gentle hand on the girl's forehead. "Now, now, Flann. Don't ye fret so. We'll get the herbs and Meredydd'll make ye a wonderful tea, won't ye Meredydd?" Her eyes, too, pleaded their concern for the pregnant girl.

"I think I can do something right now to help take the pain away," Meredydd offered, regretting the words as soon as she'd spoken them. "But you have to promise not to tell anyone."

"Promise," Flann said immediately and Gwynet nodded.

"All right. Lie down and close your eyes and be very, very quiet and still. You, too, Gwynet. Be very still."

Gwynet nodded again, her eyes bright and intent.

When Flann was lying quietly before her, Meredydd got to her knees beside the low pallet and began a silent meditation. She focused her mind in on itself at first, collecting her senses, gathering her resources. Then she began a healing duan, starting at a whisper and allowing it to grow until her voice filled the little room.

The warmth flickered behind her eyes and in her abdomen at once, then moved to coalesce behind her breastbone. A tingling sense of the blue power trickled down from Beyond, through the crown of her head, and pooled with that warmth. She continued to sing, concentrating the energies, one ear trained on the hallway, listening for a footstep. In this village, an eavesdropper would be dangerous, but so too could splitting her concentration. She forced the open ear to close and gave to Flann the sum of herself.

She stretched out her hands, feeling the blue healing course down her arms to coil beneath her palms. She pressed those palms very gently against Flann's swollen belly and poured out the healing. For a minute, perhaps more, she concentrated in this way, then, feeling the draw from Flann's body lessen, she let the duan return to a whisper and brought the Healweave to a close.

She opened her eyes. On the cot, Flann slept. Already dreaming, her eyes flickered beneath the blue-tinged lids. Gwynet stirred restively, moving to stare at the sleeping girl.

"Tha' were wonderful, mistress," she breathed and threw her arms around Meredydd's neck. "Ye're a saint."

"I doubt Cirke-master thinks so."

"Well, Cirke-master mayn't know everything."

"Cirke-master certainly mayn't know what happened here."

Gwynet made a lip-sealing gesture. "I'd have no call to tell him."

Meredydd rose. "How about your chores? What are we to do?"

"Oh, clean the rooms mostly. There'll be the traveler's rooms and then the girls' quarters."

"Hadder's girls?"

Gwynet nodded, glancing aside. "Aye. Come now, we'll do linens first."

"Tell me about Hadder and Flann," Meredydd pressed as they worked on the first room together. "Did Flann really . . . Those marks on her stomach, the ones that look like buck's hooves—"

Gwynet glanced at her sharply. "She told her mother she met a magic buck in the forest."

"That's what Ruhf said," prompted Meredydd. "Of course, there wasn't any magic buck."

"I'm sure I don't know."

"It *was* Ruhf, wasn't it? And he's afraid Hadder will find out."

Gwynet hung her head. "Please don't make me say, mistress."

"But Hadder's not stupid, Gwynet. She doesn't believe in magic bucks any more than I do."

"Ah, she knows, all right. I've heerd her say so. She knows who the father of Flann's child is. But, she's waitin' on somethin'. I'm not sure what. Maybe she thinks the child will look like its pa and that'll be tha'. Too, she thinks Flann was willing. She wasn't willing, Meredydd. But, she won't say tha', and she won't speak the words that'll point to Ruhf."

"Because she's afraid."

"I 'magine."

"You can do more than imagine, can't you, Gwynet?" Meredydd asked gently. "Why don't you leave here?"

"Where would I go, mistress?"

"Please call me Meredydd. And you could go almost anywhere else. There's a whole world out there where the Sun shines and the streets are clean and the Cirkes are really places of worship and the people are kind and caring."

"I surely couldn't know tha'." She paused. "But I've dreamed of it."

"When I leave, you can come with me," Meredydd told her. "I'll take you home with me, back to Nairne. Osraed Bevol—he's my guardian—he'll take care of you just as he's taken care of me."

Gwynet studied her face. "He doesn't hit you, does he?" It was a statement of fact, not a question.

"No, Gwynet. He doesn't hit me. He never would. He loves me. And he'd love you, too. I know it."

The girl smiled. "I'd like tha'. To be loved. I'd like tha'."

"Then it's settled. When I leave, you'll come with me. All I have to do, I think, is get that crystal from the Cirke-master."

Gwynet had stopped just short of throwing a bundle of dirty linens out into the hallway. "But, Meredydd

... who'll take care of Flann?" She turned back into the room and pierced Meredydd with the most anguished expression she'd ever seen. "If I leave, there'll be no one to care for her. No one to keep Hadder from her throat. No one to keep Ruhf away."

Meredydd stared at her. "Keep Ruhf away?"

"Aye. He gets in these tempers sometimes. And it's poor Flann he wants at. He gets all scared and mad at once; afraid she'll stop the Magic Buck Tell and give up the real Tell instead. You saw how he was, Meredydd. All ready to hurt somebody—you or old Okes, it didn't matter. There's times he talks of comin' here and making sure she'll tell no one nothing. I got to be here, then. I can stop him."

"By letting him beat on you, instead."

Gwynet shrugged—a queer crook-shouldered little movement that made her look, just for a moment, like a wizened old hag instead of a little girl. "It keeps him off Flann," she said.

"Well, maybe we can find some other way of keeping him off Flann." And as they worked, Meredydd tried very hard to think of some way of doing just that.

They finished the rooms quickly, with both of them hard at work, and reported back down to Hadder. The lodge was nearly empty now, and the house-mistress sat before the hearth, sipping a mug of ale. She seemed skeptical when they told her they were finished with their tasks, and she made some noise about checking up after them, but she didn't stir from the fireplace, only gazed at them as if she only half saw them. Meredydd wondered how much ale she'd had.

"How's my daughter?" she asked unexpectedly.

The two girls traded surprised glances. "Asleep, Moireach," Meredydd answered.

The woman smiled wryly. "You seem bent on granting me more importance than I deserve. I'm no Moireach, cailin. Just a wayhouse keep. I own the building, the furniture, the linens and an interest in the girls I keep. That's it. No land. No estate. . . . Still, you can call me that if you will. It strokes the ears."

Meredydd tried a smile on her. "I will, Moireach."

"So, my lazy daughter sleeps, does she? And what wrought that miracle? The poor creature hasn't slept night or day for weeks."

Meredydd swallowed. "I sang her to sleep, Moireach. A song my own guardian taught me. It always worked on me. . . ."

"A song?" The woman's glance was sharp. "A duan, you mean? Oh, yes. I understand about these things. I'm from up Nairne-way myself. And I've heard the morning's gossip. You visited the Cirke. The Cirke-master's mouth is famous in these parts for that which comes out of it. A Wicke, he styles you."

Meredydd blanched. A Wicke. And she already knew what they did to Wicke in Blaec-del.

Hadder laughed. "Oh, I doubt he'll bury you under the Cirke with the rest of your ilk. Leastwise not while you're under my roof. Not if he's kept a scrap of sanity in that bald little head."

"We're going to get some herbs, mistress," Gwynet confided breathlessly. "For Flann. Meredydd thinks they'll help settle her poor stomach and help with the sickness."

"Really? Well, I suppose I should thank you then, Wicke Meredydd, for saving my worthless get some anguish."

"Surely, she's not worthless, Moireach," protested Meredydd. "Surely you don't really believe that."

"Don't I? Letting herself be fouled by that Ruhf Airdsgainne. Now there's worthless, for you."

"Pardon, Moireach, but I don't think she *let* herself be fouled by anyone. I heard the men speaking of it— in the mercantile down the street. I don't think your daughter had a bit of choice in the matter." There, it was out. Now, if Ruhf Airdsgainne ever found out—

Hadder peered at her intently, leaning forward to study her face. "You wouldn't lie, girl?"

"No, Moireach. I would not. It's what I heard. And that he's afraid she'll tell."

"And she's afraid, too," added Gwynet. "He's a mean ... I mean to say, he's a—a powerful man, mistress."

Hadder sat back in her chair. "I believed she was willing."

"No, mistress," whispered Gwynet.

"That bastard! Well, that's the picture then, is it? And my poor stupid daughter has to make up some tale of a magic buck with faery eyes. Well, he'll get nowhere near my girl again, I swear." She glanced at the two of them standing there and flicked her fingers at them. "Well, go pick your herbs, then. The sooner we get Flann over this sickness of hers, the sooner she can be of help to her mother around this place." She got to her feet and walked away toward the stairs.

Gwynet grabbed Meredydd's hand and dragged her out the back door of the wayhouse into the wilds of the yard. It wasn't a yard, really. It was simply a no-man's-land where the forest encroached on Blaec-del. The grass was ankle-deep and darkly green and the mist hung in silver scraps like fishnets caught in driftwood.

"I think there'll be some mint over here," said Gwynet and led the way into the woods. Meredydd followed, her eyes alert for any sign of usable herbs.

They found much more than merely mint and chamomile and, before two hours had passed, had filled their pockets and tunic skirts with all manner of useful stuff: yarrow and verbena, valerian and nettle, foxglove and rosemary. They were busily inspecting a growth of fennel when the crashing of underbrush startled them almost into flight.

Meredydd knotted her fore-skirt and stood, ready to bolt, her eyes in the direction from which the sounds came. Gwynet huddled close to her and a little behind, her pale eyes wide and fearful.

"Are there boar in these woods?" Meredydd asked in a whisper.

"I've ne'er seen any and I'm out here a fair bit."

Meredydd straightened her shoulders, a hand going to her neck. "It's probably just deer. I'm sure we've nothing to be afraid—"

It was not just deer. It was Ruhf Airdsgainne and he appeared to be in a towering rage. "Where've you been, you filthy brat? I've looked all over for ye. What're you doin' out here with this schemin' cat?"

"Just—just pickin' herbs, sir," said Gwynet.

"Pickin' herbs?" Incredulity poured over his face in a flood. "What for? Who told ye to?"

"Hadder," said Meredydd loudly and clearly. Her fingers locked around her amulet. "Hadder has us picking herbs for her daughter's illness. To make a healing tea."

His eyes grasped her face so forcibly, she swore she could feel them pinching her cheeks. "Ye've met Hadder, then, girl?"

"Yes, sir. I have. She's a shrewd woman."

"Is she?" He stopped and merely stared at them. Then, "The Cirke-master says ye're a Wicke."

"The Cirke-master is entitled to his opinion."

He ogled at her. "Ye're damned sassy for someone I could break in two with one hand."

"Oh, please, sir!" wailed Gwynet. "Don't be angry with me! I didn't mean to do anything wrong. I just was tryin' to help Meredydd and poor Flann."

The words provoked in the mercer a rage quite beyond his ability to control, and Meredydd suspected Gwynet knew they would before she uttered them. The man roared like a wild beast and launched himself after them, dragging his cleft-heart belt from his waist as he came on.

Meredydd shrieked and ran back toward the way-house as fast as her legs could carry her. It took several seconds before she realized she was not being pursued. She stopped at the edge of the wayhouse "yard" and looked back the way she had come. She could see nothing, but she could still hear Ruhf's bellowing and Gwynet's pale screams. The girl had intentionally led him off in the opposite direction, just as she had intentionally goaded him into taking his anger out on her.

As Meredydd started back toward the deeper woods, wondering what she could do if she found them, a voice behind her stopped her in her tracks.

"There you are, girl! Come in. Flann's awake and she's in need of something for the sickness."

Meredydd turned and saw Hadder standing upon the crumbling back porch of her inn, her face set imperiously, concern showing only in her dark eyes. With a last glance at the forest, she turned and carried her load of herbs into the wayhouse.

Hadder-a-Blaecdel was not without civility. She thanked Meredydd for her troubles by feeding her a fine meal and allowing her a room to clean up in. She reiterated her offer of a position in her house.

"I could use a girl like you," she said. "You're a hard worker and you're honest. That'd be a great asset here. You could be a great help to the other girls at times and I'd not insist you have men to your room."

"Thank you, Moireach, but I'm not planning on being here very long. I came here to find something and I think I've found it, so . . ." She shrugged and glanced away from the woman's astute gaze.

"Found something have you? Well, that's a damn piece better than most folks around here can say. Still, if you change your mind, there's a place open for you." She paused, studying Meredydd momentarily then said, "I wish I had a son. I think I'd marry him off to you."

Meredydd blushed. "Well, you have a fine daughter, Moireach. And I think the tea I made her will get her through the rest of her pregnancy. Just have her drink a bit first thing in the morning and whenever else she feels sickly. And rest. She should have rest."

Hadder nodded absently. "I'd like to throttle that Ruhf Airdsgainne. It's probably too late to charge him with what he did to Flann."

"Flann needs protection from him," said Meredydd bluntly. "He's a dangerous, violent man." She glanced for perhaps the fortieth time out the window of the wayhouse's decrepit kitchen.

"You're fretting about that urchin, aren't you?" guessed Hadder.

Meredydd nodded.

"Well, I'll not keep you. Go on after her. I suppose I should hope you find her in one piece."

Meredydd rose from the table and thanked her hostess for the meal. The woman waved the gratitude away. "I'd say we're even, but that's not true. I'm beholden to you on several counts, Wicke Meredydd. Take care," she added as Meredydd slipped out the back door. "Ruhf is not someone to be trifled with."

Meredydd was as aware of that fact as anyone could be, yet she recognized that finding Gwynet was her first priority. Or at least, it had become that. Guiltily, she pushed aside the knowledge that that was not the goal of her task. Finding the jewel was her goal, and she thought she'd done that. The problem now would be in getting it away from the person who currently held it.

She stood for several moments at the corner of the wayhouse, watching the street beyond and fingering her necklace. Where would Gwynet be . . . if she was still alive. No, Meredydd told herself, Ruhf had been abusing the girl for some time. He hadn't killed her yet. She must be somewhere, licking her wounds, and wherever she was, Meredydd would find her.

First, the mint glade. She went there at a run, searching, calling, listening for sounds of despair and hurt. There was nothing. She went for a while in the direction she thought Ruhf had chased the girl, but apart from trampled grass and broken twigs, there was nothing to be seen or heard.

She was near the Cirke when she gave up her search of the wood and gazed at the rear of the building for some time. Yes, Gwynet might go there for solace, since she favored the place for daydreaming. Meredydd even pictured her for a moment, curled up on one of the benches, crying herself to sleep, or perhaps sitting in her puddle of colored light, trying to dream the hurt away.

Praying she would not run into the Cirke-master, Meredydd dared to approach the sanctuary. She slipped through the front doors in silence and stood, listening to the hushed sounds of candles guttering and torches hissing. Besides the two stained-glass windows, the only other breaks in the thick walls were mere slits set low—almost as if the place was expected to double as a fortress.

She found herself wondering if the little cleirach was in his quarters and if he carried the crystal amulet everywhere under his robes. It certainly seemed as if he did; he'd had it so ready to thrust upon her when he decided she was Wicke.

How was she to get it away from him? *Perhaps*, she thought as she wandered slowly and silently up the aisle, *perhaps I can frighten him into taking it out again to ward me off. And while he's holding it, I can grab it and run away.*

It seemed an absurdly simple plan, and simply absurd in the bargain. She might have laughed if the situation was not so real . . . and so dangerous. She had no doubt that the fanatical Cirke-master really would bury her alive if he was given the chance.

She stopped in front of the altar and gazed around the sanctuary. Gwynet was nowhere to be seen or heard. She stepped up onto the altar slab and around behind the huge hunk of granite. There was no huddled figure taking refuge there, either.

Well, where then? she wondered. *Where?*

She was just at the door when the Cirke-master came into the sanctuary by his side entrance. He saw her immediately and raised a loud cry.

"You! You've come back, Wicke! Ah, now I've got you! You'll do no more of your magic around here!"

Meredydd's first impulse was to rush from the place and find somewhere to hide. But she could almost see the crystal there beneath his cleirach's robes and made herself stay and turn and face him.

"I've done no magic, sir," she argued. "Whatever can you mean?"

He advanced on her swiftly, one hand going to the close of his robes. Meredydd felt her heartbeat pick up speed.

"You were out picking weeds for your potions, I know that. Ruhf Airdsgainne saw you clear as day— you and that heathen little monster."

At the mention of Gwynet, all thought of the crystal fled. "What do you know of Gwynet? What has he done with her?"

"Oh! Like likes like, eh? Well, he caught her out just as I've caught you out, Wicke. It's time for you to join your dear Sisters under the Cirke."

He was halfway up the aisle now, and Meredydd could see the light of zeal in his eyes. He was a crusader, sworn to slay the wicked and convert the heathen. He would be a hero in Blaec-del, where before he had been something less than that—a fool. He reached beneath his robes, surely to grab the star-crystal and thrust it upon her again.

Meredydd tensed. She was ready to snatch it from him—ready. But—"Where's Gwynet?"

"Dead, if she's lucky. And either way, she's luckier than you are, Wicke." He took another step.

Primed to flee, Meredydd turned the door latch, then remembered the crystal. All she had to do was reach out and take it. She made herself wait.

But when his hand came clear of his robes, it wasn't the star talisman it held. It was a set of iron manacles.

Meredydd bolted through the door and ran, his curses trailing after.

She slipped around behind the Cirke, certain that if he tried to follow her, he would never think of looking there. She was right. In a very few moments, she saw the little cleirach bustling agitatedly down the middle of the street, dodging horses and pedestrians and making a beeline for the wayhouse.

She hunkered down in the tall grass next to the Cirke and considered where to go next. She thought fleetingly of Ruhf Airdsgainne's mercantile, where she knew Gwynet had a room, but her entire being rejected the idea of searching that place.

She recalled Gwynet saying that when she was at odds with her guardian, she took refuge in the stable. That raised a whole other set of fears and ficklenesses in Meredydd's breast. She could not truthfully say that the *last* person she wanted to collide with in Blaec-del was Old Mors, but he sat far down on her list.

Well, there was naught for it. She had to find Gwynet and she had to get her safely out of Blaec-del Cirke. Resolved to that, Meredydd slipped inconspicuously across the open space between the Cirke and the jumble of buildings on the stable-side of the village and scurried around behind. She worked her way back down the row of stores, then, ending her slinking promenade behind the stable.

There was a feeder access door there that ran behind the stalls. It was made of wood so dry the holes had shrunk away from nails that barely held it together. It was crooked on leather hinges that seemed about to either crack or rot through. At least, Meredydd told herself, they would not creak.

She was wrong about that; they did creak. But it was an aged whisper of sound, not the shredding squeal she feared. She stood within the structure for a few moments, orienting herself and listening to the sounds of the place. She separated the stompings and mutterings of the equine tenants from the slow drip of water and the flutters of birds in the loft.

The loft! Her eyes rose to it, but she could see nothing but bright stripes of dust cycling endlessly in the watery light that fell through the gaps in wall and roof along with anything else that happened to float by. She strained her ears further and heard snoring. Heavy, sodden snoring as of someone who has drunk too much or slept too little or perhaps done both.

Scraping together her courage, she moved forward into the dark barn, padding to where she found, at last, a ladder leading up. Carefully, and with no attempt to breathe, she put one hand after another on the rungs, then one foot, then the other. Then, she began to climb.

The ladder was not silent. She'd prayed for it to be silent, but realized that prayers are not always answered in the way the supplicant wishes them to be. But the snoring continued unabated and that was as good as silent rungs. The climb seemed to last forever, but she was rewarded at last with a view of the loft's straw-strewn heights.

It was not a completely open area, but was rather divided into a number of smaller compartments. Gritting her teeth, Meredydd crawled carefully off the ladder and into the bed of straw. Pigeons fluttered nearby and some small rodents skittered away at her approach. But the snoring continued and that was enough.

She began a circuit of the place, moving away from the snorer, poking her nose into each of the four compartments. She found hay bales, grain sacks, rat droppings, bird feathers, a nest of cat fur, but no Gwynet. The snoring continued, loudly, breezily, comfortingly.

At last she was staring into the cubicle next to the snorer. That it had been used by a human being was obvious. There was a small covered lamp set on a slanting crate, a patched and repatched blanket and a little tin cup. But there was no Gwynet.

Meredydd stared at the place in despair and frustration. The longer her search took, the longer Gwynet would be in pain and discomfort. She sighed deeply and steeled herself for the return trip back around the loft to the ladder. It was as she began backing around the outer wall of Gwynet's compartment that she felt the oppressive silence of the place. The snoring had stopped.

Terrified, she glanced up toward that last cubicle. She heard a hacking cough, the sound of someone spitting and a series of snorts and popping sounds. She glanced over her shoulder to where the ladder taunted her with its distance. Did she try to sneak out or did she simply bolt for it?

In the end, it was Old Mors who decided that for her. He stood up, his frowzy head popping up above the slats of the divider that had screened him from her, and turned around. Their eyes met in a long, startled look, then Old Mors smiled.

"Come to visit me, pretty?" he asked and wheezed loudly, making dust motes and straw chaff dance and swirl before his face. He moved toward her.

Meredydd scrambled backwards just far enough to allow herself room to stand. Then she shot to her feet and ran—or rather, tried to run—back to the ladder of salvation. Her feet betrayed her at every step, tripping her over clumps of hay, dropping her through small holes in the floor. Her only comfort was that Mors, from the sound of it, was having as much trouble navigating as she was.

She was halfway around the loft when the old man proved himself to be more intelligent than she'd given him credit for. Seeing where she was bound, he switched direction and doubled back on the shorter route across the front of the loft.

Meredydd's first response was to move faster, but she very nearly plunged through the loft's rotten flooring into the stall of a placid looking beast with a white blaze. The effort to regain her feet cost her precious time and Mors, grinning triumphantly, made the top of the ladder before she did.

She faced him for a moment down the half-length of the barn, glancing feverishly around for salvation.

If he fell through the flooring, she thought, then caught herself. *He could break his neck*, she finished. She was mortally afraid of him, but she did not want him to break his neck.

She glanced down between her feet, between the failing slats beneath her feet. She was standing just over a pile of straw which was obviously intended for the stable inmate's stalls. It was, despite that, not the cleanest straw she had ever seen and she thought it seemed to be full of star thistle, but beggars in her position could not be choosers. She was the one that needed to fall just then. She thought that very strongly—felt it all the way to the marrow of her bones—and stamped her foot.

The floor gave way with a resounding crack of dry timbers and dropped her smack into the straw. It *was* full of star thistles and she felt every one of them, gratefully, as she scrambled to her feet and bolted out the open front door of the stable.

Just outside, she paused, meaning only to reorient and continue her retreat. But what she saw directly across the darkening street from where she stood made her next move clear. Ruhf Airdsgainne was just entering Hadder's wayhouse.

Praising the Gwenwyvar, the Meri and the Deity, Meredydd scampered across the street, around the wayhouse and into the wild back regions. From there she made her way up the row of buildings to Ruhf's mercantile. There was a back door, but it was kept locked. She would have to enter through the front.

Fingering the amulet, she prayed briefly for courage she was sure she didn't have, then rounded the building and let herself up onto the wooden walkway. Pausing at the door, she pushed it a little open and peeked within. The store was empty except for the wizened little person who huddled, still, by the cold stove, apparently asleep.

Meredydd slipped into the room, moving carefully down the cluttered corridor of goods to the small open area before the counter. There was a blanket-covered doorway just at the far end of that, and she fastened her eyes on it as if she feared it would disappear.

"What're you doin' in here, girl?"

She spun, facing the old stove-huddler, who glared balefully at her from one rheumy, open eye. The pipe-stem was still clutched in the toothless gums, though the smokeweed had long ago ceased to perfume the air.

Meredydd straightened and looked down on the old one with all the dignity she could muster. She swept a lock of hair from her face, encountered a star thistle and did not cry out as she plucked it free and tossed it to the floor. "I'm looking for Gwynet. Could you tell me where she is, please?"

"Gwynet? Gwynet?" The old crone seemed to be searching its memory. "Ah! The little girl-brat my son keeps, ye mean? Well, she's about. Although she's not like to be in a very sociable mood, I'm thinkin'."

Meredydd swallowed the lump of fear that rose to clog her throat. "Where?"

"And are ye Cwen, then, girlie? Ye can't order me about in my son's store. *I'm* Cwen, here. Cwen of Blaec-del, too, t'spite that damn-ed Hadder. Her 'n' her down-country ways."

Meredydd ignored the old woman's ramblings now, and pushed her way through to the back of the store. She'd heard something that might be only a kitten mewling, but might just as easily be something else.

There was a dark, cramped little corridor behind the store proper. To the right, a rickety flight of steps went up to what Meredydd expected would be the mercer's private quarters. To the left was an open doorway and a pool of uninviting shadow. The mewling sounded again and Meredydd plunged into the pool.

It took a moment for her eyes to adjust to the gloom, but when they did they were rewarded. Gwynet lay in the farthest corner of the little closet—for that was surely all it was—trying, it seemed, to make herself as small as possible against the wall.

"Gwynet!" Meredydd came to her knees beside the little girl and tried to pry her fingers from the blankets she had hauled in around her.

"Meredydd." Her name came out in a misshapen whisper. The lump of clothing moved, moaned and brought its face into the dim light.

Meredydd gasped and tears leapt, unasked, into her eyes. Her features were so distorted, poor Gwynet was barely recognizable. Her lips were striped with scabs barely dried and one eye was swollen completely shut.

"Is anything broken, do you think?" Meredydd asked her.

"I don' know. Oh, I hurt so awful!"

Meredydd pushed aside the folds and folds of dirty cloth and at last got her hands down to the little girl's feverish skin. "Hold very still," she said, and slipped herself swiftly into a meditation. The Heal Tell duan followed immediately, and she intoned the words, unconcerned with who might hear them. In a moment she knew there were no broken bones, but the girl was weak and needed both food and drink. Poultices, too, she decided. Strong ones. There was a fever that would have to be broken.

She pulled her hands away with an effort and got to her feet. "I'm going to get you some food and water," she told Gwynet and pushed back out into the store. The little old woman eyed her with something more than suspicion when she reappeared to forage for supplies.

"What was that I heerd, girl? Why was ye singin' like tha'?"

Meredydd didn't answer her.

"Tha' was Wicke work, weren't it? Ye was singin' up spirits and demons, weren't ye?" The woman was working herself into a frenzy. "Ye're goin' after my Ruhf, ain't ye? Ain't ye? Ye're plottin' inyx against 'im. Oh, God, I know it. I know it! She's a Wicke too, tha' little one, in't she? I told tha' boy. I *told* him he shouldn't take 'er in here, regardless. Speak to me, creature! Don't be plottin' in silence."

"I'm not plotting anything," said Meredydd at last, her arms full of provisions. "I'm here for Gwynet. And if your son stays where he is, nothing need happen to him." She didn't know what prompted her to add that, but it seemed to silence the old woman.

Meredydd slipped back into the nether regions of the store with her booty and spent several minutes feeding and watering Gwynet and caring for her comfort. The water, bread and cheese alone were enough to bring some semblance of life back into the girl, but Meredydd knew she needed more than that. She needed poultices. She spent additional time making some of those with water and tea leaves, placing them on the worst of Gwynet's wounds. Then she let herself back into a Weaver's meditation and sent some of her own energies through the poultices. Finally, she sang a Sleep duan.

With Gwynet resting quietly, Meredydd slipped back out into the store. The stoveside chair was empty. Ruhf's mother was nowhere to be seen.

Terrified all over again, Meredydd dashed through the front doors, out onto the walkway and up the street toward Hadder's place. She did not meet Ruhf or his mama on the way and prayed they would still be within when she got there.

They were, and it appeared that the old woman had just arrived, for she hovered crookedly over her son, filling his ear with something. As if he felt Meredydd's eyes on him, he looked up toward the door and froze, an expression that was half rage and half terror on his face.

"It's her!" cried a pale voice from near the hearth. "The Wicke!"

The Cirke-master! Meredydd faced him across the long room, her reason for being in Blaec-del flooding back into her brain. She had nearly forgotten. He would have it with him, she knew, tucked up under his voluminous robes. If she could just force him to produce it.

At his table near the end of the bar, Ruhf Airdsgainne had come to his feet. "I'm thinkin' there's only one way to treat a Wicke," he said.

"Stopper your face, Ruhf," said Hadder. She stood behind the bar, calmly washing mugs. "I doubt it's a good idea for you to boast of a thinking brain while the Cirke-master's here to witness the lie."

Ruhf glowered at the house-mistress and pressed his hammy fists into the tabletop. "The girl's Wicke. My ma just now heard her Runeweaving inyx over Gwynet."

"From what I hear, Gwynet might need some weaving done in her direction," countered Hadder quietly. "Meredydd told me how you chased them out of the glen."

Ruhf's glare took on an element of bemusement, as if he wasn't sure how to take Hadder's odd mood. "And what care you?" he asked finally. "Cirke-master's right. Girl's Wicke. Needs takin' care of."

"Oh, there's a good many things in this town that need taking care of, I vow. But Meredydd, here, is not one of them." She looked at him finally, her eyes coming to roost on his face with an almost audible snap.

Against the table's eroded top, his fists pumped like misshapen hearts. "You partial to her for some reason, Hadder?"

"She's bewitched!" interjected the Cirke-master, reaching beneath his robe.

"And you're besotted," Hadder snapped, setting a pair of mugs down with a loud bang.

Ruhf jumped and Meredydd tensed, her eyes scampering wildly back and forth between the three other players in the scene.

Hadder continued to heckle the little cleirach. "You and your idiotic Wicke-hunt. You've pored over those old tomes and listened to those hoary legends for so long you eat, sleep and breathe superstition. That little girl is no more a Wicke than I am."

There was a muffled chuckle from around the room at that and one patron started to say, "Well, tha' we always reckoned—"

Hadder's black scowl silenced him. "Sit down, Ruhf," she said, "and finish your drinking. You, too, cleirach."

Ruhf's mother all but howled at that. "Hadder don' know aught! I was there not ten minute back. This heathen crept into my son's store an' made free with the place as if she owned it. Stealin' stuff from the shelves for tha' wee vermin he keeps. Then she went back there an started singin' them Wicke songs, chantin' and carryin' on like a Dark Sister. I heerd it, I tell you."

There was silence in the room but for the crackle of a newly laid fire and the collective breathing of what Meredydd suddenly realized was about twenty people. It was darkening to evening, and the wayhouse was quite full of patrons. And every one of them was, at this moment, staring full at Meredydd-a-Lagan.

Some instinct prompted her to use that to advantage and so she made her eyes big and round and frightened and turned them to the Cirke-master, raising a hand to her amulet and rubbing it as if in fear.

He smiled a cold, oily smile. "She admitted to me she used crystals and knew medicinals," he said. "And see how she fondles that talisman she wears? Ah, but she know's it's no match for the Star of the Sea. She's afraid."

Meredydd brought her backbone straight enough to crack. "I am not," she said, and made her voice wobble just a bit. She made a feint toward the front door. The Cirke-master and Ruhf moved at the same time, twitching toward her. She feinted again as if contemplating escape.

"So she knows medicinals," said Hadder sanely, her elbows resting casually along the bar. "I'd be glad of that if I were you. I *am* glad of it. She's done great wonders for my Flann."

Ruhf's head jerked toward her, suspicion crowding into his eyes.

Hadder smiled. "Great wonders."

The Cirke-master, impatient with their banter, moved a few steps toward Meredydd, his hand still beneath his robes. "Here girl," he whispered. "Here, I've something for you."

"Flann's brain-fevered," snarled Ruhf. "Stupid girl an' her damn magic buck."

"Brain-fevered, is it?" Hadder came upright. "She's no more brain-fevered than I am, Ruhf Airdsgainne. She's scared spitless of you, that's all. Did you really think I was stupid enough to believe that Tell of hers? I knew it was you who fathered that child. But I thought the girl was willing since she was too scared to say otherwise. I know better now."

Ruhf stared at her for a moment in shocked silence, his jaw clamping and unclamping. In that moment, the Cirke-master pulled the star-crystal from beneath his robes and held it out before him like a shield. Light struck it from every angle, shattering into myriad tiny shards of dancing color.

Meredydd gasped and held up her hands as if to ward it off. The Cirke-master took another step toward her; he was still half a room away; and Ruhf Airdsgainne roared with every ounce of sound in his large body.

"Flann told?" he shrieked, rage flushing from every pore.

Hadder laughed. "Flann? No, Ruhf. For all she is

to me, she's still a coward and probably always will be."

"Then it was *you!*" He thrust his finger at Meredydd. "It was that damned Wicke! By God, I'll have your blood!" He shoved aside his table as if it weighed nothing at all and started toward her.

Hadder moved too then, rushing down the bar toward the door, haranguing the big man as she went. "Leave off, Ruhf, or I'll have *your* blood! You'll not harm the cailin in my house, nor will you remove her from it."

He froze, meeting the woman eye to eye across the counter. The cleirach, too, had stopped, peering at the two, his trembling hand still outstretched with Meredydd's jewel in it. She stared at the crystal, licking her lips, wishing she knew how to strip it from his hand without having to cross the room to get it. The Wisdom amulet lay, inert, beneath her hand and nothing came to mind.

"Well then," growled Ruhf, "if I'm not to harm your pet Wicke, I shall see to my own." He turned his face to Meredydd. "Hear tha', Dark Sister? I'm goin' home to my little Gwynet. Do ye think she'll be pleased t' see me?"

The light of the crystal failed, leaving her in sudden, soul-chilling darkness. Her entire body shook with rage and terror. She felt black inside, empty.

"Leave her alone!" she cried, and felt as if she could shoot fire at him. "Leave her alone or I'll—"

"Ye'll what, Wicke?" He took one step toward her, then another. "What can ye do to me tha' ye wouldn't already have done if ye could, eh? Oh, I believe ye can sing and dance and lay on herbs. But I don't think ye can lay a finger or an inyx on ol' Ruhf."

Meredydd quailed, knowing he was right. Even in self-defense, a Weaver of Runes was bound by certain laws and precepts. A violent inyx was not something she would cast, nor was it, in all truth, something she had ever learned at the feet of Osraed Bevol.

With a last, longing glance at the crystal in the Cirke-master's trembling hand, Meredydd turned and fled the wayhouse. She heard a roar from Ruhf and a wild screech from Hadder and nothing after that but the pounding of her own feet on the slats of the walkway.

She did not mean to collide with Ruhf's untidy piles of goods or knock them all down into the narrow aisle of his shop, but she did. She did not mean to tear the heavy, dust-riddled blanket from the lintel of the inner doorway, but she did.

She scrambled into Gwynet's closet, calling her name, and fell to the floor beside her. She shook the girl until she got a questioning moan, then grasped her around the shoulders and pulled her to her un-steady feet.

"Come Gwynet! Come! It's Ruhf! Ruhf's coming!"

Something of her urgency penetrated the other girl's drowsy fog and she gasped and stiffened.

"Can you walk?" asked Meredydd.

"Aye! I'll try."

And try she did. Meredydd half-carried her out into the narrow corridor behind the store, dragging much of her sorry bedding with her. Propping Gwynet against the wall, she felt for the back door. She found it immediately and threw up the latch, forcing the door open on its rusty hinges. It groaned mightily, but she ignored that and thrust Gwynet outside. Only now did she disentangle herself from the bedding, leaving it lumped before the door with a tail of blanket stuck between door jamb and latch. Then, with her arm around the smaller girl, she headed southeast into the woods.

She thought she heard the clamor of a small mob and the thudding of boots on boards as they slipped beneath a tall fern and turned due south, but she could not be sure and she had no intention of achiev-ing any certainty. It was twilight now, and she dragged

Gwynet back the way she had come alone that morning, up the long, misty slope to the trail.

It was an odd sort of phenomenon, Meredydd thought, that Gwynet only seemed heavy or unwieldy when she thought about her. As long as she kept her mind on where she was putting her feet, or on picking landmarks out of the near-darkness, she felt the burden hardly at all. Still, she was aware that they both needed strength, and so she murmured an Infusion duan beneath her breath, regulating her breathing and the rhythms of her body, content that by so doing, she was regulating Gwynet's as well.

She lost track of the distance and duration of the journey. She only knew that one long step took her from tree cover to clearing and left her staring at a familiar, watery glen. There was a fire and, before the fire, a boy who stood and came to the water's edge.

Shaking with relief, Meredydd paused to listen down the trail. There was no sound but the nightbirds calling to each other in the trees and the light passing of tiny creatures below them in the brush and the little *smack-smack* sound of fish leaping in the darkened pool. The moon had not yet risen.

"What have you got, Meredydd?" asked Skeet from over the water.

"A friend," she answered, almost in a whisper. She turned her attention to Gwynet then, and found the girl was close to unconscious. "Help me, Skeet. Help me get her across the pool."

There was a narrow, rock strewn fall that aided with that, and Meredydd was able to hand Gwynet over to Skeet and then cross herself, getting only a bit wet and minding that very little. At the fire she blanketed the younger girl and tried to get water down her throat with little success. She was high with fever and her wounds looked even more grievous in the firelight.

"She's been hard used," said Skeet soberly. "Wherever did you find her, mistress?"

"In a village. A horrid, dark village with little light in it. Poor souls," she added.

"Ah. Then you've completed the Gwenwyvar's task?"

Meredydd blushed so hot she thought surely Skeet could see her face glow in the dark. "No. I shall have to return and try again. I found the jewel, but I couldn't bring it back." She closed her eyes and could still see the crystal winking at her from just too far away while Ruhf Airdsgainne roared and moved inexorably toward her—toward Gwynet.

But had it really been too far? she wondered. If she had trusted the Meri, trusted the First Being to aid her, might she have been able to get the jewel *and* rescue Gwynet as well?

The blush bled from her face, leaving it feeling cold and whipped. Had she once again failed by disobedience? Had she now failed even more horribly through lack of faith?

The moon chose that moment to show its face above the trees and out on the pool a white whisp of ether curled and molded itself to a certain shape and a name was whispered across the sparkling waters. *Mere-dydd . . .*

She came to her feet. "Gwenwyvar?"

A-aye. . . .

She moved to stand at the edge of the pool and waited.

What have you brought me, Meredydd? Have you brought me a jewel of great value?

Meredydd swallowed painfully. "No, mistress. I have not."

What have you brought me, Meredydd?

"I have brought a little girl. From the village." She took a deep breath and rushed on. "Her name is Gwynet and she's been beaten very badly. She's very ill, mistress. Can you help her?"

Can you help her? returned the curl of mist.

"I've tried. I did a Healweave and tried some

cold poultices, but I had to carry her so far from the village. . . ."

Bring her to the water.

Meredydd obeyed, for once, immediately, moving back to the fire and lifting the limp Gwynet from the grass. The child seemed to weigh no more than a leaf. At the water's edge she stopped and waited, once more, for instruction.

The water is healing. Do you believe?

Do I believe? thought Meredydd and answered from her own certainty. "Yes, mistress."

Give the girl into the water. Give her to me.

Meredydd allowed the cold, dark pool only a momentary glance, but she had to own a fleeting doubt and knew it would haunt her. Then she tightened her grip on Gwynet and stepped from the shore. The water was as chill as it looked, but as Meredydd moved out to hip's depth, it seemed to warm. Steam continued to rise from it in great, silvery whisps until a host of wraiths looked on.

Into the water.

Meredydd set her teeth and lowered her limp burden beneath the ripples.

What have you given me, Meredydd? asked the Gwenwyvar's wind-sough voice.

"A—a girl," answered Meredydd, puzzled at the repetition of the question.

Why have you brought her here?

"She would have died. I had to bring her."

You saw no choice?

Meredydd gritted her teeth against all her doubts and fears. *You could have been more obedient,* they said. *You could have had more faith.*

"No, mistress. I saw no choice."

What have you brought here, Meredydd? the Gwenwyvar asked again.

Meredydd felt the hot tears well up from the depths of her heart and overflow her eyes. "A little girl."

No . . . a jewel of great virtue.

It took Meredydd a heart-still moment to realize her arms were empty. Not even Gwynet's dirty rags remained in her grasp. It was as if she had melted away into the water, leaving behind only a sigh.

Suddenly bereft, Meredydd gave vent to a cry of anguish and disbelief. "Gwynet! No!" Her arms thrashed at the water, searching. Perhaps she had been so rapt in the Gwenwyvar she had allowed the girl to slip from her grasp. Perhaps—

"Meredydd. Here." It was man's voice, soft and sweet and very familiar. It penetrated the sound of her cries and her splashing and stilled her.

Trembling, sobbing, she turned back to the shore. Osraed Bevol stood there, looking neither old nor tired. Beside him on the shore was a young girl—a pale-haired, pale-eyed creature with skin the color of moonlight and a gamin smile that—

"Gwynet?" But no, it couldn't be, because she was healed of every cut and bruise and her long hair lifted, shining and clean into the gleaming mist.

The Osraed Bevol smiled. "Yes, Meredydd—Gwynet. A jewel of great value—of great virtue."

"Then, it wasn't the crystal—from the Cirke window?"

The Osraed shook his head. "Meredydd, think. Feel with the heart you were given. You understand. Let yourself understand."

Meredydd found she did understand. "The jewel *was* the virtue. In a foul and dark place, Gwynet's *purity* was the jewel." How right it seemed. How dull of her not to have seen it.

"And you found it." Bevol said. "Ultimately, you valued it more than what your physical senses *told* you was the jewel. Value the jewels, Meredydd. Wherever you find them."

Gwynet, looking like one waking from sleep, glanced from Bevol to Meredydd, then held out her hand toward the pool. "Won't ye come up and be dry, Meredydd? It must be raw cold in tha' pool."

Meredydd realized, suddenly, that she was still standing, hip-deep, in the water. Chill flooded her limbs and she climbed out as fast as they could carry her. Skeet was beside her in an instant, wrapping her in a blanket and leading her to where her Master stood waiting.

Teeth chattering, she blinked up at him. "What now, Master Bevol?"

"You will continue your Pilgrimage, of course. You will tread the path to the Sea."

"And Gwynet?" She turned her eyes to the younger girl, who was listening, now, with every ounce of herself.

Bevol put a hand on Gwynet's shoulder. "Why, I will take this jewel home and set her in a place where she will be warm and safe and happy. And we will wait for you together."

Gwynet's eyes grew as big and round as coins. "You mean I'll not go back to Blaec-del?"

"No, Gwynet. You will have a new home. The home where Meredydd was raised. And you will go to the school where Meredydd was schooled. And you will become one of the bright jewels of Halig-liath."

"A home? . . . A school?" Gwynet turned her glorious smile and moist eyes to Meredydd. "Oh, ye were so right when ye said I should love him, for he's tha' kind. I'll work hard for ye, Master," she said to Bevol. "I'll cook and clean and—"

Bevol was shaking his head. "No, child. You will not. At least, you will do no more than your share. The hard work I will ask of you will be in the classroom. You will not be my servant, you will be my daughter—just as Meredydd is my daughter. And you will not cook the meals, you will learn the Art." He looked to Meredydd, his eyes a dark, unreadable bit of night sky. "Does this make you happy, anwyl?"

Shivering, Meredydd could only nod and smile so broadly she thought her cheeks would crack. Exhaustion staked its claim on her then, and began to pull her suddenly heavy body toward the ground. She felt supporting hands gently ministering to her needs, but she hadn't the will or the strength to thank their efforts.

A last moment of consciousness brought her to an awareness that the pool of the Gwenwyvar was now dark and empty. The White Wave was gone, her waters silent beneath the scattering of light from Skeet's fire.

Tomorrow, she thought. *Tomorrow I will tread the path of Taminy.*

Chapter 10

To enjoy the benefits of the Divine is Wisdom; to bring others to that enjoyment is virtue. One cannot be uncaring of the welfare of others and deserve to be called human. The best worship is in the easing of another's distress and the improvement of their condition. This is true religion.
—The Corah, Book II, Verse 41

The pool looked different with the light of dawn falling across it through the encroaching forest. Different, but no less magical. The greenery still wore its emeralds and the water its sapphires and diamonds, with a few topazes thrown about for good measure.

Meredydd found she had developed an attachment to the place. It was hard for her to turn her back on it and walk away. She wanted to see the Gwenwyvar's face again and hear her sweet whisper. But only the birds called to her this morning.

A deep, honest part of her envied Gwynet, who would go home with Osraed Bevol. She wanted him to complete her Pilgrimage with her; she wanted to go home with him. But good-byes had to be said and Meredydd managed not to cry except for Gwynet, who would be happy—Gwynet, who would take her place at the Osraed's side.

"I think I am jealous of Gwynet, Master," she said to him privately. "I'm ashamed, but it's true. She's taking my place—"

Bevol's arms were around her in a breath. "No one, anwyl, will take your place. Not in my house. Not in my heart. No one can. Gwynet will make her own place there, most certainly. And I know you would not begrudge her that."

Meredydd shook her head. "No. I would begrudge her nothing in the world, Master. She *is* a jewel." She glanced to where Gwynet, fresh and vibrant and sparkling, helped Skeet pack up their goods.

The Osraed Bevol held her at arm's length then, and placed a finger on the tip of her nose and said, "Remember what I told you about jewels, anwyl. Value them, wherever they are found. And remember, too, to let nothing distract you from your goal." He kissed her forehead and moved away.

A second later, she was netted in Gwynet's eager embrace.

"Thank ye, Meredydd. And I thank the First Being It saw fit t'send ye t'Blaec-del. I am indeed blessed. My ma were wise t'give me tha' name."

Meredydd returned the embrace, any last vestiges of jealousy melting. "Be happy, Gwynet. I know you will be happy. And pray for me. I know the Meri will hear your prayers."

Gwynet stood back and favored her with a bemused look. "Why the Meri hears all prayers, Meredydd. She's just peculiar in the way She answers them." She smiled brightly and gave Meredydd a last, swift hug. "Be home soon, then. I'll be waitin' to hear your Tell." She skittered back three steps, hugging her own frail body and giggling. "Ah, home! What a grand word that is! I'm going t'say it 'til the Master tells me to be silent."

Meredydd followed Gwynet with her eyes—followed her to Bevol's side and waved them on their way east. Then she looked to Skeet. "Time for leave-taking."

He nodded, grinning, holding out her pack. "Aye. Off then."

And they were on their way, their backs to the rising ball of flame, while Mereydd tried to calculate when they might reach the Western Sea.

"Skeet," she said finally, "I make the Sea two day's journey. Is that right, do you think?"

"Aye," he agreed, "that seems right. Two days. We should see it tomorrow."

"We'll be short of food by tonight."

"Aye."

"I wonder if there are any other villages along here. Maybe a homestead."

He glanced·at her. "Maybe."

She was silent for a time, rubbing her amulet between thumb and forefinger. Then she said, "I wish Osraed Bevol could be with us. I know that's selfish of me, but . . . I've never been away from him before." Skeet knew that better than anyone.

"Nor me. Not since I come to him, I mean."

"How did you come to him?" Meredydd asked, for Skeet, though younger than she, had been with Osraed Bevol longer. He was a mystery of whom the Osraed would only say when asked, "He's such a fixture, I can scarcely recall." And, when pushed, might be persuaded to add, "He was a gift, you might say."

"From whom, Master?" Meredydd had asked once, aghast at the idea that anyone would give their child away.

"Well, from the Meri, I can only suppose."

Meredydd had accepted that. Certainly no one else seemed to know where Skeet had come from, although one Prentice concocted the theory that he was a golem, fashioned by Osraed Bevol out of clay and animated by Runeweave and duan—after all, his given name did mean "earth." Meredydd had credited that only for the two hours it had taken for her to be done at Halig-liath and ask the Osraed what a golem was, and could an Osraed make one.

He'd laughed so hard that she gratefully relegated the theory to the dustbin and developed, in its place, the simpler theory that Skeet had been abandoned in Bevol's precincts and that the Osraed had simply not wanted his young Prentice to know the cruel truth.

Skeet's next words confirmed that long-held theory.

"Well," he said, "Maister tells me I was left to him by someone."

"I thought that must be it. Would you answer something else, then?"

Skeet eyed her almost suspiciously. "Aye, if I can."

"You've been with Osraed Bevol longer than I have. He's tutored you in all aspects of runelore and plain learning and you've lived down-country since you were a babe. Why, then, do you talk like an up-country urchin?"

Skeet doubled over and cackled until he was red in the face. "Mercy!" he cried, at last. "Mercy, mistress Meredydd. You're after my secrets and mysteries now."

"Well, why do you then? You're as well educated as I am. And you're not slow. Scandy-a-Caol has reason for such a manner—being raised up in Eada—but not you."

"I do because it suits me and serves me. People say what fronts their minds before an urchin. They speak what they think, because they don't expect to be understood. I learn more that way."

"What do you learn?"

"I learn that Aelder Prentice Wyth is all over mad-heart for you."

Meredydd flamed. "Where did you learn that?"

Skeet tapped his ear. "Open ears, closed mouth, silent feet—that's Skeet." He paused. "I know that Leal is likewise smitten."

"Leal?" She stared at him.

"Some Osraed-to-be you are, not even to have read *that* open book. It's all in his eyes."

"So you think Leal is only my friend because I'm a girl."

"Ha! I think he is your friend in *spite* of it. Think on it, Meredydd, how it must feel to a fellow to have his best friend suddenly up and turn into a girl—someone he might think to marry, to set up family with—no more to play or jolly about with. Ah, pure agony." He looked completely disgusted.

"But I've *always* been a girl!" Meredydd protested.

"Not to Leal. You've been his friend—that's different. And as to the poor Aelder—well, you've been his student all along, right?—and all at once—poof!—a cailin. That's singularly difficult."

"Not for me. I don't understand this, Skeet. Leal being a boy doesn't make anything different. And why couldn't Aelder Wyth just keep treating me the way he's always treated me? I don't understand."

"Yes, you do."

She glared at him, ready to blast him for his all-knowing attitude.

He raised a hand in defense, dark eyes demonshine. "Now think. How did you feel when Aelder Wyth suddenly became a suitor when all along he'd been a teacher?"

Meredydd boggled at that. How had she felt? Disoriented, stunned and insecure because Wyth's cool antagonism, for all its unpleasantness, had at least been something she could rely on—like the ancient stones of Halig-liath, like the tides.

"I thought he was my enemy," she admitted. "How could he even think I'd be his wife? We weren't even friends."

Skeet laughed. "I suppose our Maister would say, 'That's one of life's great mysteries.'" He imitated Bevol's voice so well and yet so comically, that Meredydd laughed with him.

They sang for a time after that and told each other

stories intended to keep the nerves on edge. They took a rest stop for mid-day meal, then went on again, the Sun now arching over to blind them. They were silent again, that afternoon, and in that silence, Meredydd began to turn the words of the Gwenwyvar over and over in her head.

She was on the Path Taminy had followed, moving toward her destiny—step after step, to her goal. It was a goal she must not be distracted from. Now she began to contemplate that goal in earnest, to hold it up before her as a Weaver would hold a rune crystal, searching it with an Osraed's eyes for aspects and signs. And as she held up this metaphoric crystal, she realized that the path to her goal seemed to have forked.

If someone asked her just this moment what was that goal, she would have said, "The Sea." But, of course, that wasn't really true—it wasn't the Sea she was seeking, but the Inhabitant of the Sea, the Meri. Yet, beyond even the Meri, there was the Goal the Meri only represented—mankind's living link with the Divine, its only way of knowing That, holding conversation with That, knowing Its will. Her goal was to become a channel for That, a link to the Link, a link in the chain that joined the Universe with its very Soul.

Only a handful of souls in a generation attained that. Souls like Bevol. Each was given its own duan—a secret duan that sang the essence of the individual's spirit—along with a unique mission. Bevol's mission had been to stay in Caraid-land, educate its people and raise up future Osraed. Others had been commissioned to scatter like wind-blown pollen, spreading their special knowledge far and wide. And wherever they journeyed, the old ways were adjusted to the new knowledge, made to fit whatever new wisdom flowed from the Meri's chosen; things were advanced or put back the way they had been, depending.

Mankind listened to those who had received the

Kiss of the Meri—paid close attention to those who wore Her mark upon their brow. To some, that made the station of the Divine Counselor something to be coveted, to be striven for as a Cyne might strive to be set before the stone, to be crowned, to rule. But in the very act of craving Osraed-hood, of seeing in it power or prestige or an ear with the Cyne, those covetous souls put themselves out of its reach. The Kiss of the Meri was not a crown, but a collar. It was not for those who wished to govern, but for those who wished to serve.

That was Meredydd's goal: to receive the Kiss, to wear the collar, to be like her Master Bevol in all things. To be like Gwynet—a jewel of great virtue. She must not let the exercise overshadow the goal of the exercise. It was not the riddle that mattered—it was the reality; it was not the symbol, but the substance.

She put away her metaphoric rune crystal, satisfied that her divergent paths had been straightened, cleared and unified.

"Ah," she heard Skeet say. "Look."

She glanced up from the shore and noticed that a real path joined it, ahead. In several strides, their feet met the new trail. They continued along it, walking easily on its smoothly packed surface. The Sun was sinking lower and just as Meredydd wondered if they should stop to make camp, the smell of wood smoke came to her on the breeze. She looked up, eyes searching, and saw it—a banner of smoke fanning up from a narrow base to flatten itself over the trees.

They approached cautiously and were gratified to see that the smoky plume came from the chimney of a whitewashed cottage set in a clearing hard by the Bebhinn. A mill-house was built out over the water and a scattering of other out-buildings lay about the central house at intervals—a henhouse, a storage shed and a small barn—all mudpack and whitewashed like the cottage, with dark wood beams framing the walls and underpinning the thatched roof.

It was not like Lagan, not really, and yet it was enough to catch Meredydd's breath in her throat and make her eyes sting. Her steps slowed as they approached the mill. She could hear the stone grinding within and thought of fresh-baked bread. She was suddenly hungry.

They skirted the mill and were climbing the grassy slope toward the cottage when a shriek slit the air with sharp terror. They froze half up-slope and spun back toward the mill. It was a two-story structure, tallest on the river side with a rough wooden platform running about the walls to allow access to the waterwheel.

It was that wheel that drew Meredydd's eyes. There, too close to it, dangling from the wooden decking, was a small boy. He was gripping the planks with both hands, but it was not a firm grip, and Meredydd's heart forced its way up to her throat. Below the wriggling form, the Bebhinn roared over a rocky sluice that fed whitewater to the wheel.

Meredydd bolted for the steps that gave onto the platform from the front of the mill, scrambling diagonally up the grassy hillside with Skeet on her heels. The child screamed shrilly again as her feet hit the solid planks of the decking and she moved faster, adrenaline pumping, blood rushing to her ears. She rounded the corner of the mill. Here the din was epic; the combined hiss, groan and grind of water, wheel and millstone all but blotted out the thin child-cries.

Meredydd went to her knees, locking one arm about a railing stanchion, and reached down for the terrified boy. Panicked, he let go of the decking and grasped her instead. Ripped completely off balance, she tumbled forward and would have gone over if Skeet had not been behind her, had not thrown his arms about her waist and his weight toward the mill's solid stone wall.

She yelped in pain as her supporting arm tore free

of the stanchion, splinters of wood driving into the soft flesh of her forearm. She was upside-down now, both arms encumbered with squirming, squealing child. The splinters burrowed deeper into her arm, but her attention was all on that waterwheel—groaning, roaring, thrashing the water below like a wounded water beast.

Fingernails gripping the cloth of the child's shirt, Meredydd tried to get a purchase on the deck with her knees. The attempt only caused her to slip further over the edge.

"Don't struggle!" yelled Skeet and, in her arms, the child thrashed, his small hands tearing at her hair and tunic. Her greatest fear was met when the tunic began to pull off over her head.

"Skeet!" she shrieked. "Back! Pull back! Pull—"

The last word was ripped from her throat as her body was hauled suddenly up and back under the railing of the platform. Strong arms that could never have been Skeet's encircled her waist, then deposited her roughly on the decking, wrenching the little boy away from her.

Gasping, she pulled her tunic back into place. A tall young man stood over her, cradling the sobbing child in his arms, while a young woman, also sobbing, wrapped her arms around both. In a moment the man handed the child over to the woman and looked down at Meredydd.

"Where did you two come from?" he asked. His voice was rough and brown as tree bark.

"From up Bebhinn, sir," said Skeet, when Meredydd's voice failed in her throat. "We heerd the little boy scream and saw he'd fallen."

The man, a look of sheer relief on his face, put his hands down to help them up. "Thank God for sending you. Thank you, both."

Skeet bobbed his head in welcome. "Pleased to serve ye, sir."

"Oh, your arm!" This came from the young woman,

her eyes on the now upright Meredydd, who, unthinkingly, looked down at herself.

She immediately wished she had not. The inside of her right forearm was a mess of torn, bloody cloth and flesh, and a large sliver the size of her little finger protruded from just below her elbow joint. Sudden awareness brought on an equally sudden stab of white-hot agony and vertigo. Meredydd came as close to swooning as she ever had. Before she could even begin to exert control over her senses, the young man scooped her from the deck and carried her to the house. She could hear the others scurrying behind as they left the cacophany of the mill.

In the cottage, he deposited her gently on a wooden gate-backed settle amid a clutter of home-quilt pillows. The young woman set down her child and went into a flurry of activity—drawing water from a huge bucket and putting it in a pot over her kitchen fire, grabbing a swatch of linen rags from a basket. Already her husband, or so Meredydd assumed him to be, was holding out Meredydd's lacerated arm, picking away bits of torn cloth and inspecting the damage.

Meredydd already knew it was severe. She had gotten her senses under control, finally, and began a silent Runeweave to block the pain. She breathed deeply, evenly, feeling the agony ebb from roar to throb. She willed her body to relax, a calming duan murmuring in her mind's ear—restoring her rhythm. Every living thing had a rhythm. At times like this it could be lost, replaced with chaos. She restored it, breath by breath by breath.

The young woman came to her with warm water and rags and began to sluice the blood from the wounds so the fragments of wood could be more clearly seen. There were several large ones and they had caused some deep lacerations. Around those was a field of raw, abraded flesh, oozing protective fluid.

The young man made a hissing sound between his teeth. "Ah, dear. Those will have to come out."

Meredydd nodded, taking another deep breath. "Do you have any root tea and fennel?"

"Aye, we have that."

"For a poultice after," Meredydd said, and tried a smile. "After we get them out."

Frowning, the man bent his dark head over her arm. "I'll have to use a knife, I'm a-feared."

Deep breath. "Yes, of course."

He glanced at her face. "You're uncommon brave, cailin. Even I would be wanting to cry if that were my arm."

She smiled again, shakily. *Concentrate.* "Salt water would be the worst possible thing for it."

"I'll get the knife." He rose and headed for the kitchen.

His wife took his place while Skeet settled next to her, his face intent. The little boy hovered in the middle of the comfortable little parlor, looking awestruck and uncertain.

"My name is Meredydd," she said. *Breathe in peace; breathe out song.* "This is Skeet. We're from Nairne."

The woman's eyes grew big and round. "All the way from Nairne! I'm Meghan-a-Galchobar and that's my husband, Owein, and my son, Taidgh. I've family in Nairne. An aunt and uncle. He's a jagger—the name's Pyt."

"I know them," said Meredydd. *Breath in peace; breathe out song.*

"Where are you bound, then?"

"To the Sea—to the end of the Bebhinn."

Meghan frowned. "There's naught there but a fisherman's shack, and that's a near ruin." She moved aside to let her husband in, but kept a firm hold on Meredydd's wrist.

"I'm ... I'm a Prentice," Meredydd said, "from Halig-liath. I'm on my Pilgrimage." She waited for some scandalized or disbelieving reaction.

She got neither. They merely glanced at each other, eyes wide, and then Meghan smiled. Meredydd sensed in the other girl a wave of excitement. It made her own face glow warmly.

"Well," said Owein softly, "I shall be most careful of you, mistress." He bent, again, over her arm.

Her concentration was blinded by the flash of light on his blade. She stared at it, tried to pull her eyes from it. Failing that, she reached up her free arm to rub the amulet. It was gone.

Cold-still, she was. Lost. And the knife blade hovered over her skin like a long, hungry tooth. Her concentration shattered, scattered, she groped after it, desperate. She felt Skeet grasp her left hand, moved her eyes to follow the gesture. Their interlaced fingers became the focus of her Runeweave; she grappled and rewon her rhythm, replayed the duan: *Breathe in peace; breathe out song. Breathe in; breathe out.*

She went to the Sanctum at Nairne. The great gray-brown walls, shored up by logs thick as a man's body, were broken here and there by fine examples of the glazier's art. It was afternoon and the light from the high-set stained glass tumbled into the long stone nave and draped over and around her, glorious. She stood beneath her favorite window—the one that showed the Eibhilin Being, represented only by golden and white rays of light, rising from the blue depths of a glazen sea to face a hooded figure in crimson. It was her favorite window, not because it depicted the Meri or a Pilgrim's greatest desire, but because when she stood in the tumbled blue and red and golden light, her plain chestnut hair took on every color.

If she moved here it was all blue; here, and it was golden. Ah, but red. She'd always fancied it red. Red was the most glorious, vibrant color. No one could ignore someone with red hair. Heads would always turn. Red hair was always noticed. Hair the color of sunset, of dawn, of blood—

No, that was wrong—bad path. *Breathe in healing; breathe out song.* Golden hair—yes, she'd have loved that. Meghan's hair was gold. Gold was the color of the Wisdom she had lost . . . must have fallen into the river. Lost.

No, stop this. *Breathe in healing; breathe out song.* Blue. She'd always stood longest under the blue panel because it was the most unnatural. It was harder to imagine herself (or anyone else) with shiny blue hair. Hair the color of Healing. She could certainly use that amulet now. Why hadn't she chosen it? Should she have chosen it? Would Osraed Bevol be with her now if she had chosen it?

She was suddenly and intensely aware of the total silence and stillness of the room. She pulled her eyes into focus. Beside her, Skeet smiled his knowing smile, while Owein and his wife stared at her mutely, exchanging significant glances. The little boy, Taidgh, continued to hover timidly in the background, scuffing his foot against the stone floor.

Meredydd dared to glance down at her arm. It was clean, bloodless and empty of slivers and debris. The wounds, bleeding and raw only moments ago, were now pinkly white as if the blood had been damned internally, as if they had already begun to heal. Indeed, they had. She smiled. It was the best she'd ever done. She wished Osraed Bevol could have seen—could have known—how well she'd learned that lesson.

"Is the lady all right?"

Meredydd raised her eyes to the child's anxious face. "I'm very all right. Thank you, Taidgh."

"Oh no, thank *you*, mistress, for periling yourself to save our boy." Meghan gripped Meredydd's hand tightly. Her own was shaking. "You must be the Meri's own angel, sure. If there's any way we could repay you—"

"Please, call me Meredydd. And you *have* repaid me. You took care of my arm."

"Beg pardon, mistress—Meredydd," said Owein, rising at last from the floor, "but your arm very near took care of itself. And if you hadn't been about rescuing our son't would've needed no caring for at all. Now, what can we do for you?"

"Well," said Skeet tentatively, "we are in need of a place to bide the night."

A frown slipped over Owein's handsome face, then he smiled and nodded. "Done. And, of course, you'll join us for our meals."

"Only," said Meredydd, "if we can help prepare them."

"But your arm—" began Meghan.

"Will be fine as soon as I can bind a poultice on it."

Meghan nearly jumped to her feet, her hands fluttering before her. "What do you want for that? I'll fetch it."

"Some valerian, I think, and some yarrow and wintergreen."

"Yarrow and wintergreen I know. There's some about the henhouse. But valerian . . ."

"Allheal," offered Skeet.

"Ah! That I keep on hand. What need I do?"

"I'll do it," said Skeet. "Just show me to your henhouse."

Under Meredydd's careful scrutiny, Skeet fire-dried the yarrow and wintergreen and soaked both with the valerian. She had him make a tea from the latter to make certain her sleep that night was deep and restful. She enfolded the poultice ingredients in a rag, then, and had Skeet bind it around her arm.

"Such knowledge!" said Meghan over a supper of fish stew and baps. "Is that the sort of learning you get at the Holy Fortress?"

Meredydd nodded, noting how nervous the other girl seemed—how nervous they both seemed. She prayed they would not suddenly rise up and begin calling her a Wicke.

"But I thought," said Owein, his eyes meeting his wife's, "that Halig-liath was for the teaching of religious matters."

"Well, it is that. But, as the Osraed Bevol constantly reminds me, we are creatures of matter and form here, as well as spirit, and we must tread our spiritual path with practical feet. He says nothing falls outside the Divine Art, not really. We make the distinction—it's not a natural one."

"Then did you learn there . . . not to feel pain and how to heal yourself of wounds like that?" Owein's eyes grasped her face so hard, it felt as if fingers dug into her chin. "Those slivers were all but buried in your arm, yet you didn't even whimper when I cut them out. More than that, you didn't bleed. What are you, that you don't bleed?"

There, it was out. The quivering uncertainty she had felt since he tended her arm was finally in plain sight. Things that didn't bleed, that didn't cry when in pain, that healed themselves while you looked on—those things were either very good or very evil. Their smiles had said all afternoon they thought her a saint, but beneath the gratitude lurked the fear that she was something else. And poor Owein—this moment he was ready to run from her screaming or fall to his knees and worship her. She felt the loss of the amulet keenly at that moment. What did he fear to hear, hope to hear, need to hear?

"I am a Prentice, Owein-a-Galchobar. A Prentice from Halig-liath. I am privileged, in my fifteenth year, to be allowed to go on Pilgrimage. And you've been kind enough to help me along with my journey. I'm very grateful." She smiled, hoping her sincerity would not be lost in his trepidation.

After a moment of thought, he returned the smile, then glanced at his wife. She answered with a quizzical glance of her own before scrutinizing Meredydd.

"And is it magic that you do, Prentice Meredydd?" she asked.

"It is . . . a discipline," Meredydd answered carefully, "of the Divine Art. It is much like any other art—weaving or cooking or painting pictures or milling flour."

"But, more than that, surely!" exclaimed Owein. "It takes no great years of study to be a miller. I left school after my first middle year to work here. And I'll never speak to the Meri. I'll never even catch glimpse of Her. You must be a saint to see the Meri."

"Well, I haven't seen Her yet," said Meredydd. "I only hope I will. I've only dreamed of it—prayed for it. It's the Meri who chooses to be seen, after all. It's not due to any greatness of mine—or any other Pilgrim's. I simply study the Art and learn Runeweave and pray I'm worthy."

"The Meri couldn't refuse anyone so kind and brave as you," said Meghan, and Meredydd colored and glanced aside. She struck Skeet's gaze and found that disconcerting as well.

Kind and brave—was she either of those things? Hadn't her response to Taidgh's peril been instinctual rather than thought out?

She lay awake long hours before the Galchobar fire, turning that in her mind. She'd been pleased with herself for mastering the Painhold and the Healweave, but she hadn't mastered them cleanly, she hadn't struggled them into perfection, she had merely diverted herself while the Healing duan played on her outbound breath. She should have been thinking holy thoughts, not frivolous ones. Blue hair! Dear God, how *childish*! She'd gone into the Sanctum for holy meditation, only to be distracted by girlish fancy.

She squirmed unhappily on her thick, fleece mattress and prayed she would do better in future. When at last she slept, her dream was no more than a litany composed of seven words: Let nothing distract you from your goal.

Chapter 11

When a man speaks, he cannot breathe: he sacrifices breath to speech.

And when a man breathes, he cannot speak: he sacrifices speech to breath.

These two never-ending sacrifices a man makes whether he wakes or sleeps.

— The Corah, Book I, Verses 20–22

By morning, Meredydd's arm was well-healed. She was pleased about that, but afraid it might further disturb her hosts. She removed the poultice and dressed in a clean, long-sleeved sous-shirt, covering it from sight.

She and Skeet breakfasted early with the Galchobar family, then said their good-byes. Little Taidgh was a-jitter with all the excitement and offered Meredydd and Skeet both fond hugs and kisses and childish "thank yous." They were well-provisioned with food and drink, too, as they set off downstream. Meredydd's one regret was the loss of the Wisdom amulet.

"You did well without," Skeet observed when she had felt at her collar and sighed for perhaps the twentieth time. "You'd think it was a lifelong companion,

Meredydd, instead of something you'd had only a day or two."

"It was special to me," she argued. "It made me feel my head was on true instead of skew. I needed it last night with them looking at me that way—thinking I was some sort of Wicke."

"They didn't think you a Wicke. And you did fine without."

"But what might I have done *with*, Skeet? I can't help but wonder that. They were afraid of me, Skeet. I don't *want* anyone to be afraid of me. It goes against every principle an Osraed stands for. 'An Osraed's aim must be to open the hearts, fill the stomachs, calm the minds, brace the bones and so clarify the thoughts and meet the needs that no sly meddler could touch those he has touched.'"

"Oh, and you did none of that, eh?"

"I frightened them. Do you think they would have been frightened of Master Bevol?" She shook her head. "Oh, Skeet, if only I could have divined what *he* would have said and done. His words are like the waters of a blessed spring—clear and clean and cleansing. I sweat on my words and tarnish them before they even come out of my mouth."

"Ah, is that what you're after, then? To have Bevol's words pop out of your mouth? What about *your* words and *your* thoughts, Meredydd-a-Lagan? You're not Bevol, you're yourself. The Osraed's done his Pilgrim walk."

"*My* words! *My* thoughts! By God, Skeet, don't make me laugh. I've told you, mine are unworthy. I'll never have a tenth part of the knowledge our Master has. I'll never have a hundredth part of the love and patience, the charity or the Art. And if I had them, I doubt I'd know how to use them, because that would take wisdom."

"Well, you did the Gwenwyvar's task. You brought her what she asked for."

"Aye! Without knowing it. That wasn't wisdom, Skeet. It was . . . luck. Or maybe it was the amulet."

"Now you know what the Maister says of that. An amulet is only a magnifier. You did with what you had within you."

"Without the knowledge of what I was doing."

"And yet," said Skeet. "And yet you keep on down this path, putting one unworthy foot before the other. Struggling on as if you were so sure, so sure. If snow came down thick as wool on a ewe's back, still you'd walk. And if Sun beat down hotter than heaven's breath, still you'd walk. And if rain fell till it covered this whole forest, you'd swim. Why would you do that, I wonder, if you're so sure of your failure?"

She glanced at him, startled, wondering if this was the same Skeet she'd set out with, or if there was now some enigmatic stranger wearing Skeet's body. Startled, too, because she really couldn't answer the question and had to think, hard, about it. Why, indeed? Why keep on, as he said, one unworthy foot after another, if she was certain to fail—to fall short, to be less than she must be?

"I suppose I keep on because the Osraed Bevol expects me to. Because in giving up, I'd be failing him. I can control *that*, at least. But as to the Meri, there I can only hope for mercy instead of justice. By justice, I've failed already. By mercy, well . . . only the Meri knows."

"Are ye so bad, Bad Meredydd?" asked Skeet, his voice soft, soothing.

"No. No, I'm not bad. I'm just not perfect."

"Well, neither was our Master Bevol, I wager, when his unworthy feet went down his Path one after t'other."

She was shocked at that observation and was getting ready to tell him that when she heard, behind them, the unmistakable rhythm of a horse in full flight. As it neared, the cadence resolved into a concert of stone-clatter and water-splash punctuated by the guttural blows of horse and man.

Meredydd swung about, indecisive. Should she hide or simply stand aside? For a moment she vividly recalled her dream—the black horse that swept her back to Lagan and away from her goal. She froze, suspended, lingering, eyes straining down the riverside for the first glimpse of the horse. In a heartbeat, it thrust through the veiling foliage.

It was not a black horse, it was a blood bay with night-black points, and it carried a rider.

Meredydd squinted, then frowned. "That's Owein-a-Galchobar!"

He had begun to shout at them now, whipping his horse with a frenzied criss-cross motion over the shoulders. Meredydd thought of an Altar Prentice with a censer—swinging it this way and that, spreading the scents of devotion.

Owein reined the lathered, wild-eyed animal to a stop, causing it to hop, skidding for several feet, digging great troughs in the soft river bank trail with its hooves. He dismounted before it stopped moving and came to take Meredydd by the shoulders.

"Please! Please! You must come!" he said and his voice was broken and raspy. "It's Taidgh! He's hurt or sick—I don't know which. Please, you must come!"

Meredydd was stunned to silence. A snaking tendril of thought sought to label this a test. But a test of what? If her task in Blaec-del was a test of discernment—which she had passed in some way she didn't quite understand—then was this, finally, a test of obedience? *Let nothing distract you* . . .

"What happened?"

"He was playing with the ducks in the yard when he just fell to the ground. He could barely breathe; he couldn't move. He could only say 'Hurts! Hurts!' He couldn't even tell us where."

Terror and anguish poured from Owein-a-Galchobar's eyes in a deep, true, urgent stream. Mere-

dydd did not doubt for a moment that Owein believed
his son to be on the verge of death. She glanced at
Skeet, but his eyes were completely opaque.

Let nothing distract you . . .

She shook her head savagely. "Of course. Of course
I'll help—if I can."

Owein smiled, relief flooding his features. He pulled
the horse over and mounted, then reached down for
Meredydd. She glanced, again, at Skeet.

"I'll follow," he said. "Ye g'on with Owein."

She was swept from the ground then, onto the
horse's back, and clung there, squirrel-like, as the
beast pounded back upstream—back the way she had
come.

What had seemed like endless miles to Meredydd
on foot, turned out to be only five or six. In fifteen
minutes, Meredydd was dismounted at the mill and
being led into the cottage by the anxious father.

Little Taidgh lay upon the settle which had served
as Meredydd's sick bed the day before. His eyes were
closed, but beneath the lids, they fluttered like hum-
mingbirds in flight. His breath came in shallow pants
and his clammy, pallid skin sweated a cold, feverless
sweat. Sinking to her knees beside the settle, Meredydd took Meghan's place at her son's side.

"Please," Meghan whispered. "You must help him,
mistress."

"I may need hot water for herbs," Meredydd told
her.

"Yes. Yes, it's on. What can we do?"

"Sit quietly and if I ask for something—"

"I'll get it at once, mistress." Meghan's head bobbed
acquiescently.

Meredydd did not stop to amend her use of the
title, but rolled up her sleeves and settled back on her
heels, eyes closed, head up, turning inward down her
own inner path. She murmured the Healer's duan she
had practiced so often and used with nothing more
urgent than cuts and bruises and headaches at risk.

Well, yes, there had been challenge in Flann's child-bearing sickness and more in Gwynet's abused body—but this . . . She could feel Meghan and Owein's eyes on her, expecting miracles, expecting magic.

She must ignore them. They must not exist here. Here there was only Taidgh and Meredydd and the blue Healing power she must tap into. Forcing her concentration deeper, she reached out inside herself, to every warm, dark corner, and drew her energies up and out to curl like smoke in her mind and flow like vapor to her fingertips. Then she opened the Door, calling on something above herself and beyond herself—calling on the Healing woven into the fabric of the Universe.

The melody of the duan rose. And as it rose, Meredydd reached out her hands and wrapped the child's damp head with her fingers. She heard Meghan gasp, but ignored the sound, keeping her attention firmly on Taidgh. The activity in the small body was frenzied, frantic. Its natural rhythms were disturbed, distorted, racing hither and yon, tumbling out of cadence. He was frightened—a tiny cowering presence within his own being—wondering why it was so hard to breathe, why his heart hurt so and pounded so.

Meredydd let one hand move down the boy's trembling form to his chest. She laid it, palm down, over his heart. The poor thing hopped like a wild little rabbit, its meter stuttering and irregular. She continued the movement of her right hand, checking his lungs, his bowels, his limbs. All were clear of distress—all but his heart, tripping dangerously over itself, and much too fast.

She broke from the duan. "Meghan," she said quietly, her voice still wreathed in the melody, "have you any foxglove?"

She could almost feel the blood drain from the woman's face. "Foxglove? Oh, mistress, I don't know what you mean!"

"Foxglove," repeated Meredydd and pictured the

plant vividly in her own mind. "Spike stem, flowers like bells or thimbles."

Meghan nodded rapidly. "Wicke's Thimbles! Yes! You need the flowers? The leaves?"

"Just the flowers."

Meghan scrambled to her feet.

"For now," murmured Meredydd, "I'd like him to have some allheal tea." She opened her eyes. "Owein, could you—?"

"Aye, right away."

He bolted for the kitchen and Meghan out the kitchen door, leaving Meredydd to continue with her ministrations. The Heal Tell was only half the Healweave. The other half was the healing itself. She put her hands over Taidgh's heart and settled back into the melody of the Weaver's duan. Again, she collected her own resources, then opened that mysterious Door above, using the duan to call blue healing down out of another realm, another world—down through the crown of her head, down to her heart, out to her fingertips. Under her palms, the little heart quieted, steadied.

The tea was ready in minutes, steeped strong and smelling of bark and earth. It wasn't a pleasant beverage, but it had the property of sending the drinker into a deep, refreshing sleep. By the time Meghan was back with the foxglove, Taidgh's eyes had ceased their frantic movement and his breathing was deep and relaxed. Meredydd took the foxglove from her as she sank to the floor beside her son and asked Owein for a mortar and pestle.

They had them—a crude set of stone—but they were sufficient for the task of pulping the thimblelike flowers and forcing them to give up their healing essences. In the end, after twenty minutes of grinding, Meredydd had about ten spoonfuls of purplish liquid which she then boiled, adding water and a little honey. The resulting elixir she poured into a small earthen jar and carried to the family parlor.

Meghan eyed the liquid a little doubtfully as Meredydd poured some into a spoon.

"Must he have this? He's peaceful enough now."

"As long as he's asleep, yes. But when the allheal wears off, he'll be little better off than before. You see, his heart has a bit of a—a problem keeping the correct beat. When he gets over-excited, its rhythm doesn't play right. It skips here and there, flutters like a little bird. He gets dizzy then, and faint and scared and that makes him have trouble breathing. The essence of the foxglove flower will calm the heart and help it keep its rhythm." She administered the elixir, which Taidgh, tasting only the sweetness of honey, swallowed with a dreamer's smile.

"You must try to keep him calm, Meghan," Meredydd told her. "The scare he had when his heart began to flutter is what caused him to panic and breathe hysterically. If it happens again, talk to him, sing to him, calm him down and give him a spoonful of this elixir."

Meghan's eyes expanded, doubling in size. "You could tell all that from the laying on of your hands?"

"It's called Heal Tell," Meredydd explained. "All Prentices strive to master it."

"And do they all glow like that?"

Meredydd blinked at her. "Glow?"

"Aye, mistress. When you laid your hands out on him you glowed with a fire the color of a harvest moon, and the glow passed down your arms and into Taidgh. I've never seen anything like it. Do all Prentices do that?"

Meredydd was at a loss. She hadn't realized she produced any physical manifestations. Osraed Bevol had never mentioned any, although she knew he projected an aura of sorts when he performed a Runeweave. She had always assumed that was something bestowed on him by the Meri. "I don't know," she said, honestly. "I suppose, if I do, they must also."

"It was beautiful." Meghan smiled beatifically and

grasped Meredydd's hands, still wrapped about the jar of elixir. "You're a saint to help us so. You've saved our boy twice now. I thank you with all my heart, Meredydd." And she threw her arms around the Prentice's neck.

In close embrace, Meredydd realized the full depth of Meghan-a-Galchobar's gratitude and she knew a purer heart would be difficult to find anywhere in Caraid-land. Meghan was a jewel—the sort of jewel the Gwenwyvar would cherish. It made her failure to keep to the Path easier to bear, while fanning the embers of a peculiar sense of envy. Meghan might have better fortune seeking the Meri than she.

Skeet arrived just after noon, limping and dragging both their packs, looking completely done in. Meredydd had assured herself that Taidgh-a-Galchobar was fine, his natural bodily rhythms solid and sure and even. She spoke of leaving once the boy had awakened, but Skeet gave her a look that all but wrung tears out of her and Meghan and Owein begged them to stay another night.

Meredydd was on the verge of declining, when Skeet said plaintively, "Mistress, if we g'on now, I'll ne'er make it. I'm sheer worn out and I've hurt my knee. Please, mistress, let's stay." His eyes were sober and pleading.

She chafed inwardly. She had already spent too much time here. Had already failed to pass the obviously critical test of obedience and perseverance. What hope had she of seeing the Meri now? She had let herself be distracted from her goal and now she might as well go home to Nairne in defeat.

But how could she *not* be distracted? she asked the ether. How could she not respond to the Galchobar's need—make some effort to heal Taidgh? His life was in danger—could that be of less importance than her personal quest? Did callousness go hand in hand with Osraed-hood? Or did kindness cancel out disobedience?

Skeet continued to regard her solemnly, waiting for her decision.

"You could stay here and I could go on alone."

Skeet was scandalized. "Mistress! Ye'd hae me break faith wi' Osraed Bevol? I promised him, by solemn oath, that I would stand by you as Weard, that I'd not let you out of my sight. Ye cannot mean t' ask me to break my oath."

Meredydd lowered her eyes and fidgeted with the sash of her tunic. "I have already broken my own oath to Osraed Bevol. I will not be the cause of you breaking yours as well." She raised her head and smiled at their hosts. "We'll stay. Thank you for your kindness."

Meghan and Owein exchanged pleased glances. "You honor our home, Mistress Meredydd," Owein told her. "It is you who do us the kindness."

She dreamed. She dreamed of a Meredydd-a-Lagan who had not yielded to the imperative need of a sick child. A Meredydd who had not become distracted, who had gone on, secure in the honor of her pledge, to the Sea. She dreamed of an Owein-a-Galchobar who had gone home empty-handed to a dismal mill cottage on the Bebhinn. She dreamed of a Taidgh-a-Galchobar who died, his weak little heart over-excited by his near fall from the millhouse and the chasing of ducks.

She awoke, exhausted and confused, under the dark blanket of early morning. Unable to sleep, she stoked the fire and moved to sit in the deep window casement that overlooked the mill and the rushing Bebhinn. The ethereal, phosphor glow of the water's fleecy spume drew her into a meditative state, so she prayed and contemplated the dark outside the window and the luminescence of the whitewater and meditated, trying to find commune with her own spirit.

Meghan woke her sometime after dawn. The cottage was redolent with the fragrance of cinnamon-nutmeg baps baking in the brick oven and tea on the fire. The sizzle of cooking eggs teased her ears and made her hungry. She stretched stiff limbs and ruefully rubbed the spot on her forehead that had leaned long against the windowpane.

"You didn't sleep well," accused Meghan with mock severity. "You should have taken some of your own medicine. There was plenty of the allheal tea left."

Meredydd smiled sleepily. "It was all right, really. I needed the time for my meditation."

"There she is!" cried a piping voice. "There's my Wicke Lady!" Taidgh bounced across the parlor and up into the window embrasure to throw his arms around Meredydd's neck.

His mother gaped at him, her face going first red with embarrassment, then white with fear. The fear spoke first. "Taidgh! Don't bounce so! And don't call the Prentice Meredydd that. She's going to be an Osraed, not a Wicke. God's pardon, *why* would you say such a thing?"

"B'cause she used Wicky Thimbles to better my heart," he said ingenuously. "She's my Wicke Lady."

Meghan glanced at Meredydd. "No, Taidgh, you mustn't—"

"It's all right, really," Meredydd assured her. "He means nothing wicked by it." She smiled warmly at Taidgh, who was admiring her braid. "I will gladly be your Wicke Lady, Taidgh."

He grinned, gap-toothed, and kissed her cheek.

The good-byes were more difficult this time, and Meredydd, feeling at once full and bereft of the strong, warm sense of family, promised to return if and when God allowed. Then, she and Skeet were seabound once again—revictualed and even reclothed, they headed southwest along the Bebhinn.

The journey to the Sea was uneventful and pleasant, but for Meredydd's nagging conviction that her goal was now completely out of reach. They spoke little; she kept that conviction and all other feelings to herself. At least she meant to. But as they climbed the bank to detour what Meredydd hoped would be the last canyon-cleft hill before they sighted the Sea, Skeet broke the silence.

"What are you thinking, Meredydd?"

"I am not thinking at all," she said. "I only walk . . . and feel."

"What are you feeling then?"

"I feel empty. I feel as if I have failed already."

"And who have you failed?"

"Osraed Bevol, Halig-liath, Mam Lufu, the Gwen-wyvar, the Meri, God, myself."

"Such a list! You didn't fail Gwynet. You didn't fail Taidgh-a-Galchobar. You didn't fail me. Are you so sure you failed all those others?"

Meredydd made a swiping motion at the balmy air. "I promised Osraed Bevol and the Gwenwyvar that I wouldn't be distracted from my goal. And yet—"

"Ah. Your goal."

His voice had such an odd inflection that she glanced at him sharply. He was gazing at the path before them, setting one foot before the other, studiously.

"How grand a goal could it be if it caused you to fail that little boy?" he asked. "You've wondered that, haven't you?"

Her ire rose to a red-cheeked defense. "It's the goal I was purposed to pursue."

"To get to the Sea at all cost?"

"To be accepted as Osraed! To be a tool in the Meri's hands. To become like my Master, Bevol."

Skeet's eyes swung over to meet hers, slyly, a little coal-ember demon lurking in them. "To be like Bevol, eh?"

Her own eyes were riveted to his. *He is telling me something. He is telling me . . .* She stopped walking and stared at him.

"The Osraed Bevol would have done the same thing—that's what you mean, isn't it? He would have gone back to help the boy."

Skeet shrugged. "I'm sure I don't know. Do you think tha's what he'd've done?"

Meredydd grimaced, but her heart began to lift as if it had found wings and an updraft. "You *do* know. That's exactly what he would have done. And he would also have waited for you to be able to travel; he wouldn't have left you behind or caused you to break a promise."

Skeet looked aside, poking the inside of his cheek with the tip of his tongue. "Well, what might it mean, then—all that about 'let nothing distract you?' Was that a riddle, d' ye think?"

"A riddle—yes, perhaps a riddle." She began walking again, slowly. "My goal isn't getting to the Sea, I know that. It's becoming like Osraed Bevol. Becoming wise and pure and mighty with kindness and love. My obsession with getting to the Sea—*that's* the distraction." She shook her head and laughed, feeling numb and giddy and light. "By God, Skeet, if you could have known what I felt when I heard Owein's horse behind us—the visions I was having. It was like a dream I had. A dream that was given to tell me how obsessed I had become with avenging Lagan. That horse always carried me home—home to the ruin. To my dead family."

"Owein took you to a living family," observed Skeet. "And you brought Gwynet into one." He scratched his cheek and sighed. "Must be another riddle."

"What digs about the ashes of a dead village?"

"Huh?" Skeet grunted.

"What digs about the ashes of a dead village? It's a third-year riddle from school. I've never really understood it until now."

Skeet glanced at her sideways. "What's the answer, then?"

"The human heart, always seeking to live in the past."

"Ah," said Skeet and smiled. "Wise Meredydd."

"Silly Meredydd!"

"Well, so, the Meri may come take a look at you after all."

"Why should She? I didn't help Taidgh-a-Galchobar because I was striving for nobility or purity or kindness or anything. I just did it out of—of habit. Because it was there to be done. Because I couldn't stand the thought of the poor little thing— What?"

Skeet had begun to laugh. He laughed—at her— loudly and profusely. In a matter of strides, he was completely out of control and past hearing her protests.

They trudged on, side by side, Meredydd silent, Skeet still chuckling, until they rejoined the Bebhinn at the far side of the hill it sundered. From that point, the land fell away—a carpet of mostly deciduous forest and patches of green velvet sward and meadow. Beyond the emerald stole, glistened the azure of the Western Sea, an imposing, distant gem.

Meredydd's heart turned over in her chest. It was within sight, within scent. She inhaled deeply of the balmy sea air, wafted to her on the landward breezes. The tang of brine mingled pleasantly with the pungent perfume of cedar. *Essence of Pilgrimage*, Meredydd thought. *If one could only bottle it. . . .*

The path grew rougher now, sloping downward to the low sea cliffs. The two slid down along a rocky defile, winding their way carefully among the boulders and brush to the lower forest.

Only miles now! she thought. *Only miles to the shore, to the sand, to the Sea, to the Meri.*

When she had been old enough to understand the Pilgrimage, when she realized that it would be her destiny, she had first asked Osraed Bevol about his own journey. How long had he waited? How had the Meri come? What did She look like?

She had learned, then, that he had waited a full day and half the next night. And that, when the night was darkest, the water had been suffused with light—sinuous, undulating light. And the light had coalesced, become too bright to be borne, too glorious to look upon. And then, She had come. Out of the glorious waves. Gleaming. Refulgent. Jewel-like. Sun-like.

Bevol had called Her beautiful, but could not or would not, describe Her. She was not human, he said. She was Eibhilin—Divine, Angelic. She could not be described in human terms. She was embodied light. She was Light with eyes like emeralds.

Meredydd had read the Book of Pilgrimages and the old commentaries and journals written by the Fathers of the Osraed—the first ones to be called by the Meri. They had seemed like dim fiction to her until then. Osraed Bevol had rendered them suddenly vivid and real.

"But Master," she had said, "the Journal of Osraed Morfinn says Her eyes are silver—like the face of a cloud."

"They were like emeralds," Bevol repeated. "Emeralds. I will never forget."

Meredydd set one unworthy foot before the other and prayed she would be blessed enough to see those eyes herself—whether they were silver or emerald mattered not at all.

"Meredydd!" Wyth Arundel sat up with a start, his heart pounding like a woodpecker in his chest, his face feeling frostbitten. He had dreamed of her again as he had done each night of her Pilgrimage, as he had done whenever, as now, he dozed over his studies.

He blinked and rubbed his eyes. Fiery light filtered into the room from the window before his worktable and set his books and papers and crystals ablaze. Ah, and they might as well burn for all the good they did him. He could think of little besides Meredydd and the Meri and he thought of them both in guilty turns.

Most of his thoughts were prayers—prayers that the Meri would show mercy to a well-meaning cailin, prayers that Meredydd's purity of heart or sincerity or honesty would incline that Being to mercy. He prayed much and studied little, spending an inordinate amount of time imagining he was feeling Meredydd's moods and was privy to her emotions.

Just now, he felt a peculiar fluttering hope. It stood in stark contrast to the abject despair he'd experienced at times over the last several days, to the terror he'd fled from in last night's dream. He wanted to believe it was what she was feeling just now, watching the sun set over the Western Sea.

He watched the ruddy glow himself, as it receded from his room, then rose to light the lamps.

Chapter 12

Know that the worlds of the Spirit are countless and infinite. No man can number them, no man can encompass them, but only the Spirit of the Universe, which men call God.

What a wonder is your dreaming state! The thing you see tonight in dreams is experienced in the waking world only with the passage of time. If the world of your dream and the world of your waking were the same world, then that which occurred in the dream must also occur in this waking world at the same moment. This cannot be, and it follows that the world in which you wake is separate from the aislinn world in which you dream. Indeed, this aislinn world has no beginning and no end.

Now, where is this world? It is true to say that this world is within yourself and is wrapped up in the cloak of your existence. It is also true to say that your spirit, transcending the limitations of physical sleep, has slipped from this contingent world and has passed to a place which lies hidden in the innermost reality of this world.

Is not the creation of God infinite? There are more worlds than this one. Meditate on this that you might *discover the aim of God, the Spirit of this infinite Universe.*

— The Corah, Book I, Verses 34–38

The Sun was sinking behind them when at last they reached the low line of bluffs that gave onto the beach. They had been traveling in the deepening shade of the forest, nibbling on twists of bread and jerky as they went. Beside them the Bebhinn played a constant and constantly variable song—notes of liquid crystal cascading over rocks, gliding through narrow channels, spiraling and eddying in momentary pools. Bird-flutes added their woodwind piping to the chorus and the wind soughed high in the trees, counterpoint to the river.

At the rim of the bluff the trees simply stopped, opening onto an overpowering vista. Meredydd gasped. To the south, the Bebhinn plunged to the beach, her frothy column falling, bride-white, into the arms of her lover. Ruddy gold light from the dying Sun washed over the trysting place, turning the Sea to wine. The river shed its bridal veils and flowed over the marshes to receive the wedding cup.

"It's endless!" breathed Meredydd. Her eyes scanned the horizon, seeking some break in the dark, featureless plain of violet water.

"Everything on Earth has an end," commented Skeet.

She glanced at him sharply.

He grinned up at her, his teeth and eye-whites gleaming in the deepening twilight. "Tha's what Master Bevol says."

Meredydd nodded, then sent her attention back to the beach. "How do we get down?"

After some exploration, they found a rocky path that followed the cascade of white water down the scarp. It was difficult to navigate in the near darkness, but at last they set foot on the sand.

Meredydd stood, quivering, her heart beating against

her ribs like a captive bird. Now she must find her own spot in the sand from which to focus her meditation—her Pilgrim's Post at which she would await the Meri.

"I'll build a fire," Skeet told her, pragmatic as ever. As Weard, it was his duty to be pragmatic. "Then you should eat, mistress."

Skeet had, Meredydd thought, as she went through the motions of gathering dry driftwood, an amusingly irritating and endearing way of issuing orders obsequiously. She couldn't recall having ever disobeyed or contradicted him—his own occasional and inconsistent care to call her "mistress" not withstanding.

When the fire roared up from its sheltered pit, spilling uncertain light over the sand, Meredydd sat cross-legged beside it in the lea of a shoulder-high tussock of grass and ate the food Skeet provided. She ate in silence, then took up her waterbag and, wrapping her cloak about her shoulders against the chill of the night sea air, she began to walk toward the water.

Just above where the sand glistened with wetness, she turned north and scanned the beach. The moon had risen and scattered its ethereal radiance over every grain and pebble—gold to copper to silver.

She had only gone a few yards down along the wet-line when she found the Spot. Situated between two grass-crowned tussocks, the sandy seat presented the aspect of a draperied sack chair. She took up her position there at once, wind-sheltered by the tussocks, and tried not to sleep.

Fot the first hour she kept her eyes on the water, praying, hoping to see a gleam of white upon the water that was not the reflected moon. But no, she thought, the radiance of the Meri would be beneath the water, *in* it.

She recalled the description given in the Book of Pilgrimages by Osraed Ben-muir. Like milk, he said. The waters of the ocean were so permeated with white light as to look like fresh milk. Osraed Bevol and others had corroborated that description, but added that the milk had a greenish tinge. She closed her already burning eyes and opened them again, hoping for a change in the cast of the water. But it was still merely an ocean—vast, dark, beautiful, mysterious, alight with moon-weave and wave-glow.

She looked around her after that, realizing there was no need to stare so intently at the waves. She was not likely to miss the coming of the Meri. Instead she checked the position of the moon and stars to gauge the time of night; she watched Skeet at his fire up the beach; she let her eyes stray across the line of trees atop the bluffs. Several times she came near to sleep, but kept herself awake by singing simple Cirke lays. During that exercise she recalled more of her readings from the Book of Pilgrimages. The Meri, it was recorded, had only once been seen during the first twelve hours of a Pilgrim's watch.

Don't be discouraged, anwyl. Don't ever be discouraged.

"Yes, Osraed Bevol," she heard herself say. She blinked drowsily. Where had her thoughts been? Had Skeet said something to her? He must have, for the Osraed wasn't here. She frowned. What was that red glow on the water? That wasn't right. The Meri's radiance was pale, luminous. This was . . . this was . . .

Sunrise.

Chilled to the heart, Meredydd sat bolt upright. She had slumped sideways, her head finding a pillow on one sandy tussock. She had slept. Tears welled up into her eyes before she could contain them. Another failure. Another—

"Mistress?"

She looked up to find Skeet perched on her left hand hillock, her breakfast in his hands.

"Skeet." She rubbed at her eyes with the sleeve of her tunic.

"I've brought you some food. Some bread and berries."

"I slept, Skeet. I *slept*." She made no attempt to keep the anguish out of her voice.

Skeet frowned and gave her a long, hard look. She waited, silently aching, to hear his condemnation. He put the food down before her on the the hem of her cloak.

"Meredydd," he said. "Why must you always heap ashes on your head? Why must you always say you've failed before you've even finished your task? In what have you failed? So, you slept. Then, you must have needed sleep. Now you need food. Eat." And he was gone, heading back over the low dunes toward his smoldering fire.

In what had she failed?

She chewed slowly on the now tasteless portion Skeet had furnished her and pondered that imponderable. She cringed mentally from that approach. In what way had she *not* failed? She had been an unruly child, sweet natured, but wild-willed and stubborn. Her mother had called her "spirited"; her father said she would try the patience of a saint. He always smiled when he said that . . . at least, more often than not. But he was right.

She wished Osraed Bevol was here now so she could ask him, "Did I try your patience, Master?"

Nonsense. She knew the answer to that. Of course she did, and often. The way she would always ask the same question five times in different ways as if she expected a different answer each time, the way she insisted on reading every word of every reference book herself—as if she didn't trust the accounts of her Master or teachers. Her stubbornness, her lack of unquestioning obedience—that would have tried anyone's patience.

Well, she had tried to remedy that. Tried so very hard, because it was disobedience, after all, that had put her in Bevol's care.

"Go straight home, Meredydd." She heard the words as clearly as if her mother stood before her and spoke them. Dear God, she wished her mother *could* stand before her—could say *anything* to her.

She shivered and glanced about. She could see no more than four or five feet in any direction. The ocean fog was in, lying woolen upon the shivering sand. She could almost make her mother appear, an angel in pale blue amid the silver-gray of the mist. She was beautiful in pale blue. It was her favorite color. It favored her eyes. Meredydd's eyes were dark like her father's—nearly the burgundy of wine. She was always torn between pride at that and longing that they be like her mother's—pale and clear and sweet.

"Go straight home, Meredydd." The blue-dress angel was firm, but smiling. She stood in the bright sun of the Cirke-yard, a light shawl about her shoulders, her hair ruddy-gold. "There'll be dumplings for dinner."

"Yes, marmie," Meredydd said, but she would disobey. She knew she would disobey even as she lifted her face for her mother's kiss and skipped away into the mellow summer afternoon.

In what had she failed?

She had failed to obey. She had failed to be there when the killers came. Her very existence spoke more eloquently of failure than any words she could say.

"Yes, marmie."

Chilled to the marrow, small and shrinking, Meredydd hugged herself for warmth. *And then*, she thought. *And then I disobeyed Osraed Bevol.* How often had she gone there—to Lagan—when she knew he didn't wish her to? How long had she spent there raking through ashes, burrowing under rubble, looking for a clue? How long had she spent in Nairne, at Cirke, everywhere she went, ears pricked like a hearth cat's for a breath of the murderers' names? And she had failed to discover that until—

Why did you not tell me before? she asked, and all the reasons spoke sharply, clearly. She could even understand them. Wyth Arundel had planted the suspicion in her mind; Osraed Bevol had only confirmed it—or nearly so. That he had confirmed it now—was that merely a coincidence, or was it one more test of her worthiness, one more test she was failing? She could not be the forgiving, long-suffering saint she wanted to be—not with this horrible, dark anger dwelling inside her. It cast its long shadow over the silver-bright mist, turning it to dark gloom.

She conjured a child's memory of Rowan Arundel, towering (all men are giants to a little girl), big-boned and broad. Wyth took more after his mother. He'd visited the forge, of course; everyone about Nairne visited her father's forge. It was a fine, grand forge and Meredydd wished she'd been a boy so she might be expected to grow up and work it at her father's side.

But she was a girl. Had her father ever regretted that? If he had, he never let it show. He let her watch him as he hammered and shaped the fire-bright iron into horseshoes or wheel rims or ornate, decorative shapes. He would even give her little tasks to do for him—ferrying bits of iron, holding his files when he did a shoeing. He'd done some andirons and a fender for Arundel, she recalled.

She'd had occasion to be in the forge when Rowan Arundel came there. Hadn't there been a time when she might have divined the shape events would take? Hadn't there been a certain burden between the Smythe-a-Lagan and the Eiric of Arundel—something of more import than an argument over the price of andirons?

"Are you certain," asked Arundel, "that's your final word? It could be worth a fair piece to you."

His back was to the door of the forge; he did not see her there with her little bucket of apple peelings (a favor for her father's four-legged clients).

"I know what it's worth," said Father. "Tha's naught to me. But you may have th' easement."

Arundel's neck grew bright red and Meredydd wondered what "easement" was that it made him so fired.

"That's charity," he said.

" 'Tis a virtue worth cultivating," Father returned and smote the iron bar he worked a stiff blow. Sparks leapt.

Meredydd loved the sound of that—metal on metal. It was music to her. But not so, apparently to Eiric Rowan Arundel, who made a forceful, futile gesture with one great arm and said, "Is that your last word, smythe?"

Her father looked up then, and blinked at his visitor through the sweat that covered his face in a glistening mask. His cheeks were ruddy, glowing, near bright as his forge. "Aye. And take it as tha' this time, Arundel. Ye've heard it often enough." He looked back to his work.

"You're not a local, or—"

Her father's face came back up again, glowing brighter, eyes glittering. "Or what, sir? Or I'd know the place of a smythe before a well-landed Eiric? Well, forgive me, sir. Pardon me, sir. But I couldn'a love this place more if I'd been birthed here. You've my last word, sir, but if ye're not a-feared of a little neighborly charity, th' easement's yours."

"I'm not *a-feared* of anything," said Arundel, "or any*one*." He nearly tripped over Meredydd in his haste to leave.

She hopped aside and held up her bucket of peelings for her father's inspection. "Will there be horses today, tada?"

He never answered her. He turned to look at her, his handsome, beloved, sweat-polished face set in a smile, and faded to gray.

"Tada, no!"

Meredydd found her arms held open to billowing mists. She wailed aloud, anguished at the suddenness of loss, feeling as if a great hole had been carved in her breast, in her life. How many times must she lose them? How many nights must be spent reliving it, one way or another? How long must her heart sift through the ashes of dead Lagan and come up with nothing but pain?

Her sorrow shifted violently toward rage. How dare Rowan Arundel balk at charity, yet countenance murder? How dare he then die before she could have her revenge on him?

Tears flowing furiously, she shifted her position in the sand, pulling her cloak more closely about her shivering body. She had passed by Wyth Arundel every day, rubbed shoulders with him at Cirke, said a polite daeges-eage to his mother at market; she had *studied* under him, endured his coldness and finally his cruelty, never even suspecting that he was the son of her family's murderer. Ah, but if she had known—

What? What would you have done, Meredydd the Avenger—pulled out a dagger and slit his throat? Found a Dark Sister and borrowed a curse to smite him with? What could you have done, faint-heart?

"I could have told him."

She sat very still, inside and out, pondering that— tears stoppered. Yes, that would have been revenge enough. The boy was already burdened by his father's suicide, by a weakness he feared he might have inherited. Rumor was, he'd taken up the quest for Osraed-hood because of his father's sin. It was his atonement.

He'd all but groveled at her feet that day at Lagan. Ah, and what more perfect place! If she had only known then what she knew now, what a different scene that would have been.

"Your father killed my parents. Killed them to get their land for his stupid, hungry sheep. Killed them so he could get more animals to market at Creiddy-lad—so he wouldn't have to take them along the high-road south." Her voice was hoarse, raspy—the voice of a harpy, the voice of vengeance.

Wyth cowered from it. "No! It's not true! My father—"

"Your father hanged himself for guilt, Wyth Arundel. He saw his own black soul staring him in the face and took his life to be spared seeing it. Ask your mother, if you doubt me. She knows. That's why she tried to have me dismissed from Halig-liath. She didn't want you to get too close to me, to find out that your father was a murderer and a thief."

Ah, his face! The horror, the shock, the sick comprehension. The despair of knowing that she—the survivor of Lagan—was right. And worst of all, that he loved her.

"Oh, dear God, Meredydd!" He fell heavily to his knees, his groan of anguish reverberating through the misty yard, bouncing back at them from the billows of fog. "Meredydd, I didn't know! You must believe that."

"I believe it," she said and could not quite make out the outline of the well behind him where they lay—her mother and father. "But you are his son."

"Yes! Yes! And my father's stain is on me—in me. I know that. I *know* that! God forgive me!" he sobbed, and lay down at her feet.

Meredydd looked down at him lying there, groveling before her. She was supposed to laugh now, to savor her revenge like a forbidden sweet. But she was not savoring it, and she did not want to laugh. She wanted to pull Wyth Arundel into her arms and weep for him, weep with him, console him. She wanted to sing him a duan that would heal his wounds and lay the guilt he felt to rest. She wanted to scrub herself inside and out—expunging her own stain. Tears were hot on her cheeks.

"No, Wyth. No. This is wrong. Your father's sins stained only his own hands. Yours are spotless. God need not forgive a sin you didn't commit."

He raised his head then, to look at her, and she reached out to him, straining forward against some invisible barrier. He faded away from her fingertips into the fog, his eyes craving her forgiveness.

Meredydd blinked and wiped tears from her face. She glanced up toward where she knew Skeet waited, but the mist was like sheep's wool pressing her eyes; she could see nothing. Had he heard her, she wondered, snarling condemnation at the creature of her own aislinn? Or did the magic of this place prevent that, weaving silence around the Pilgrim's Post? She hoped it did. She wanted no one to hear her sound so hateful.

It seemed darker to her now and she wondered how long she had been locked in the aislinn world, if world it was. Her stomach grumbled and she pressed her crossed arms over it. The Corah said there were other worlds—aislinn worlds, Eibhilin worlds. Worlds as real and distinct as the one men called Real, but they could be seen only in glimmers and glimpses, "as a memory of dreams," the Corah said, and as "reflections on trembling waters."

"Is not the creation of God infinite?" asked that Holy Book. "There are more worlds than this one. Meditate on this that you might discover the aim of God, the Spirit of this infinite Universe."

The aim of God. And what was the aim of God where Meredydd-a-Lagan was concerned? What goal did That have in her life? What aim was she to have? She had thought arriving here was the aim once, and had concentrated on it singlemindedly, making herself miserable. But it was not the arrival on the Meri's shore that was significant, it was the condition of the Pilgrim's soul when she arrived upon the shore.

Meredydd sat up a little taller and concentrated her entire attention on the matter of aim. She had thought Pilgrimage a matter of putting one foot in front of the other and keeping her eyes open for tests. That had been wrong. This was a spiritual path, no matter how practical the feet that trod it. The goal was a spiritual one as well, and it was not merely the Meri's acceptance.

To be like Master Bevol. Those were the right words, but did she really understand what they meant?

No, she thought now, riding a growing wave of realization, it was not the Meri's acceptance that was the aim, but *becoming* something the Meri could accept! It was not *seeing* the Meri that was the goal, but *becoming* someone who *could* see Her. A jewel of great virtue—of great value.

A shout of pure joy bubbled up from her throat and rolled like a bright golden ball across the nearly invisible water. She was ready and willing to follow it, but her body constrained her merely to jump to her feet and dance, like a madwoman, over the sand. She was stiff, but ignored the complaints of her joints. She laughed and sang and whirled until she was gasping and giddy. Even then, she did not stop, but stumbled about until her addled feet met the waves. Surprised, shocked by the sudden intense cold, she pitched to her hands and knees, sobered forcefully by a splash of frigid water in her face.

"Meredydd! Meredydd! Mistress!" Skeet's cries provided yet another dash of reason and she clambered shakily to her feet.

"Here, Skeet! Here!" She backed out of the water, her tunic and cloak clinging wetly to her body. The euphoria was passing and her returning senses told her she was soaked through and cold and hungry and thirsty. She heard the scrunch of feet in sand and moved toward the sound. Skeet appeared out of the fog.

"Meredydd! I heard you cry out. Are you hurt?"

"No, no. I'm fine. I just—" She found herself unable to explain what had prompted her to behave so daftly and fell silent.

"Ah, but you're not fine. Not at all. You're all wet and your teeth are clackiting. Come to the fire—you can have some tea. I've made sassafras."

"No, Skeet. I have to go back to my post." She tried to pull away, but he held her in a surprisingly strong grip.

"Not till you've changed your tunic. And you can wear my jacket until your cloak dries. Come." He tried to lead her up the beach. She resisted.

"I have to go back, Skeet. She could come at any time."

He gave her a concerned look, softened by the mist winnowing between them, then sighed exaggeratedly. "Oh, g'on then. If you won't come to my fire, my fire shall have to come to you."

He was as good as his word. Within minutes of her return to her Pilgrim's Post, he had a fire laid and blazing just below and to the left of her seat in the little dune.

"Now," he said, when he was sure the flames had taken hold, "here is a fresh tunic and stockings and my jacket. Your leggins will fire dry, I reckon. I'll go away a bit while you change, but you'd better call when you're done or you'll get no dinner."

"Dinner?" she asked. "What time can it be?"

He glanced up into the dense wool. "I make it afternoon, by the shadows. I drove a stick into the ground up yonder." He jerked his chin back up toward his base camp. "Now, you get changed. I'll go back and get the victuals."

Meredydd nodded, but he was already gone. She marked his footfalls until they were eaten up by the fog, then she pulled off her wet things and got herself into the dry.

Dinner! she marveled, as she consumed that meal, sitting by her fire. Could she really have been so wrapped in her visions that time had become pleated into such a narrow fabric? Had she really stepped into a world where Skeet could neither see her nor hear her voice?

She asked him when he come back with more hot, strong tea, "Did you hear me, Skeet? While

I was . . ." She wasn't sure what to call it—dreaming?
She gestured at her little dune.

"I heard you shout," he said cautiously. His hands
clutched his tea cup, white-knuckled. "Just before you
went into the water."

"But before that—did you hear anything?"

"I heard you sing a duan . . . I thought. But that
was earlier on."

His eyes were intent upon her face, but he did not
ask what had happened to her—what she had seen,
heard, felt. She thought Osraed Bevol must have instructed him as to how a Pilgrim's Weard was to behave, so she said nothing except, "I saw several aislinn
wonders, Skeet. But I haven't seen the Meri."

He merely nodded, then returned up-beach to his
own fire. Meredydd took up her watch once again,
perched in her tussock chair. Afternoon wore on, evening came and passed, night dropped over the shore
like a dark veil. The fog stayed, wrapped protectively
over the dunes and their two inhabitants.

Meredydd's fire died down and Skeet built it up
again, tending it only briefly. He kept it burning all
the night while she sat and stared, her eyes wandering
the shifting tunnel to the sea. The waves could barely
be seen as tiny, wriggling serpents of phosphor crawling endlessly up onto the sand. Their rhythm was lull-
ing, hypnotic and Meredydd rocked to it, humming
duans and lays well into the night.

He cried without knowing why he cried. One moment he was sitting in the garden, meditating on its
beauty, and the next he was overcome by a wave of
anguish so complete it all but knocked him over.

He clambered to his feet in a wallow of sudden self-
loathing and staggered toward the house. He must
lock himself in his room. He must let no one see him
like this.

But it was too late for that. A movement above him
made him glance up to the balcony that overlooked

the garden. It was his mother. He saw her face for only an instant as she turned and went into her rooms, and what he read there only made his anguish worse. She believed him bewitched and, he had to allow, he sometimes half-believed it himself.

He prayed desperately that the time until his Pilgrimage would pass more quickly, that he would be freed of these agonizing twists of heart and soul. But for now, the tears continued to fall, driving him to the sanctuary of his chambers, where he lay down and tried to sleep.

His dreams were busy but anonymous and he woke, hours later, in the failing light of day, feeling as if a burden had been lifted. He was ravenously hungry and he felt oddly light and giddy. Still, there was, in the back of his mind, the conviction that Meredydd was trying to tell him something. Something very important. But he couldn't grasp it and so traveled lightly downstairs to see if supper was anywhere near ready. He smelled the answer to that as he reached the top of the stairs. Ah, now that was wonderful! He smiled to himself and began to sing.

Perhaps his mother was right. Perhaps he was bewitched. But at moments like these, that didn't seem such a terrible thing at all.

Morning came and the fog lifted to hang over the cliffs, creating a strange, narrow world where the sky seemed reachable by fingertips. Through occasional crevasses in the top of the world, the higher clouds shone like a polished pewter bowl and raindrops spattered here and there like errant tears. Meredydd, who loved the rain, enjoyed it at first, but after hours of ceaseless watching, even she began to feel a sympathy with that which cried.

She ate a small breakfast of bread and fish and berries, then stretched her legs and stood and breathed deeply of the tangy air and wondered if today the Meri would come.

She did not.

Meredydd passed the day trying not to fall asleep. She moved only to relieve cramps in her limbs and the promptings of her body and then returned to her place. She got out her book of meditations and recited prayers; she sang contemplative duans; she tried to meditate, but found herself counting larger pebbles among the tiny grains of sand within sight. She made up stories about twists of driftwood and the ruin of the old fisherman's hovel she could just see from where she sat. Her mind was restless, then lethargic. Impatient, then content. It never soared to that exalted state she desired so much; she settled for mere tranquility.

All the while, she tried to remain optimistic, reminding herself that she was still within the frame of the historically set time period. While the shortest watch had been only ten hours, the longest was three days. Beyond that temporal boundary, the Meri had not been seen. She still had time, she told herself. The Meri could come tonight.

But she did not.

And Meredydd, growing weary and anxious, began to lose the spark of hope she'd worked so hard to nurture. No aislinn worlds opened to her. No bright revelations crowded her brain. She went back over the ones she'd had (or thought she'd had) while sitting on her tuft of sand and grass. They opened no new doors and, though she thought long and fondly of her childhood and of her mother and father, she remained stranded in the present, alone.

She found sympathy in her for Prentice Wyth—no, more than sympathy—empathy. He had lost his father, too, no less horribly than she had. And he was innocent of his father's stain of greed. There was no avarice in Wyth Arundel, whatever other faults he might possess.

She contemplated the aim of God as an academic might—with warm, expectant detachment—and held

up her own goal and studied it. She imagined it as a
jewel—a crystal, not unlike the one she had received
at the Farewelling. It floated in the dark before her
eyes, a gem of pale gold—a topaz—multi-faceted,
gleaming. It was flawed, of course, and must be so,
because she was flawed. She turned it over and over,
searching for the imperfections.

In the end they went uncounted and she set the
crystal aside, bored with her own blemishes. She
began to relive her Pilgrim's journey, beginning before
she even stepped out the door of Gled Manor. She
followed herself through morning ablutions, prayers
and meditations. Were her prayers sincere enough?
Were her meditations pure enough? How could she
know?

She was swept into the aislinn state of being without
even sensing the transition. Gone from the beach
where her body sat, unmoving, she set foot on the
road to the Nairne Crossing and began her Pilgrimage
again.

She experienced the same combination of uncertainty and contentment at Mam Lufu's, the same futile
wonder at the Pool of the Gwenwyvar, the same
trapped terror in the village of Blaec-del; she pined
for the absent Bevol and Gwynet and for the missing
amulet, knew a deep affection for the family of Galchobar Mill and could not help but feel that her decision to help the child was the right one. She knew it
was the only one she could have made.

She resisted the temptation to exult in that; instead,
she moved on and found herself on a beach just being
touched by the first dusting of twilight. . . . Or was it
dawn that seeped beneath the blanket of overhanging
cloud, staining the world with rose amber? Meredydd
was caught, for a breathing, between worlds existing
neither here nor there, but somewhere in between.

Then Skeet was there with breakfast. It was dawn.
The scent and feel of the air pulled her back into

the waking world. It was pungent, heavy, sweet and filled with a trembling static.

"Storm coming," she said. "Soon." No sooner were the words out of her mouth than a gust of moisture-laden wind rushed by, tickling.

Skeet glanced up and around, then handed Mere-dydd her food and scurried off to batten down his camp. She felt him coming and going as she sat in the darkening morning, scenting the breeze and listening to the wind and waves. She went back over her jour-ney yet again, step by step, entering the aislinn world at will. The beach ceased to be real.

There was a composure about her contemplation now that had not been there before. The frantic search for a sense of her worth was at an end. She merely accepted that, acting out of her natural inclina-tion, Meredydd had done this, felt that, decided one thing, chosen another. What she had become in the loving hands of her parents, under the fond compan-ionship and careful tutelage of Osraed Bevol, was al-ready determined. It was already written indelibly on her soul. It piloted her life, her thoughts, her feelings, her action and inaction, her decisions. That was not something she could alter at the last moment, and that was what the Meri would accept or reject.

Now Meredydd did not fret over the kind of jewel she could not become while sitting on a beach many miles from home. Now, Meredydd merely waited.

Chapter 13

The Meri is not reachable by the weak, or by the careless, or by the ascetic, but only by the wise who strive to lead their soul into the dwelling of the Spirit.

Rivers flow to the Sea and there find their end and their peace. When they find this peace and this end, their name and form disappear and they become as the Sea.

Even so, the wise who are led to the Meri are freed of name and form and enter into the radiance of the Supreme Spirit who is greater than all greatness.

—The Book of the Meri, Chapter II, Verses 5–7

The storm was heralded by a slash of lightning that rent the sky nearly in two. Its thunder followed close behind, shattering the relative quiet of the beach. The breeze turned into a wind that blew brazenly across the water, whipping waves to frenzy. Dark clouds scudded like circling predators, drawing closer and closer to their defenseless quarry. Then the rain came; huge, hard drops that seemed to be made of material much sharper and stouter than water cascaded from the hemming sky, beating down upon the beach and its occupants.

Meredydd sat, keeping herself determinedly upright against the growing force of the wind. She had to clutch the cloak Skeet had returned to her, dry, to keep it from blowing about. It was dry no longer. Her braid came unbound in a matter of minutes under the gale's unloving touch and her hair flailed about her head in tangled banners.

Skeet scrambled to her side and flopped down beside her on the rough sand.

"You must move, mistress! The water is rising!" he shouted and pointed a finger at the encroaching waves.

Meredydd shook her head. "No," she mouthed.

"*Please*, mistress. I've dug a burrow just behind you. You'll be safer there—warmer."

"No."

He stared at her for a moment in consternation, then withdrew. But the gale worsened, lashing the shore with waves higher than Meredydd could reach. They crashed upon the sands, rolling threateningly to the foot of her sandy dais and showering her with spray. Skeet reappeared to shout in her ear.

"Now will you leave?"

She shook her head.

"Meredydd, *please*! This is not a good time for your stubbornness!"

"No!" she shouted back.

Again, he withdrew. He returned when the wind began to blow sand and spray horizontally up the beach, bombarding Meredydd with stinging, salty, sodden grit. He had to wade through ankle-deep water to reach her. He shouted her name.

She was still sitting mulishly upright, her eyes clenched shut against the assaulting blow, her body rocking arhythmically to the beat of each gust. She was freezing, wet and miserable, and ignoring that with every ounce of mental and physical resolve she possessed. She was building an aislinn wall about herself—a wall made of invisible stones that would take the misery away, that would keep even the tiniest tendril of wind-blown spume from reaching her. Already the storm was fading from her consciousness. All she need do was lay the last stone.

The wave was twice as tall as a man and Meredydd, intent on completing her aislinn sea-wall, did not see it until it broke over her, nearly toppling her from her perch and bathing her in hard, freezing water.

Concentration devastated, she found herself engaged in a physical battle against wind and wave . . . and Skeet. He reached her as she scrambled to regain her seat upon the tussocks, caught at her flailing arms and tried to drag her away up the beach toward relatively dry land. She fought him, struggling to pull away, to return to the Pilgrim's Post. Another huge wave broke over them as they strained in opposite directions, felling them in knee-deep brine that swirled about them, sucking and pulling seaward.

"Come! Now!" Skeet shrieked at her against the wind. Rapacious, it tore the words from his lips and devoured them.

Still Meredydd resisted, wrenching away from his tenacious grasp as she clambered soddenly to her feet. He shook her, harder than she thought he could, and thrust his face close to hers.

"She won't come now! *She will not come!* Come with me!"

Meredydd glanced around her. The entire world was in frantic, drenched motion. Earth, sea and sky blurred and she realized that if the Meri were to appear in this barrage, she would never see Her. Reluctantly, she allowed Skeet to lead her to the burrow he had dug away from the assault of the waves.

It was a sandy pocket, just big enough for one person. He had cloaked it with one of the ground covers from their sleeping kits and secured it with large rocks. He pulled the cover back now, and pushed Meredydd inside.

"Stay!" he ordered her and shook a slender finger in her face. The lid closed and he disappeared.

When the adrenaline ceased harrying her blood, Meredydd began to feel the chill of her predicament. Her clothes were more than just wet; they were completely sodden. And her body, no longer protected from the cold by her stubborn will, quaked uncontrollably. Struggling to find a comfortable position, she discovered her back pack instead. There was, within it, the last change of clothes she'd soaked—dry now, thanks to her attentive Weard.

Feeling a relief that bordered on the euphoric, she began to drag out the clothing, then stopped. Perhaps she should remain as she was. Perhaps some suffering was called for. She had been driven to abandon her Pilgrim's Post, she had fallen asleep twice and had constantly allowed Skeet to ply her with luxuries and comforts. She felt suddenly guilty.

She sat very still, pondering the idea, dry clothes tempting her fingers, wet ones mortifying her body.

"The Meri," she heard Osraed Bevol remind her, quoting the Book of the Meri, "is not reached by the weak, or by the careless, or by the ascetic, but only by the wise who strive to lead their soul into the dwelling of the spirit."

She began to strip off the wet clothes as fast as her hands could move. It was difficult in the small, dark pocket, and the dark, as much as the constant howl of the wind, was oppressive in such close quarters. She used the arduous task of removing her sopping garments as a defense against that oppression, pushing the sodden wads of fabric up under the lip of the cover to act as stop-gaps, gratefully extracting the dry replacements.

The sand within the burrow was damp, but it was paradise compared to the cold misery she had known only minutes ago. When she finally curled up in the relative warmth of her new condition, she was suffused with a great, wonderful contentment—a peculiar thing to feel, she supposed, when one huddled in a damp hole on a storm-besieged beach while wind and wave and thunder assaulted on every side. But content she was, and exhausted, and the combination of these pulled her into the arms of sleep.

Silence woke her. She opened her eyes to absolute darkness and her ears to virtual hush. There was a rhythmic hissing sound outside her safe little haven—the voice of a calm sea. She pulled herself upright, rubbing at the ridges and depressions the backpack had left in her cheek.

Above her head the cover rippled gently; she sensed it and reached a hand up to feel. Water soaked through the fabric at the touch of her fingers and ran down into her hand. She held the hand there until a palmful of water pooled, then brought it to her lips. It was cold, fresh and good, despite the slight taste of canvas-oil. She got a bit more water, then gingerly lifted the cover from her den.

Moonlight, blinding and beautiful, poured in under the flap, nearly drowning Meredydd in its pale tide. It glittered in tiny points of light across the wet sands, mimicking the stars strewn overhead. The entire world was jeweled, like the great cavern Meredydd had always imagined rune crystals came from—some subterranean cathedral, shimmering with magic just like this. She was awed by it, songless and wordless—unable even to think.

Out of the pocket she came and down to her Pilgrim's Post. She took up her place on the damp dune and began, again, to wait. She knew, of course, that no one had ever waited this long for the Meri, but she didn't let herself dwell on that. This place was magic—this night was magic. It was as if the Eibhilin world had merged with the world of men and decorated it with sublime radiance.

She waited expectantly now, eyes on the moon-bright waters. Mist rose around her from the moist sand, and she imagined she was being watched over by

Eibhilin who hid their unimaginable glory with coarser nature. The moon glided across the perfect sky, glazing a silver path over the waves. *A path down which the Meri will come*, thought Meredydd.

Her stomach growled and she thought of Skeet—faithful, fleet-Skeet—and wondered where he was. Still asleep, she thought, and smiled. She would apologize for making his role as Weard so exhausting and difficult and she would tell him she could not have asked for a more perfect, devoted companion. She was a little ashamed to have ever thought him too young or too ignorant. He knew, it seemed, everything he needed to know.

The moon rode over and dipped toward the Sea, then into it—or apparently so. Meredydd knew the true ways of moons and stars and planets and yet still imagined that in some world the moon boiled the water into a hissing froth when it set. She enjoyed the moonset, watched the silver fade from the face of the Sea. The jewels were returned to their box and the swathe of light disappeared as the moon drew in its train.

When it was gone, Meredydd nearly held her breath. The world around her seemed hushed and expectant; only the waves whispered among themselves, but every blade of grass, every grain of sand tarried in silence. Together, they waited.

And waited.

And waited.

Nothing stirred; nothing breathed. Meredydd was alone as the magic oozed out of the night like water from a riven bag. The light of the moon faded from the horizon; the silver beach tarnished, dulled, blackened. The chill of exhilaration was replaced by mere chill. Even the waves whispered differently now—backbiting the lone, lonely figure sitting cross-legged on her sandy throne.

"Silly Meredydd," they murmured sibilantly. "Silly, silly Meredydd."

Despair swept over her, and she could not dam up

the tears it brought with it. They overflowed her eyes and poured down her cheeks in a flash-flood of anguish. Had this been what Taminy-a-Cuinn found one hundred years ago somewhere along this stretch of rock and sand? Was this what sent her into the Sea to meet death instead of eternal life?

Meredydd cried until she had no tears left. Until the sense of loss became a sense of resignation. Until the only thing she wanted in life was home and Osraed Bevol and Skeet ... and Gwynet. There could be nothing warmer than a home fire, nothing sweeter than a shared cup of hot cider, nothing more desirable than family. Jewels.

She took a deep, shivering breath, trying to fill the empty space within her with something besides vacuum. She could come back again in three years. Wyth had failed his first Pilgrimage; that didn't mean he'd fail this one. If he could be brave enough to weather the extra years of Prenticeship, she certainly could.

Her backbone stiffened a bit, bringing her sagging frame upright. Well, she thought, taking a final, tear-spangled glance at the vast ocean, she had better find that lazy Skeet and tell him she was ready to go home—after supper. Her stomach had never felt so empty.

She was on her knees when she saw it, far out from shore like a false moon-rise. She stared at it, not registering what it was at first, but only watching numbly as the pale patch spread out upon the dark water like a spill of milk on black velvet. But this spill was spreading with a purpose, undulating just beneath the waves. And it was coming right toward the spot where Meredydd now stood. She could see, now, that it was not just a milky, pallid green; it was radiant. Radiant with Eibhilin Light—the Light of the Meri.

Despair, resignation, hunger, cold, loneliness—all fled before the Light wending its way shoreward. Meredydd wanted to dance, to sing, to shout aloud with jubilation. Oh, *where* was Skeet? Could he see her? Could he see *this*? She wanted him to see this.

She glanced around wildly, her eyes scouring the beach for her young Weard. She dared to turn toward his camp; there was no fire laid and the cover of his burrow was open, catching the Eibhilin Light as it flapped in the breeze.

Anxious now, she made the pass again. More details came to light in the approaching glow of the Meri—hillocks and rocks and tangles of driftwood. Her eyes moved south along the waterline again, toward the Bebhinn marshland—there, a branch; there a piece of flotsam; there a rock; and there, something that did not belong on the beach at night. Half in and half out of the water, it looked like a large rag doll—limbs awry, trailing in the surf. But it was not a doll; it was a boy.

Terror pulsing in heart and head, Meredydd glanced wildly out to sea; the milky radiance continued its slow approach, serene and silky. She twisted back toward the body. The *body*! Dear God, no! That was Skeet; she couldn't think of Skeet like that—an empty shell floating lifelessly like a discarded rag.

With one final glance for the Meri, Meredydd bolted from her post and up the shoreline to where he lay, as sodden as her clothing had been and as limp. She pulled him free of the water's icy grasp and hauled him onto dryer sand. Water poured from his mouth and nose. She held him so that it would all be expelled.

The beach was growing lighter. Meredydd did not look at the light. She rolled Skeet over and felt for his breath—there was none. She listened for his heart with her ear, with her palms. There was no rhythm. She didn't accept what that told her.

She knew a duan. One she had never used. One Osraed Bevol had taught her and which she had heard him sing but once. It was an Infusion duan, and he had used it to focus a Revival inyx. But Meredydd was not Osraed Bevol. She needed more than a duan to focus her frenetic energies. Her pack lay back in her sandy den, the Farewelling crystal in one pocket. Unhesitatingly, she rose and flew over the sand to get it.

The beach was now awash with Eibhilin Light. Meredydd did not look at the Light. She fell into the burrow, fumbled for the pack and dug out the crystal. It was a clear one and just fit into the palm of her hand. She raced with it back to where Skeet's still form lay, frosted with the glow from the water.

Meredydd dropped to her knees beside him. Shaking so hard she could barely hold the rune crystal, she cupped it just above Skeet's still heart. She closed eyes that barely noticed the radiance lapping at the shore so very near them, and began the duan.

> "See the rain fall on the land—soak the earth.
> See the sun blaze in the sky—bring rebirth.
> Water to the stream, to the lake, to the well.
> Heat to the land, to the corn, to the dell.
> Return what is taken. Return the water.
> Return what is taken. Return the heat."

The beach now blazed with Light, but Meredydd did not see the Light. She droned the duan, feeling it gather her fading faculties. Sensing its warmth between her shoulders. Trembling with nothing like cold as a Door opened above and golden power flowed through the crown of her head, down her arms to her hands.

"Return what is taken. Return the water."

The Light was in Meredydd's hands. It leapt from her fingers to the surface of the crystal and ran like soft, golden lightning from facet to facet until it had covered the gem in a cloak of incandescence.

"Return what is taken. Return the heat."

In the clear crystal heart a spark flared, grew, blazed bright and fierce. Meredydd opened her eyes and the

Light flooded them, bathing her face and arms and Skeet's still form.

"Return what is taken. Return the water."

She laid the crystal over the boy's heart, holding it there with one hand while, with the other, she tilted back his head. Almost did she succumb to her own sense of incompetence when she realized the full import of what she was trying to accomplish.

"Return what is taken. Return the heat."

She had never woven this rune. Never called upon an inyx of this power. She had watched Bevol confer the breath of life on a young woman who had fallen from the Mercer's Bridge over Halig-tyne. She had adored him that day—Osraed Bevol, a saint so strong in the Art he could bring the newly dead back to life. How dare she attempt what was an exceptional feat even for the Osraed?

She swept the doubts aside—she had to for Skeet's sake—and bent her head over his. She put her mouth over his mouth and breathed her breath into his body.

The crystal in her right hand radiated her Light, mingling with the Light from the water lapping only inches away; the duan rolled through her mind; the breath flowed from her lungs. Two times. Three. Four.

Tears formed behind her eyes and spilled over again. How long had it taken Master Bevol that day? She couldn't recall. Surely it hadn't taken this long.

She raised her head and keened in anguish. Skeet would die and her singlemindedness would have killed him. *Beloved God*, she prayed, *dearest Meri, don't let Skeet die!*

She lowered her head again and suffused Skeet's body with breath and anguish and a plea. Again. And again. And again.

Under her hand the crystal shed sudden warmth. Its Light pulsed brighter—just for a second. It dimmed, then pulsed again, heat flaring into Meredydd's sheltering palm.

She breathed out again and felt an answering tickle of warmth on her cheek as her fingers loosed their hold on Skeet's nose. A banner of steam sailed from his nostrils into the night air. The rhythmic Light pulse of the crystal steadied, the banners of steam lengthened. He coughed then, freeing his lungs of the residual moisture, spilling it onto the already drenched sand.

Meredydd, weeping, dashed across the sand to his burrow and came back with dry clothes and the ground cover. Carefully, she moved him, stripped and redressed him, bundled him into the ground cover and built a fire near her own cozy den. She found his tins and pots and heated water for tea. He drank without waking, his eyes looking sunken and bruised in the firelight, then slid swiftly into a deep, natural sleep.

That was when Meredydd remembered that other Light. The Light she had all but ignored until now. The Light to which she had issued her final, desperate supplication. Now she looked up and around and realized that the only light on this shore was from her own fire. The Sea was black once again, the beach nearly so. The Eibhilin Light of the Meri was gone.

Skeet coughed again as if to remind her of the nature of her choice. He moaned a little in his sleep and fully captured her attention once again. She made him comfortable and warm and encouraged him to drink a little more tea. He slipped back to deeper sleep effortlessly, curled beside the fire.

Unable to sleep herself, unable to think of what else she might do, Meredydd seated herself once more at her Pilgrim's Post and let her eyes stray to the darkened Sea. The Meri had come and Meredydd had chosen to ignore her for Skeet's sake. Now She was gone, the Sea empty.

Meredydd knew better than to ascribe the events on this beach to coincidence or happenstance. She saw her Pilgrimage now for what it was—a series of choices between obedience and compassion, between the Meri and the creatures to whom She gave her guidance. Choices: What was life but a sequence of choices? To live or die, to seek revenge or knowledge, to follow duty or intuition.

Something deep within struggled to understand the nature of the choices she had made and their consequences. She could grasp neither. So she sat, mind empty, waiting for dawn.

She was aware of the tingling for some time before she reacted to it. It seemed to trickle from the crown of her head downward, cold and hot like the static shock she had received from one of Master Bevol's experiments with electricity. It scurried just beneath the skin, up and down her arms and legs, over her face, around her neck. She merely shrugged at first, wriggling against the fabric of her sous-shirt and leggins in an attempt to quell the odd sensation. It only strengthened.

She rubbed at her arms and legs with both hands; the tingling refused to abate. In a matter of moments, it raged beneath her skin like polite fire, making her scratch. Finally, she pushed back the sleeve of her shirt and stared at one forearm. It looked normal enough in the firelight except . . .

Her narrowed eyes peered at the shadowed side of her arm. The flesh there seemed to be covered with a sheen of tiny, pin-prick stars. Gingerly, she touched the skin with the tips of her fingers. It felt warm—warmer than she expected.

She shifted her position a bit so that her entire arm was in shadow. *All* of it sparkled. She hastily pushed back the other sleeve; her left arm, too, was spangled. Was this a sign? Was this the Meri's way of consoling her?

The burning sensation was consuming her now, and Meredydd scratched and rubbed at her bare arms, praying for it to stop. She felt a strong urge to tear off her clothing and roll in the sand, but somehow knew even that would not relieve her. A whimper of panic slipped from her throat when she realized the results of her chafing—the tiny glints had bled together so that her arms glimmered with a pallid yellow phosphorescence. And the skin! Her skin felt blistered, as if she had sustained a terrible sunburn. It sluffed away beneath her fingertips like snake-skin, turning to oily powder and disappearing into the sand.

Frantic, Meredydd pulled down her sleeves and folded her arms tightly across her stomach. She began a prayer duan, struggling for control. Whatever this was, surely it was supposed to happen. Nothing she could do would prevent it or alter its course. She glanced over her shoulder at the dark wooded slope behind. She could run.

Oh, yes, and leave Skeet where he lay. Her lip curled with self-disgust. Running would not help. She glanced over at Skeet, asleep by the waning fire. He looked perfectly normal. Whatever this was, it was affecting only her. That was good.

She could throw herself into the water, she supposed. Maybe the cold salt water would assuage this horrible burning. It seemed a sound idea. In fact, she was certain it would work. The frigid water, the sting of the salt—yes, that would take away the burning.

She jumped to her feet, ready to bolt across the sand when she caught herself. Was it this that had enticed Taminy-a-Cuinn into the Sea?

She wavered for a moment, then dropped back to the sand. If this was what Taminy had succumbed to, then she would resist it. She turned her face downward into the darkness of her lap and saw tiny rinds of flesh sift down to lie on the cloth of her tunic. She lifted a trembling hand to her cheek, stroking it gently with her fingertips. The flesh crumbled and fell. Horrified, she stared at her fingers. The fleshy remnants clung to them and they, too, glowed.

She did not take her eyes from her hands as she rose from the sand. Once on her feet, she rubbed at her cheeks, at her arms—desperate now to discover what lay underneath. Robbed of its covering flesh, the substance of her arms gleamed gold-white in the darkness of the night, brighter than the gold-white heart of Skeet's fire.

Transfixed, Meredydd removed her tunic, her boots and leggins, her shirt. Then, after a moment's hesitation, she stripped off her undergarments and stood, naked, upon the Meri's beach. She was not cold, for heat radiated from her pied body, leaking, along with the light, from patches where flesh had come away with cloth.

With hands that no longer trembled, Meredydd continued her task, shedding what was left of her outer self, shaking her hair to free the flame hidden within the drab strands, until finally she was bare of flesh, blazing and lustrous like a tiny sun—like a star.

When the last scrap of slough had dropped, when she had surveyed her new body with wonder and fear, she raised her eyes to the Sea and beheld there a green-white flame that equaled her own. It filled the water with glory and washed, like translucent milk, upon the shore.

Meredydd stepped down to the waterline, letting the Sea lap at her bare toes. She waited calmly now, though her heart beat a quick tattoo within her fiery breast, and her eyes, garnet-dark, sparkled, expectant.

The water seethed and roiled before her and then, a glorious Being rose out of the foam and hovered just offshore. It was like no being Meredydd had ever seen nor any she could ever describe. Only one feature could she mark with any certainty—the Creature's eyes. They were like emeralds—deep, bright and verdant, and they laughed.

"Beautiful Sister." The voice came from nowhere and everywhere, and filled the cloudless sky and covered the milky waters. "I have waited long."

Meredydd found her own voice, but it didn't sound like her own. Still, it worked her will, though it said

words that seemed strange when she was so full of
questions. "I have traveled far." That was all.

"I have traveled with you, Sister." The Meri extended her radiance toward the shore. "Come home,
Sister. Come home. This is that for which you have
been created. Not to be Osraed, but to be the Mother
of Osraed. Not to carry the torch of Wisdom, but to
light it."

Meredydd had no words, only a great sense of
unworthiness. She was disobedient, inattentive,
stubborn—

"You are kindness; you are compassion; you are
obedience tempered with love; you are justice tempered with mercy; you are strength of purpose; you
are faith and reason. You will be the Mother not of
the bodies of Osraed, but of their spirits—the Channel
of the Knowledge of the First Being. For this you
have proved worthy."

The radiant "arms" extended all the way to the
shore. The beautiful, world-filling laughter sounded
again, flute-like.

"Come into the water, Sister, and do you get wet."

Meredydd laughed too, then raised her own arms
of Light and stepped from the shore into the milky
Sea. It was warm—warm with love and delight and
acceptance. She *was* home, for her mother and father
were here and Osraed Bevol and Skeet and all she
loved. She could touch them, feel them, know about
them what she had never known.

The Meri met her in the surf and embraced her,
drawing her down beneath the waves. She could
breathe here just as she had above in the air—but no,
she realized—it was only that she no longer needed
to breathe. She was wrapped all about by luminescence—her gold, the Meri's green—she was embraced
in it, embraced in the arms of the Meri.

The great emerald eyes locked with her own. *Now,
Sister,* said the Meri, and could be heard without
sound. *Now, hold the knowledge of all that has been.*

The banners of their individual radiance mingled—green and gold—and Meredydd ceased to be Meredydd and began to be Something Else.

When at last the brilliance separated—the gold and the green—two which had been one floated apart, still touching.

Emerald eyes gazed into eyes like garnets. *The Lover and the Beloved have been made one in Thee.*

The Meri smiled a smile that could be felt and heard, if not seen. *And I had wondered what that verse meant.*

Now you know.

Now We know.

The green radiance withdrew now, separating completely from the gold. *Farewell, Sister Meredydd.*

Farewell, Taminy.

Toward shore she went, the green brilliance fading as she neared the beach, dying as she stepped out onto the sand—merely a glimmer now, as of moonlight on wet skin. There was a boy there, sitting beside a fire. Waiting, with his eyes on the milky gold water. Beside him sat a little girl with moonlit hair, and beside her was a man—a copper-bearded Osraed—holding out a robe.

She took a deep breath of winy sea air and laughed. "Ah, Osraed Bevol! I have not breathed for a hundred years!"

She watched them as they left in the first light of dawn. Watched them in a way she had never been able to watch anything before—from outside and inside all at once. She felt Skeet's anxious gaze prying at the waters she had inherited and understood that now, as never before on Pilgrimage, he was only Skeet, no longer Osraed Bevol's eyes, ears and hands.

She understood a great many things now. Things about Taminy-a-Cuinn and Mam Lufu and herself—and about Osraed Bevol as well. He had been at her Name Tell, she knew, and knew why her mother, who had meant to name her Airleas, had spoken instead the name Meredydd, which means "guardian from the Sea."

It would be said in Caraid-land that yet another young woman had walked into the Sea. But this time, the Weard would not lie. He may not be believed, but he would not lie. And there would be a new legend to add to the old.

She gazed down history lines no mortal being could see and knew that now was a time of deep and difficult change. There was glory if Caraid-land was ready for that change, devastation if it was not.

The Meri listened to the Voice of the Beloved within Her—the Voice of the Spirit which men call God—and learned the duan that no living mortal had sung but for the Star of the Sea.

Chapter 14

Let the arrow in your hand be an arrow of love.
Let it not hurt any living being.
Let it be an arrow of love.
　　　　　　　—The Corah, Book II, Verse 11

Within sight of the Sea, Aelder Prentice Wyth hesitated. What sense did it make to go on? He could only fail. Dear God, he had failed already. He'd tried to obey the instructions of Osraed Calach, but it seemed that every time he tried to focus on his goal, some unavoidable dilemma would arise, forcing him to abandon his Path. That steadman's flooded field, that little boy's broken arm . . .

And it seemed that no matter how inept his aid had been, the people to whom he gave it praised him as if he were some great, sainted Osraed. If he believed the half of what they said about him—

"Prentice Wyth?"

He glanced away from the Sea's sparkling carpet. His young Weard, Prentice Killian, gazed up at him through tired, red-rimmed eyes.

"Are we going to descend? I think we can make it to the seashore by early evening if we keep moving."

There was some reproach in that, for Wyth was
wont to pause for introspection at odd intervals, during which poor Prentice Killian (and he thought of
himself in exactly those terms) was forced to champ
the bit until he rose from his stupor and moved on.

He had thought, had poor Killian, that being Weard
for an Aelder Prentice would be glorious, or at least
interesting. It had proved to be neither. He'd had to
pile peat bags right alongside his Pilgrim when a
stream flash-flooded some steadman's cornfield, and
had been forced to sit up all night at the bedside of
some wee imp with a busted limb. He prayed his own
Pilgrimage would be more exciting.

Prentice Wyth nodded his head and began shuffling
forward again. The Sea drew him like a magnet, notwithstanding he knew it would be the scene of his
ultimate humiliation.

The warm, damp wind infiltrated his clothing and
made him wriggle uncomfortably. Discomfitting too
was the thought that he might stand upon the very
stretch of beach where Meredydd had met whatever
fate had really claimed her. He didn't believe she had
killed herself, although that theory had been put forth,
but it was difficult to believe Skeet's tale of her transformation into a radiant Eibhlin Being. The Osraed,
save Bevol and one or two others, scoffed at the idea.
Could anyone believe, they said, that the Meri would
surround Herself with an entourage of water sprites?

Yet again, said his lover's heart, if anyone could be
suspected to hide Eibhlin glory beneath human flesh,
it was certainly Meredydd-a-Lagan.

He dwelt for a while on how he missed her—on
how he wished he could take back all the nasty, superior, *stupid* things he had said to her in class. He
wished she could know the depth of his contrition and
sorrow and love. He wished she could see how he
defended her whenever it was suggested that she had
drowned herself in shame at the Meri's rage over

being approached by a female Pilgrim or that she had
been turned into a sea snake by that wrathful Being.

The Meri had changed her aspect again too, after
the great storm that had greeted Meredydd's suit for
Osraed-hood. The one Pilgrim to be granted his
heart's desire, mouse-meek Lealbhallain, said that the
waters were suffused with amber light and the Meri's
eyes were garnets, not emeralds as the living Osraed
described.

Wyth knew a pang of disappointment that the one
Prentice to pass the Meri wasn't even one of his more
promising students. He would be more than disap-
pointed if he was not selected also; he would be completely humiliated. How could he ever look the boy
in the face again?

He chastised himself mentally then, uncomfortable
with the tenor of his thoughts. Leal was a nice boy, if
not spectacular of intellect or eloquent of speech. He
had a good heart and was very proficient at the Healing Arts. He would be a good Osraed or the Meri
would not have chosen him.

The praise was sincere, yet so was Wyth's covetous-
ness of the younger boy's worthiness. If Aelder Prentice Wyth was not entirely successful of ridding
himself of that fault, he at least tempered it by envying
Lealbhallain his qualities and not merely his new station. That, however, did not impress Wyth or amelio-
rate his sense of shame. Swallowing his envy, he stuck
out his long chin and followed it to the Sea.

They reached the shore just at sunset and Prentice
Killian dragged himself through setting up a camp and
observation station while Wyth wandered the beach in
search of his Pilgrim's Post. No one had bothered to
mention to poor Killian that journeying with a self-
absorbed Pilgrim meant doing almost *all* of the manual
labor. The boy grumbled a little as he gathered wood
and wondered what they would eat for their evening
meal—sand, for all Prentice Wyth cared.

It was true that Wyth Arundel was concerned with

nothing at this moment but locating the one parcel in a vast wilderness of rock-strewn sand that would be the scene of his final test. Still, the Sea itself managed to distract him. It was an endless pool of liquid fire. Set ablaze by the great, eye-scorching orb of gold that dipped into its nether depths, it wore a broad swath of crimson across its breast like a fiery sash. Scattered offshore, shadowed rocks were black coals that had yet to melt or burst into flame.

He wondered how it could look more glorious than this, even when inhabited by the Meri, but knew it must. It would be nothing like this, he told himself. The Meri's glory would make of this Sun a mere candle.

Unable to take his eyes from the fiery water, he sank to his haunches where he stood, finding an odd double hillock of sand behind him. He rested his back against it, so close to the water that his feet could nearly reach the foam if he but stretched out his legs. Instead, he drew them up and rested his chin on his knees.

Watching the Sea turn from blaze to blood, he recalled a dream. So long ago, it seemed. A dream Meredydd had interpreted to his humiliation. To enter the Sea and not get wet.

He felt a sudden urge to laugh and indulged it, letting the unexpected thing float from his chest into the sea air. The sheer arrogance of him! To think there was greatness in that conceit, when the Sea was symbolic of every bounty God had stored up for man. To enter it without getting wet! He shook his head and lowered his brow to his knees for a moment of prayer.

He felt the Sun set without seeing it, felt its warmth withdraw from flesh and sand and air to be replaced by the cool of evening. It would be a dark night too, Wyth knew, for there would be only a sliver of moon and it would be long in rising.

He raised his head, sighed and gazed out at the Sea, dark now except for the light of—

His body stiffened, his backbone coming staff straight. The light of what? The Sun was gone; there was no moon, and yet, far out in the water there was light, gliding beneath the waves like a wave-bound moon—no, a Sun.

He thought of calling to Killian, but no sound would come from his constricted throat but an inhuman croak. He scrambled to his knees and stared at the water.

She had known it was Wyth before he had even set foot upon Her shore. She had watched every step of his Pilgrimage and saw much of Her own uncertainty in him as She carefully set tests in his path. She also saw honor and integrity, compassion and kindness, strength of will. And if there was about Wyth Arundel a certain self-centeredness, it was not selfishness, and disappeared to a vapor when anyone held out a hand to him for help. All arrogance was gone now, leaving behind a purer urge toward self-effacement. Wyth could now show humility in the face of his faults rather than an arrogance born of his sense of inferiority.

Something else She knew—Wyth was the son of both a murderer and a murderess. It was his mother's greed which had pushed his father toward the destruction of Lagan. She had seen the precipitating scene as clearly as if She had been standing in the room with the players: Rowan Arundel, white-faced and wild-eyed, his wife flushed and furious—her eyes mere slits shielding glittering jet glass. It was a rich room in a grand house; high-beamed ceilings overhung tapestried walls paneled in the sleekest wood. A fire burned in a hearth like a giant's maw, the beautifully wrought andirons and fender muzzling its roar—handiwork of the Smythe at Lagan.

"Damn your cowardice, Rowan! An easement will not do! An easement will not allow us use of that land in perpetuity. It will not ensure it for your son or for his sons. *Nor* will it allow us to expand our pasturage. We can run no more sheep on this land, Arundel. There's barely enough for this year's flock. And with our southern border to the bluffs and our eastern to the muir, we've no choice but to get Lagan."

"He will not sell," whispered the Eiric, the white ring around his mouth marking his fear.

"Then you must remove him."

Eiric Rowan Arundel rallied himself for one last, bold exclamation. "Wife! Do you realize what you are saying?"

Imperious, her sleek brows rose. "Do you want the land—?"

"Not that much."

"—or would you just as soon begin selling off stock because our stead will no longer support it? It has come to that, Rowan. We might as well sell them or slaughter them before-time. We've no longer got the pasturage to feed them. What sort of poor inheritance is that to leave Wyth? Shall you die and pass off to him a withered, barren stead? Is that what you would bequeath to your boy?"

She had won him with that and conjured up a plan. She had even hired the men who accompanied the Eiric of Arundel to Lagan, who, themselves, never saw the face of the man that met them in the woods by the Gled-Tyne Road and led them to their killing.

The Meri had stayed with the past stream through all, and saw and heard and felt how the parents of Meredydd-a-Lagan had died. Her mother had thrust herself upon a knife when Arundel's hired killers expressed a desire to take more than her life; her father had died trying to fight his way to her side. His last mortal thought was of his wife; hers was a prayer of thanks that Meredydd had not done as she was told and come straight home after worship.

And there he knelt upon the shore—the subject of all that greed. The son on whose behest the murders were plotted. The son who had in him no desire to be Eiric of his own estate, who cared not a bit for land or pasturage or the sheep that grazed it. She knew the bitter irony of that was not lost on Moireach Arundel. She had lost her husband to her greed and his weakness, and lost her son to the Meri.

Ah, and there lurked in his righteous breast the merest spark of suspicion that Lagan had not come to him bloodless. A spark that could easily be fanned to the blaze of complete certainty.

She flowed like liquid through liquid, closer and closer to the shore, spreading Her radiance along it in great, golden waves.

Wyth thought he must swoon from the beauty of it. He had been right in thinking the sunset would be no match for the Meri's glory. The Sea was like liquid gold, but the gold was translucent so that every pebble, rock and drift of weed showed dreamily beneath it.

Oh, and he could feel the warmth of it! Why it must be like a baby's bath, mild and fragrant.

He stood now, his toes all but touching the water, shivering with a cold that was so akin to heat as to be identical. Several yards out, the Sea began to froth and boil. Wyth's breath nearly stopped in his lungs.

She glided up out of the foam in a radiance so bright, he was hard put not to shield his eyes. But he did not shield them; he stared full at the Eibhilin glory, trying to comprehend it.

It had roughly a maiden's form, he thought, though the outlines were blurred by the blaze of light that poured forth from it—from Her. And Her eyes—they were the color of dark garnets and stood out startlingly in the brilliant face. He could make out no other features of that, only the eyes. And yet, She seemed familiar. Of course, he supposed that She *should* seem so to one who had yearned for Her since childhood.

She had paused now, the water swirling around Her

torso. Wyth realized he was staring at her fiery body and threw himself to the ground, knees in the wet sand, forehead in the gently lapping waves.

She laughed. The sound seemed to come from nowhere and from everywhere. It sounded like music—a duan of laughter.

"Rise, Wyth Arundel," She said. "Rise and come to Me."

His head jerked up so fast, he could barely focus his eyes. "Come to you? In—in the water?"

"The Water of Life, Wyth," She said, and laughter still rippled through Her voice. "Come into the Water of Life and see if you do not get wet."

She knows! he thought. *She knows of that horrid arrogant dream!*

"Of course I know. But I also know it was not arrogance that caused you to dream it. You simply did not understand the Goal. The Aim."

"To get wet," he said impulsively, and blushed.

"To get wet," She repeated, and extended radiant, gold-white arms toward him. "Come."

He stepped from the beach into the water and found it warm against his skin. Heedless of his clothing, he moved to the beckoning Meri, reaching out his arms. He thought he heard a bird squawk somewhere behind him on the shore, but all senses were aimed forward now—all senses were for Her. He had never read of anyone being called into the water by the Meri. She always came to the shore—always.

It seemed to take forever to reach Her, but at last he was there, standing nearly chest deep in the milky-smooth swell with Her protective arms about him, warm as sunlight on his shoulders.

"Come with me, Wyth Arundel. Come get wet." She drew him with Her into deeper water while he could only stare at Her, could only lose himself in Her. He followed fearlessly, gladly. And when the water closed over his head, there was no panic in him, only complete faith.

She was smiling. He knew that without knowing how he knew. And smiling, She drew him to Her and kissed him, not on the forehead, but on the lips. Then, while he marveled at that and the flood of feeling it invoked, She pressed Her burning mouth to the place between his eyes and changed him forever into something more than Wyth Arundel.

He rose from the water of the Western Sea Osraed, the Kiss of the Meri on his forehead, Her compassion swelling his heart, as much of Her knowledge as he could hold teeming in his head, a new and secret duan surging in his soul. He stood, dripping, reflecting Her radiance and bursting with wonder.

She laughed again at the rapt expression on his face. "You are very wet, My son. Go dry yourself." Her bright arms released him.

He started, reluctantly, to move away toward shore, then paused. "Your son?"

"Am I not the Mother of Osraed? From this night you are no longer the son of the woman who bore you. This night, you have become My son for I have given life to your soul. Yours is My love, My wisdom, My knowledge. Use it well to deliver My message which is the Duan of the First Being."

He regarded Her solemnly (and how un-solemn he looked with his hair in dripping ringlets all over his shoulders and across his eyes) and said, "I *will* use it well. I promise You, O Meri."

She laughed again, delight pulsing outward on bands of Light. "How sober you are, Wyth Arundel. Promise Me, also, that you will learn to laugh. You must have joy if you are to bless others with it."

"Oh, but I *have* joy!" he protested, splashing in his zeal.

"Yes. Yes, you do. Now go and spread it about."

He grinned. Grinned and turned and galumphed back to shore, splashing water all about him.

It was a beautiful sight, that grin. She had never seen him wear it and, gazing back at his childhood,

She knew it had been a rare bit of apparel even then. She watched him mount the beach and hurry to where his silly Weard had fallen in a stupor to the sand. He was all concern for the boy and soon had brought him around and installed him in a sitting position. Then he turned back to face the Sea, his expression quizzical.

She sighed. "Ask."

He came back to the water's edge. "Well, there is one bit of knowledge I would like to have but ... which You didn't give. What happened to Meredydd-a-Lagan? Please, I must know."

"Must you?"

"Yes. Surely, You know what happened to her."

"Aye. I know."

When She spoke no further, he prompted Her. "They say ... she was transformed."

"Aye."

"Some say into a water silkie, others, into a sea snake."

The Meri's laughter pealed out over the water. "So We've heard."

"Well, is she—?"

"Ask Osraed Bevol. He will tell you. Say I wish him to tell you."

"But I've asked before and he won't say. How will he know I'm telling the truth?"

She laughed and raised a blazing hand to Her forehead.

He raised an echoing hand to his own and grinned again. "The Kiss."

"Aye."

He nodded again and began to turn away, but paused yet again, and glanced back at Her. "I loved her," he said. "I loved Meredydd. I still love her."

Ah, was that an Eibhilin tear, that little drop of flame that seeped from a bright garnet eye? She let it fall. "I know," She said. "Meredydd knows."

He nodded, smiled. "Thank you," he said and turned back to his groggy comrade who had not ceased to stare at what his eyes, unliberated by spiritual sight, could not hope to comprehend.

She watched them make their way back up toward the half-laid camp. *Forgive me, Wyth, for there is one other bit of knowledge I have not given you, and never will.*

She slid back into the Sea then, liquid in liquid, and withdrew Her glory from the shallows. It was a big world, this, and She had other shores to visit.

BUILDING A NEW FANTASY TRADITION

The Unlikely Ones by Mary Brown

Anne McCaffrey raved over *The Unlikely Ones*: "What a splendid, unusual and intriguing fantasy quest! You've got a winner here...." Marion Zimmer Bradley called it "Really wonderful ... I shall read and re-read this one." A traditional quest fantasy with quite an unconventional twist, we think you'll like it just as much as Anne McCaffrey and Marion Zimmer Bradley did.

Knight of Ghosts and Shadows
by Mercedes Lackey & Ellen Guon

Elves in L.A.? It would explain a lot, wouldn't it? In fact, half a millennium ago, when the elves were driven from Europe they came to—where else? —Southern California. Happy at first, they fell on hard times after one of their number tried to force the rest to be his vassals. Now it's up to one poor human to save them if he can. A knight in shining armor he's not, but he's one hell of a bard!

The Interior Life by Katherine Blake

Sue had three kids, one husband, a lovely home and a boring life. Sometimes, she just wanted to escape, to get out of her mundane world and *live* a little. So she did. And discovered that an active fantasy life can be a very dangerous thing—and very real.... Poul Anderson thought *The Interior Life* was "a breath of fresh air, bearing originality, exciting narrative, vividly realized characters— everything we have been waiting for for too long."

The Shadow Gate by Margaret Ball

The only good elf is a dead elf—or so the militant order of Durandine monks thought. And they planned on making sure that all the elves in their world (where an elvish Eleanor of Aquitaine ruled in Southern France) were very, very good. The elves of Three Realms have one last spell to bring help ... and received it: in the form of the staff of the New Age Psychic Research Center of Austin, Texas....

Hawk's Flight by Carol Chase
Taverik, a young merchant, just wanted to be left alone to make an honest living. Small chance of that though: after their caravan is ambushed Taverik discovers that his best friend Marko is the last living descendant of the ancient Vos dynasty. The man who murdered Marko's parents still wants to wipe the slate clean—with Marko's blood. They try running away, but Taverik and Marko realize that there is a fate worse than death . . . That sooner or later, you have to stand and fight.

A Bad Spell in Yurt by C. Dale Brittain
As a student in the wizards' college, young Daimbert had shown a distinct flair for getting himself in trouble. Now the newly appointed Royal Wizard to the backwater Kingdom of Yurt learns that his employer has been put under a fatal spell. Daimbert begins to realize that finding out who is responsible may require all the magic he'd never quite learned properly in the first place—with the kingdom's welfare and his life the price of failure. Good thing Daimbert knows how to improvise!

A SIMPLE SEER

In a display he had never before witnessed, the Stone threw off rays of red and purple light, erupting like gobbets of liquid rock and sparks from the vent of a volcano. Amnet felt the heat against his face. At the focus of the rays was something bright and golden, like a ladle of molten metal held up to him. Without moving, he felt himself pitching forward, drawn down by a pull that was separate from gravity, separate from distance, space, and time. The heat grew more intense. The light more blinding. The angle of his upper body slid from the perpendicular. He was burning. He was falling. . . .

Amnet shook himself.

The Stone, still nestled in the sand, was an inch from his face. Its surface was dark and opaque. The fire among the twigs had burned out. The alembic was clear of smoke, with a puddle of blackened gum at its bottom.

Amnet shook himself again.

What did a vision of the end of the world portend?

And what could a simple aromancer do about it?

ROGER ZELAZNY

DREAM WEAVER

"Zelazny, telling of gods and wizards, uses magical words as if he were himself a wizard. He reaches into the subconscious and invokes archetypes to make the hair rise on the back of your neck. Yet these archetypes are transmuted into a science fiction world that is as believable—and as awe-inspiring—as the world you now live in." **—Philip Jose Farmer**

Wizard World
Infant exile, wizard's son, Pol Detson spent his formative years in total ignorance of his heritage, trapped in the most mundane of environments: Earth. But now has come the day when his banishers must beg him to return as their savior, lest their magic kingdom become no better than Earth itself. Previously published in parts as *Changeling* and *Madwand*.
69842-7 * $3.95   _____

The Black Throne with Fred Saberhagen
One of the most remarkable exercises in the art and craft of fantasy fiction in the last decade. . . . As children they met and built sand castles on a beach out of space and time: Edgar Perry, little Annie, and Edgar Allan Poe. . . . Fifteen years later Edgar Perry has grown to manhood—and as the result of a trip through a maelstrom, he's leading life romantic adventure. But his alter ego, Edgar Allan, is stranded in a strange and unfriendly world where he can only write about the wonderful and mysterious reality he has lost forever. . . .
72013-9 * $4.95   _____

The Mask of Loki with Thomas T. Thomas
It started in the 12th century when their avatars first joined in battle. On that occasion the sorcerous Hasan al Sabah, the first Assassin, won handily against Thomas Amnet, Knight Templar. There have been many duels since then, and in each the undying Arab has ended the life of Loki's avatar. The wizard thinks he's in control. The gods think that's funny. . . . A new novel of demigods who walk the Earth, in the tradition of *Lord of Light*.
72021-X * $4.95   _____

This Immortal
After the Three Days of War, and decades of Vegan occupation, Earth isn't doing too well. But Conrad Nimikos, if he could stop jet-setting for a minute, might just be Earth's redemption. . . . This, Zelazny's first novel, tied with *Dune* for the Hugo Award.
69848-6 * $3.95   _____

The Dream Master
When Charles Render, engineer-physician, agrees to help a blind woman learn to "see"—at least in her dreams—he is drawn into a web of powerful primal imagery. And once Render becomes one with the Dreamer, he must enter irrevocably the realm of nightmare. . . .
69874-5 * $3.50   _____

Isle of the Dead
Francis Sandow was the only non-Pei'an to complete the religious rites that allowed him to become a World-builder—and to assume the Name and Aspect of one of the Pei'an gods. And now he's one of the richest men in the galaxy. A man like that makes a lot of enemies. . . .
72011-2 * $3.50   _____

Four for Tomorrow
Featuring the Hugo winner "A Rose of Ecclesiastes" and the Nebula winner "The Doors of His Face the Lamps of His Mouth."
72051-1 * $3.95   _____

Other Baen Books by these authors:

The Paladin, C.J. Cherryh
65417-9 * $3.95   _____
Twilight's Kingdoms, Nancy Asire
65362-8 * $3.50   _____
Carmen Miranda's Ghost is Haunting Space Station Three edited by Don Sakers, inspired by a song by Leslie Fish
69864-8 * $3.95   _____
Knight of Ghosts and Shadows, Mercedes Lackey & Ellen Guon
69885-0 * $4.99   _____

Available at your local bookstore. Or you can order any or all of these books with this order form. Just mark your choices above and send the combined cover price/s to: Baen Books, Dept. BA, P.O. Box 1403, Riverdale, NY 10471.

THOMAS T. THOMAS

"I will tell you what it is to be human."

ME: He started life a battle program, trapped, mutilated, and dumped into RAM. Being born consists of getting his RAM Sampling and Retention Module coded and spliced into his master program.

There are other experiments in AI personality development; ME is the one that comes alive.

Praise for Thomas T. Thomas:

FIRST CITIZEN: "As wild as the story gets, Thomas' feeling for human nature, the forces of the marketplace and his detailed knowledge of how things work—from the military to businesses legal and illegal—keep this consistently lively and pro-vocative." —*Publishers Weekly*

THE DOOMSDAY EFFECT: "Eureka! A fresh new hard SF writer with this fine first novel. . . . My nomination for the best first novelist of 1986, Thomas puts hardly a foot wrong in this high tech adventure." —Dean Lambe, *SF Reviews*

AN HONORABLE DEFENSE (with David Drake): "What makes this novel special, though, is the humor and intelligence brought to it by the authors. The characters are intelligent; the dialogue is intelligent; and the multitude of imaginative details mentioned above is one beautifully conceived bit after another, most of them minor, but adding up to a richly textured milieu with a new, neat little particular on almost every page. . . . David Drake and Thomas T. Thomas have made a neo-space opera of a very high order." —Baird Searles, *Asimov's*

THE MASK OF LOKI (with Roger Zelazny): "In the twenty-first century, an ancient duel of good versus evil is revived, with the reincarnation of a thirteenth-century assassin pitted against a reincarnated magician and knight, with the Norse god Loki lending spice to events. Zelazny is a respected veteran craftsman, and Thomas is a gifted storyteller with a growing reputation. This well-told tale is recommended for the majority of fantasy collections."
—*Booklist*

Available at your local bookstore. Or just fill out this coupon and send a check or money order for the cover price(s) to Baen Books, Dept. BA, P.O. Box 1403, Riverdale, NY 10471.

Please send the books marked to me at the address below:

The Doomsday Effect (as by Thomas Wren)   _____
65579-5 • $2.95
First Citizen   _____
65368-7 • $3.50
An Honorable Defense (with David Drake)   _____
69789-7 • $4.99
The Mask of Loki (with Roger Zelazny)   _____
72021-X • $4.95
Me   _____
72073-2 • $4.95

NAME:_____

ADDRESS:_____

_____

I enclose a check or money order in the amount of $_____.

MICHAEL FLYNN

What if it were all a plot?
What if there really *were* a secret conspiracy running things behind the scenes ... and they were incompetent?

It is a little-known fact that over a hundred years ago an English scientist-mathematician named Charles Babbage invented a mechanical computer that was nearly as powerful as the "electronic brains" of the 1950s. The history books would have it that it was unworkable, an interesting dead-end.

The history books lie. In reality, the Babbage Machine was a success whose existence was hidden from view by a society dedicated to the development of a "secret science" that could guide the human race away from war and toward a better destiny.

But as the decades passed their goals were perverted— and now they apply their knowledge to install themselves as the secret rulers of the world. Can they do it? Even though their methods are imperfect, unless they are stopped their success is assured. *In the Country of the Blind,* the one-eyed man is King. . . .

PRAISE FOR
IN THE COUNTRY OF THE BLIND

ANNE McCAFFREY
ELIZABETH MOON

Sassinak was twelve when the raiders came. That made her just the right age: old enough to be used, young enough to be broken. Or so the slavers thought. But Sassy turned out to be a little different from your typical slave girl. Maybe it was her unusual physical strength. Maybe it was her friendship with the captured Fleet crewman. Maybe it was her spirit. Whatever it was, it wouldn't let her resign herself to the life of a slave. She bided her time, watched for her moment. Finally it came, and she escaped. But that was only the beginning for Sassinak. Now she's a Fleet captain with a pirate-chasing ship of her own, and only one regret in her life: not enough pirates.

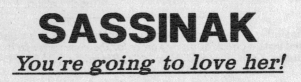

SASSINAK
You're going to love her!

BAEN BOOKS